FATHER UNKNOWN

FATHER UNKNOWN

Fay Sampson

This first world edition published 2011
in Great Britain and in the USA by
SEVERN HOUSE PUBLISHERS LTD of
9–15 High Street, Sutton, Surrey, England, SM1 1DF.
Trade paperback edition first published
in Great Britain and the USA 2012 by
SEVERN HOUSE PUBLISHERS LTD

British Library Cataloguing in Publication Data

Sampson, Fay.
  Father unknown.
  1. Fewings, Suzie (Fictitious character)–Fiction.
  2. Women genealogists–England–Fiction. 3. Unmarried
  mothers–Fiction. 4. Detective and mystery stories.
  I. Title
  823.9'14-dc22

ISBN-13: 978-0-7278-8087-1 (cased)
ISBN-13: 978-1-84751-389-2 (trade paper)

All Severn House titles are printed on acid-free paper.

Severn House Publishers support The Forest Stewardship Council [FSC],
the leading international forest certification organisation. All our titles that
are printed on Greenpeace-approved FSC-certified paper carry the FSC logo.

Typeset by Palimpsest Book Production Ltd.,
Falkirk, Stirlingshire, Scotland.
Printed and bound in Great Britain by
MPG Books Ltd., Bodmin, Cornwall.

To Mary and Bob

ONE

'**E**xcuse me.'

Suzie had been aware for some time that the large woman at the next microfiche reader was uneasy. She had seen her leaning forward to peer at the handwriting, switching between low resolution and high. There had been the occasional mutter of: 'Darn it!' Now she sat back with a sigh and turned to Suzie.

Her request was apologetic, but with a veiled determination. The accent, as Suzie had guessed it would be, was American.

She judged the stranger in the Record Office to be some ten years older than herself, perhaps in her fifties. Her hair was a striking dark brunette, carefully curled. The glossy red lipstick matched the silk scarf at the neck of her expensive-looking brown suit. The immaculate get-up made Suzie feel scruffy. She was aware that her flat pumps were scuffed, that the currently fashionable 'natural' look perhaps needed a little assistance by the time you had teenage children, and that there was a moth hole in her printed cotton skirt which she had hoped no one would notice.

She was a little relieved when the American woman disarranged her hair by running a red-nailed hand through it.

'You know, I've been going crazy, staring at this for the longest time, and I still can't make sense of it. I think it says "a base child". Would you know what that is?'

Suzie opened her mouth to answer and shut it quickly. Like every keen family history researcher, she had been itching to share her expertise with a newcomer. Not only did she have years of experience to draw on, but she knew this county and its resources intimately. All her father's family came from here, back, in some cases, to Norman times and almost certainly to Saxon.

But this question threw her on her guard. Of course she knew what a 'base child' was. She had them on her own family tree. A colourful human story, from one point of view, though annoying because you would usually never find out who the father was. But she hesitated to say the word to a woman she had only just met, from another culture.

The woman was talking on across her silence. 'I know "base" means "low". Does that mean he was a younger son? Or were these guys on the wrong side of the tracks, socially?'

Suzie played for time. 'Would you mind if I had a look?'

'Be my guest.' The woman shifted her bulk from the seat.

Suzie peered at the screen. She read aloud. '*Seventeen thirty-nine. Was baptized Adam, son of Johan Clayson. A base child. Third of August.*'

'Excuse me. Did you say *Joan* Clayson? That's John, surely. Look. There's an h.'

'No. Johan. With an a after the h. It's a variant of Joan. J. O. A. N. You get all sorts of spellings. Joane with an e at the end. Jone – like that, but without the a. Johan, with an h. Even Jane. They're all the same name, really. You sometimes get different spellings for the same woman.'

'But it has to be a man. Look at the rest of the page. It only gives the child's father. Or . . . maybe Adam's father died and this is a posthumous child. Is that what you're saying?'

'I'm afraid not. It tells you here why they haven't named the father. It's what you were asking me about. A "base child". It means Johan Clayson wasn't married to Adam's father.'

Even without looking round she felt the tension of the silence. Then the electricity exploded in a thunderous cry.

'You're telling me he was a *bastard*?'

Suzie swivelled the chair. The woman's face had turned almost as scarlet as her scarf. Behind tortoiseshell glasses her brown eyes flashed.

'That's a preposterous suggestion! Is this the way you folk usually insult someone new to your country?'

It was not the reaction Suzie had expected. Shock, maybe. People reacted differently to the discovery of illegitimacy in their ancestry. For some, the more colourful the story, the better. For others, it brought an obscure sense of shame, something that could not easily be shared with the rest of the family.

She had not thought that anger would be directed at her personally.

Then she saw the teardrop quivering in the corner of the woman's eye.

It was shock, not anger.

Suzie stood up and put a hand on her arm. 'I'm sorry. I can see it's not what you were hoping for. That's the thing about family history. We never know where it's going to lead us. Look, there's a coffee machine outside. Why don't we take a break, and you can tell me more about your Clayson family. From the sound of your accent, I guess you've come a long way on this trail.'

The woman dabbed at her eye with a tissue, careful even now to avoid smudging her mascara. 'Gee, I'm so ashamed. I don't know what got into me to speak to you like that. Prudence Clayson. And yes, I've come all the way from Pennsylvania, USA.'

'I'm Suzie Fewings. I'm sorry if I was the bearer of bad tidings. But really, it's not unusual. I've got several of them on my own family tree. Most people have. Why don't we have that coffee, and I can tell you more about them, and about being an unmarried mother in the eighteenth century. I guess your Johan had a lot harder time than she would have now.'

Prudence Clayson sniffed. A quiver ran through her large form. Then she pulled herself together. The red lips smiled bravely. 'Thank you, Suzie. That sure would be nice. I'm feeling a bit disorientated right now. I came looking for something so different.'

'I'm always being surprised,' Suzie said. 'That's what I love about family history.'

They sat in the sunlit social area. Suzie tried not to feel embarrassed by the face Prudence Clayson made when she tasted the coffee in her polystyrene cup.

She chatted away, to put the American at her ease. 'Honestly, it happens all the time. I've got some odder cases than yours. There was little William Eastcott. His mother Susan actually was married, but only a month before William was born. And the parson entered his christening in the baptismal register under his mother's maiden name. Any child born within two months of the marriage was deemed to be illegitimate. There's no mention of his father. It makes you wonder whether her husband Thomas Lee really was little William's father, or whether he was bribed to marry Susan Eastcott at the last minute and save them being a burden on the poor rate.'

She saw that Prudence's hands were still unsteady as she sipped her coffee. She dredged her memory for more stories. 'And then there was Elizabeth Radford. She came from a good family. Her father was a wealthy tanner. She bore one child out of wedlock. But that wasn't the end of it. Her father died, and only a month afterwards, she married Thomas Dimont. Her second child was born three months later.

'It's wonderful what you can tease out, just by comparing dates and putting two and two together. My guess is that Elizabeth's father wouldn't let her marry Thomas, even when she got pregnant the first time. Thomas was a Dissenter, a Presbyterian. Maybe her father refused to let her marry someone he thought was next door to a heathen. But love triumphed in the end. They had a string of children baptized at the Presbyterian chapel.

'So you see, I know you weren't expecting your search to turn out this way, but really, it's not unusual.'

Prudence's face brightened a little. 'My Adam was a Presbyterian. I guess that's why he left your England for the New World.'

'Good for him. Of course, not all my family scandals turned out that well. The most colourful one was Charlotte Downs, from my mother's family in the south-east. She bore three illegitimate children, two years apart. She never married. I went to a meeting of the Family History Society where they had a talk about illegitimacy. The speaker told us that means she was probably a prostitute. Not a bit like your Johan.'

Prudence's face registered renewed shock. She put down her coffee cup and shook her head slowly. 'You sound so cheerful about it. Almost like you think it's fun. Call me naive, but I really didn't think I'd find anything like this in my own family. Just the opposite. We're really proud in the Clayson family that we're descended from the old settlers way back in 1767. That's the oldest record I've found of the name in Pennsylvania. Adam Clayson, timber merchant in the settlement of Come-to-Good.'

'What a lovely name.'

'So you see, when I found out he was supposed to have come from these parts, I couldn't wait to find out more about him. A God-fearing Dissenter. Puritan stock. Somebody my children could really look up to. And now this. I guess I had the wrong idea about how straight-laced your Dissenters were.'

Suzie let the silence linger before she said gently, 'But he *was* all that, wasn't he? If you've got the record of his life? If he founded that chapel at Come-to-Good? Just because he was born on the wrong side of the blanket, it's not his fault. It may not have been Johan's fault, either. We just don't know. She might have been a servant at the big house and her employer, or his son, took advantage of her. It happened a lot, and the girl usually got thrown out of her job, to add insult to injury. And if you look at the baptismal registers, the first child was often born less than nine months from the wedding. It was quite normal for the young people to sleep together and only get married when the girl had proved she could bear children. Maybe Johan's boyfriend let her down. Married someone else. Or died.'

'You're trying to make me feel better, aren't you? But it still hurts.'

Suzie looked at Prudence reflectively. She was finding it easier to empathize with the pregnant Johan than with this degree of prudish shock. But the woman was out of her element, in a foreign country. She had travelled across the Atlantic with high hopes of a very different outcome. She deserved some sympathy. 'Are you staying in this area? Is your husband with you?'

'I'm a widow. Since last year.'

'I'm sorry.'

Tears were threatening behind the glasses again. 'He left me comfortable. I thought I'd use a little of the money to take myself over here and see what I could find out. I'm staying at the Angel Hotel.'

'So it's your husband's family you're researching? The Claysons.'

'That's right. Well, I guess mine sort of links up, if you go far enough back. We've got some Claysons too. I wanted to tell my children where they came from. And my husband's folks. It was to be sort of my present to them, in his memory.'

'I see. So *that* was why you were so shocked.'

'Not much of a present, is it?'

'You don't know. It could be. If we knew more about Johan and Adam. How he got from here to there. That's something to be proud of, isn't it?'

'I guess you could look at it like that.'

Suzie levered herself forward on her chair arm with a sudden impulse. 'I tell you what. You don't want to go back to the hotel and eat on your own after this, do you? Why not come back to my place for a meal? You can tell me more about your Adam, and I may be able to come up with ideas of how you could find more about your Claysons in England. Have you tried the Overseers of the Poor?'

Prudence Clayson shook her head in incomprehension.

'Right.' Suzie stood up. 'We're going to look into this, you and I. With any luck, I'm going to send you back with a story you really will want to tell your children. How are you on walking?'

The woman looked down at her medium-heeled court shoes. 'OK, I guess.'

'It's about twenty minutes from here.'

They climbed the hill above the Record Office to the ridge that overlooked the city centre. The square towers of the cathedral came into view, the metallic glint of the river, with moorland rising beyond.

As they walked down the last slope towards Suzie's road she glanced at the stranger beside her. Had she been rash in inviting her home? She realized how little she knew about Prudence Clayson. Just that she was a widow from Pennsylvania and that, way back in the eighteenth century, her ancestor had given birth to a bastard child.

Suzie pushed open the door to the wide hall of their house. She turned to invite Prudence inside. Their entry was interrupted by a commotion above them.

A teenage girl, in grey-and-white school uniform, came almost tumbling down the stairs. Her figure might be described as curvaceous. Long, waving brown hair fell about her shoulders, half obscuring her face.

Suzie saw her flushed cheeks as she hurried past, her brown eyes very bright. 'S–sorry, Mrs Fewings,' she stammered. 'Got to dash. They'll be expecting me at home.'

'That's all right, Tamara.' Suzie held the door open for her. 'You're welcome any time.'

The hall fell still again. Suzie looked up to the head of the stairs. But no one else appeared.

'One of your daughter's friends, I guess,' Prudence said.

'That's right. Tamara Gamble. She and Millie have been practically inseparable since primary school.'

Again, that questioning look at the landing, but Millie's bedroom door stayed firmly shut.

TWO

Suzie had hoped to leave her visitor in the sitting room, while she rummaged in the kitchen to see how the evening meal she had planned for three could be stretched to four. She was unsettled when Prudence rose from the sofa to follow her. She didn't like people talking to her while she cooked. It was too easy to get distracted and miss a vital ingredient or let something burn.

Prudence's large presence seemed to fill the kitchen. Suzie felt under scrutiny.

'Wouldn't you like to sit in the conservatory?'

The cushioned cane chairs she indicated gave a view of the banks of herbaceous borders that Nick had so lovingly planted. The dahlias were a feast for the eyes. You could just about carry on a conversation with someone in the kitchen from there.

The woman didn't budge. 'You have family?'

'Two. Tom's just finished A-levels. That's the exam before

university. He's away at the moment, camping in France with
friends. Millie—'

'I'm here.'

Both women turned. It was still a shock to Suzie's heart to
see her fourteen-year-old daughter. Two weeks ago, Millie had
gone off to the hairdresser's, her pale, sharp face hung about
with lank mousey-fair hair. Until then, Suzie had tried to resist
the smugness which told her that other people compared Millie
unfavourably with her still-pretty mother, whose soft brown
curls framed a rosy face almost unlined by approaching middle
age.

Millie had come back, unannounced, with bleached white-
blonde hair cropped close to her head. Her face, which had
seemed angular and sallow, now looked suddenly elfin.

Suzie had grown used to comforting Millie with the promise
that one day she would become not just a pretty, but a strik-
ingly beautiful woman. Unexpectedly, that day had arrived.

Her heart turned over again as Millie stood in the kitchen
doorway. She was seeing not just a new haircut, but a new
person. A stranger she felt she did not know.

'My!' Prudence exclaimed. 'Aren't you a beauty!'

The flush that just tinged Millie's cheekbones might have
been panic, as much as pleasure. There was something very
vulnerably in that pointed face.

'This is Prudence Clayson,' Suzie said hastily. 'From
Pennsylvania. We met in the Record Office. I've invited her
to tea.'

'Family history. Don't tell me.' Millie addressed a cool,
unsmiling stare at the American. 'She never talks about
anything else.'

'Well, yes,' Prudence agreed. 'It kind of gets you like that.
I guess I bore the pants off my family.'

Millie threw her mother a look. An appeal Suzie couldn't
interpret.

'I'm going to change,' Millie said. She swung round. A slim
girl in a grey school skirt and a white blouse. From the back
view, still a child.

But she's not, Suzie thought. Not any longer.

Prudence spoke what Suzie already knew. 'That's a stunner

you've got yourself there. Guess she'll keep you awake a few nights, worrying about a girl with looks like that.'

It was, Suzie supposed, a compliment. But one it was hard to thank her for.

Nick's intensely blue eyes laughed at Suzie over the remains of the meal.

'I'll see to the dishes. I can tell you two are itching to get to that computer and see what your detective work can turn up.'

Suzie leaned across and kissed him. She ruffled his black hair. 'Thanks. Prudence is only here for a few days. I want to find out as much as I can on the Internet, before we go back to the Record Office tomorrow to dig out documents – if there are any.'

'Really,' Prudence protested. 'You're being way too generous. You must have things of your own to do. I can't drag you back there for a second day. Just point me in the right direction and I'll go by myself.'

'Don't try and stop her,' Millie said. 'There's nothing she'd like better than an excuse to spend even more time on her old records. She lives in the past. The present might not be happening, as far as she's concerned.' For all the lightness of her words, she did not lift her eyes from the table as she spoke.

'That's not fair,' Suzie countered. 'I spend every morning in the charity office.' But she knew by the warmth in her cheeks that Millie's barb was uncomfortably near the truth.

'Just enjoy it.' Nick got to his feet and shepherded them out of the kitchen.

Suzie fetched her laptop. The two women settled themselves on the sitting room sofa.

'Let's see what we can find on Access to Archives.' Suzie opened up her search engine and selected the National Archives website from her favourites. 'Adam Clayson isn't exactly a common name. Not like John Hill. If there's anything on him, we should hit it pretty quickly.'

'You're going to have to show me how to do this. I'm pretty new to this Internet search business. I mostly leave it to my son.'

'Access to Archives is great. It has summaries of vast

numbers of documents from all over the country. I've found wonderful stuff there. You just type in the name you want, the date range, and the region. In our case, that's the "South West". Here we go. Search for Adam Cla*son. 1700–1800. South West Region. I put in the asterisk to cover variant spellings. Click. And . . .'

'You've hit it.' Prudence leaned forward in excitement.

'Yes. We can rule out the entries for Clarkson. You get more than you want when you put in an asterisk. But we've scored three records for Clayson. Adam Clayson, lease of a property in Corley called Hole, 1716. If your Adam was born in 1739, that's too early for him. Might be an ancestor, though. Even Johan's father, perhaps. That would explain why she called the baby Adam. We could follow that up. The next one looks like the counterpart of the same lease. But, hey, look at this one. Corley parish, Adam Clayson, apprenticed to Thomas Sandford for Norworthy, 1747. Is Corley the parish where you found his baptism?'

'Yes, it was.'

'Then that's got to be him, hasn't it? Eight years old and put out to work on Thomas Sandford's farm by the Overseers of the Poor. We could get the actual indenture out at the Record Office tomorrow, if you like.'

She turned to share her enthusiasm with Prudence. The other woman was silent. Her eyes, Suzie realized, had misted over as she stared through tortoiseshell-framed glasses at the computer. She reached out a hand and touched the screen gently, almost reverently.

'That's him? Our Adam?'

'Almost certainly. It's the right name, the right parish.'

'Where's this Norworthy?'

'It'll be the name of the farm where he was put to work. Most poor children were apprenticed for farm or housework. It tended to be the better-off children who learned a craft. Thomas Sandford may not even have wanted a farm boy, but parishioners had to take their turn. It kept the children in food and lodging and clothes till they were twenty-one or – if they were a girl – got married.'

'Could I go there? This Norworthy place?'

'You certainly could. *We* could. I'll get the map out. With luck, it'll still be on the Ordnance Survey.' She went to the bookshelf where the OS maps were shelved and ran her finger along the names. 'Here we are.' She spread out the map on a table. 'There's Corley. It's quite a small village. A cluster of houses and farms around the church. That looks like the village green. Now, if we trawl around it . . .'

Her eyes had caught the name she was looking for. She waited a few seconds more without saying anything and was rewarded with Prudence's cry of delight.

'Norworthy! Do you see it? Up there, between those rivers.'

'Well done. So it *is* still there. We can go and check it out.'

'I just don't know how to thank you. I'm mortified when I think how I bawled you out.'

'Don't worry. Millie's right. I'm really enjoying myself.'

She copied details and reference numbers for the apprenticeship, and the older lease as well, and printed them out. She shuffled the papers together with satisfaction. 'There. We've got plenty to go on now. I work in the mornings, but I can meet you tomorrow after lunch. We'll take the bus out to the Record Office from the city centre. Unless –' a disappointing possibility occurred to her – 'you want to get over there first thing in the morning and follow this up yourself. They open at ten.'

'No.' Prudence eased her comfortable bulk from the sofa. 'I feel I'm in safe hands with you. I wouldn't know how to go about it. And I'm dying to take a tour round your cathedral. But cancel that "after lunch". Lunch is on me. Come over to the Angel Hotel. You know it?'

'On the cathedral close. Of course. I'd love to.'

'My pleasure. Now, where do I get a bus into town?'

'You don't.' Nick had appeared in the hall when he heard their voices. 'I'll run you back.'

'You folks have been so good to me.'

'Our pleasure. See you tomorrow, then,' Suzie told her.

An hour later, she walked upstairs with a glow of enjoyment. Normally, she allowed herself one afternoon a week to follow up her family history research in the Record Office or the Local Studies Library. Not counting, of course, the hours she spent on her computer, or the Saturday expeditions to

parishes where her ancestors had lived. Prudence had given
her the perfect excuse to drop other boring things, like housework, and spend more time doing what she liked best. And
there was the extra satisfaction that she was genuinely able to
help Prudence. In a very short time she had warmed to this
plump widow, who so wanted to take back a story she could
be proud to tell her children. Suzie would help her do that.

Her children.

Suzie paused, her hand tightening on the banister. She had
a sudden picture of Millie, arrested in the kitchen doorway as
she saw Prudence. Those grey eyes turned to her mother in
what looked like a mute appeal, before she turned and went
upstairs.

Those words of reproach. *'The present might not be
happening, for all she's concerned.'*

She crossed the landing swiftly to Millie's room. She opened
the door softly.

Millie lay in bed. The blonde head looked tiny, shorn of its
familiar long hair. She seemed to be sleeping.

'Millie?' Suzie whispered, just in case.

The eyelashes, dark with mascara, did not stir. Whatever
Millie might have wanted to tell her must remain unsaid.

With a feeling of unexplained guilt, Suzie closed the door
softly.

THREE

Millie was running a comb through her short hair. Her
back view signalled haste, tension. It wasn't a good
time. She should be on her way to school by now.
Suzie tried to catch her eye in the mirror, unsuccessfully.

'Is everything all right, love?'

'Yes. Fine.' The words came fast, like gunfire.

Suzie sat down on the bed. 'You'd tell me if there was a
problem, wouldn't you?'

Millie whirled from the stool, grabbing jacket and

school-bag. 'Do you mind? That's my homework you're sitting on.'

She was gone, like a rush of wind down the stairs.

Suzie sighed and stood up. The house had fallen silent. Husband off to work in his architect's office, daughter to school. Soon it would be time to catch her own bus into town, to spend the morning in the charity office. Most of all, she missed Tom. So like his father, with his waving black hair and bright-blue eyes, but with a laughter and energy that was his alone. Millie melted invisibly into corners. Tom's presence, when he was at home, seemed to light up the whole house.

She remembered that it was dustbin collection early tomorrow. She just had time to empty the waste-paper baskets. She retrieved Millie's from under her desk and carried it downstairs with the others from the bedrooms.

She paused at the kitchen door. Since the council had got into its recycling stride, it was necessary to sort the contents. The foil from pills and cellophane packaging into the black bin for landfill; paper into the green one.

It wasn't really prying, was it? She had to check what was in Millie's basket.

Crumpled sheets. She smoothed them out. They seemed to be history notes. Tom would just have tossed his in the basket, for anyone to read. Millie's tightly-balled pages had a more secretive look. Silly, really. What would she have to hide? Suzie scolded herself for being unnecessarily suspicious.

A crisp packet. The wrapper from a CD. All normal.

She was tempted to empty the contents of the bathroom bin straight into landfill. But there were the odd bits of paper and cardboard her conscience told her she ought to remove.

A till receipt. Crumpled, like the sheets from Millie's bedroom. Suzie always dropped her own receipts in just as they were.

She teased it open. From the chemist's, of course. The next words burned themselves on to her brain.

Pregnancy Testing Kit.

She searched frantically through the rest of the bin. There was nothing there. No packaging. No used equipment. She hurried back to Millie's bedroom. If she hadn't used it yet,

where would it be? Her flustered fingers fumbled through the
contents of drawers. She peered under the bed. Stood on a
chair to check the top of the wardrobe.

Nothing.

She searched the dustbins outside.

Millie had bought a pregnancy testing kit, but there was no
sign that she had used it, or of the result.

Suzie did not enjoy her fillet of sole in the Angel's restaurant
overlooking the cathedral as much as she should have done.
It was far superior to the sandwich she would normally have
had before setting off to the Record Office. Her mind was still
racing, but it was three hours yet before Millie would be home.

She came back to the present to find Prudence ordering two
cokes.

'Not for me,' she said hastily. 'I'll just have water.'

What she really wanted was a glass of dry white wine, to
still the waves of panic which were washing over her. But she
didn't know Prudence well enough yet to judge whether
ordering wine would be a faux pas.

'Make that one coke, one mineral water.'

'Just tap water for me, please.' Better not to get into what
she thought of the bottled water industry. She forced a smile
for her generous host. 'How was your morning in the
cathedral?'

She let Prudence's enthusiasm wash over her.

It was a relief to enter the hushed atmosphere of the Record
Office's search room. There was a twinge of guilt as she felt
the tension of the present begin to slip from her. There was
nothing she could do about Millie yet. She could allow herself
to sink into the comforting arms of the eighteenth century and
the search for Prudence's family.

In the panic of this morning, she had forgotten to bring with
her the reference numbers of the documents they needed. Her
mind was beginning to steady as she located them on the
catalogue. She took the file number of the apprenticeship to
the help desk.

The archivist who took it was unfamiliar to her. He didn't
give her the helpful smile she was expecting.

'This is an apprenticeship indenture.'

'Yes. I found it on A2A.'

'You do know that all the relevant details are on the catalogue? You won't find anything more in the original.'

She felt the coldness of rejection. 'I just thought . . . My friend here is over from the States. She won't have seen one before. And there's nothing quite like seeing the actual document, the signatures . . .'

'Where are you sitting?' Still no smile.

'Table twenty.'

He turned away without a word.

Prudence's lipsticked mouth made a comic parody of reprimand. 'Guess I'm making a nuisance of myself.'

'Don't mind him. They try to avoid getting out the originals as much as they can. With so many of us doing family history now, the documents would fall apart if they didn't digitize things. But you ought to see the real thing at least once.'

She couldn't deny the thrill when the document arrived and they unrolled the long scroll.

Prudence began to read it aloud, her voice shaking slightly. '*This Indenture made the Twelfth Day of April in the Twentieth Year of the Reign of our Sovereign Lord George the Second by the Grace of God, of Great Britain, France, and Ireland King, Defender of the Faith, and so forth.* My, doesn't that sound grand!'

'And here's the names of the churchwardens and the Overseers of the Poor.'

But Prudence was running ahead of her. '*Do put and place Adam Clayson, a poor Child of the said Parish, Apprentice to Thomas Sandford of Norworthy in the same Parish to dwell and serve from the Day of the Date of these Presents, until the said Apprentice shall accomplish his full Age of Twenty four Years.* You said twenty-one.'

'I thought it was. But listen to this: *During all which term, the said Apprentice his said Master faithfully shall serve in all lawful Business according to his Power, Wit, and Ability; and honestly, orderly, and obediently in all Things demean and behave himself towards his said Master and all his during the said Term.*'

'And what does old Thomas Sandford get to do in return?'
Prudence was warming to the search. '*Find, provide and allow
unto the said Apprentice, meet, competent, and sufficient Meat,
Drink, and Apparel, Lodging, Washing, and all other Things
necessary and fit for an Apprentice. And also shall and will
so provide for the said Apprentice, that he be not any way a
Charge to the said Parish.*'

'And at the end of his time he gets: *double Apparel of all
sorts, good and new, (that is to say) a good new Suit for the
Holy-days, and another for the Working-days.*'

The two women looked at each other. Tears were glistening
in Prudence's eyes again. Suzie felt the sudden bond between
them. In the formal words of the indenture, little Adam Clayson
came alive.

'Eight years old,' Prudence said wonderingly. 'And Adam
was twenty-four when he finished. I'm going to have to do
some math to work out how old he was when he took the ship
for Pennsylvania.'

The links in the chain, both sides of the Atlantic, were
coming together.

'That guy was sure wrong, telling us we wouldn't learn
anything more from the original. It's all coming to life. Poor
little soul. I hope this Thomas Sandford was good to him.'

'Maybe it was there he learned about trees and timber,'
Suzie said. 'Wasn't that his trade in Come-to-Good?'

'It certainly was. And a fine success he made of it.'

Suzie forbore to remind her how far he had come from his
origins as a 'base child'. Instead, she followed up the lease
for that older Adam Clayson. 'We need to find where Hole
was. It wasn't on my modern Ordnance Survey map. Let's see
if they have older ones.'

'That's a strange name, Hole.'

'It's quite a common name in these parts. It means a hollow.'

They tracked the farm down on a nineteenth-century map,
and Suzie photographed it for Prudence.

They checked the catalogue numbers for the documents on
Hole.

'Look. The lease was for that older Adam's life, and then
the life of a Robert Clayson; I suppose that would be his son.'

'Nothing about our Johan?'

'No. It's a bit unusual. Leases were usually for three lives. But we can look up her baptism in the parish register. I'm sure she must be related to them.'

After a run of success, they drew their first blank. The register only went back ten years before the younger Adam's baptism. Too late for Johan's.

'Does that mean we'll never know?'

'Not necessarily. She could have been born in another parish. And there may be something else on her. We didn't run her name through A2A, did we? Only Adam's.'

'Can we go back to your place and do that?'

'No need. They've got computers here.'

She booked a machine and typed in the search criteria. 'Jo*n* Cla*son' and the date range. 'I've put in the asterisks again to allow for all the possible spellings of Johan as well as Clayson.'

There were sixteen catalogue entries. Most of them were for John Clarkson, or from places unlikely to be related to Prudence's family. There was nothing about Johan Clayson.

'Women don't show up as often as men. But somebody else is lucky.' Suzie pointed to the twelfth entry.

Prudence followed her pointing finger and read aloud from the screen. '*Maintenance of Joane Clarkson's male bastard.* What does that mean?'

'It's a bastardy bond. Joane Clarkson swore before a magistrate who her baby's father was. What a pity we haven't got one for your . . .'

Her voice trailed away into silence as the memory of Millie rushed back to her.

FOUR

'That's too bad. Hey, is something wrong?'

Suzie checked her watch in alarm. She was already rising to her feet. 'I'm sorry. I hadn't noticed the time. I need to get home.'

'Sure. Your daughter. I've been taking up too much of your time. Forgive me. I just got carried away.'

'You stay on.' Suzie smiled gamely. 'You can ask them to get that lease out for you. It might be the family of your Adam.'

'No. We'll leave that for another day – if you're still interested. I've had a great time.' Her amiable eyes grew shrewd. 'There's something wrong, isn't there? You were kind of freaked out over lunch. I shouldn't have kept you.'

'No. I enjoyed it. Really. But I have to go. Will you come back to eat with us?'

Prudence's eyes measured her. 'You've been a great hostess. But I guess there are times when a family needs to be on its own. It's OK. You don't have to tell me what's wrong. Besides, I met up with some fellow Americans at the hotel. They've invited me to the theatre with them this evening. I'll call us a taxi.'

'No. It's all right. I usually walk home from here.'

'And I could go back on the bus, like we came here. But, hey, I'm not short of money. I'm taking you home my way.'

For all her protests, Suzie was grateful to let herself be shepherded into a taxi and whirled home in a matter of minutes. She felt the warmth of the American's sympathy as they parted. Prudence had seen more from behind those tortoiseshell glasses than Suzie had realized.

The house was quiet as she hurried up the drive. But then, Millie had never been a noisy child. If Tom had been home, the walls would be thrumming with music. What Millie played was discreetly masked by headphones.

She unlocked the door. 'Millie?'

The silence lengthened. Then, a distant: 'Hi.'

Suzie climbed the stairs. She was frightened. The receipt she held in her hand could change all their lives.

She stood in the bedroom doorway. The blonde stranger who was her daughter lay on the bed, headphones on. It was hard to tell whether her expression was hostile, or just wary.

Suzie held out the paper. 'We need to talk. Would you take those headphones off?'

She sat down on the bed, not sure if she was invading

Millie's personal space, but wanting to convey sympathy, not condemnation.

'I found this when I was sorting out the bathroom rubbish. Is it yours?' A foolish question. Who else's could it be?

Millie looked at the receipt. Her expression did not change. 'Yes.'

'Have you . . . Have you used it?'

'No.'

'But you thought . . . You must have thought you might be . . . Do you still think . . .?'

Millie's grey eyes gave nothing away. 'So what if I am? Is it any business of yours?'

'Of course it is! How can you say that? You're my daughter, for heaven's sake!'

'Parents don't own their daughter's bodies.'

'We're not just talking about bodies. Though that's important, too. It's people. You. You're only fourteen, love. That's not nearly old enough to be a mother. What were you thinking of? It shouldn't even be a possibility. You've got your life in front of you. And if there's a baby, you'll have responsibilities to it. We all will. We're its grandparents. And who's its father?'

'Supposing there is a baby.'

'Well, *is* there? Why buy a pregnancy kit if you're not intending to use it? And you must have done *something* to make you believe it could happen.'

It was hard to keep her voice from rising. She hadn't meant to sound censorious. She tried to move closer, but saw Millie shrink back. Her voice softened. 'Look, love. I know this must have been a shock to you. But you need to tell us what happened. We can share it. You may have been foolish, but no one's going to condemn you. We'll stand by you and give you all the help we can. But you say you haven't used the kit. Does that mean your period came? It's all right now?'

'And it would be all right if there weren't a baby, would it?'

'Well, no. I suppose it wouldn't. You're under age. Whoever it is shouldn't be having sex with a fourteen-year-old. Is he someone we know? I didn't think you were dating anyone.'

'I'm not.'

'Then . . .' Worse thoughts were chasing through her brain. 'Did someone force you? Were you . . .'

'Raped?'

Suzie stared at her daughter, at that small, unreadable face. 'Millie. I need to know.'

'You seem to be able to imagine plenty, without my help.'

'Millie! You have to say.'

'No, I don't.'

Suzie knew when she was defeated. She got to her feet. 'I hoped we could talk about this together. Sort something out. Decide how to break it to your father. He's going to be really upset.'

'Fathers and daughters. Like we're their property.'

'How can you say that? Nick thinks the world of you.'

'And you don't?'

'That's not what I meant. You're twisting everything I say.'

'Or maybe *you* are.'

Suzie gazed at those grey eyes in silence. Then she turned for the door and made her way downstairs. She felt sick. Her attempts to help had ended in confusing failure.

Was she a grandmother, or not?

'I'll kill him.' Nick's black hair hung over his brow like a thundercloud. 'Whoever did this, I'll kill him.'

They were standing in the garden, screened from the house by a blue-flowering bush of ceanothus. Suzie crumbled petals between her fingers. 'Why won't she say? Whether she's pregnant or not?'

'It shouldn't even be a possibility, at her age.' His deep-blue eyes shot up to hers almost accusingly. 'You'd know, wouldn't you? You're a woman. There must be . . . evidence.'

'I don't mark off the contents of the bathroom bin on the calendar. It was only today. Just happening to read that receipt. Are you going to talk to her?'

'Too right, I am. I'll get his name out of her, if I have to screw her neck to do it.'

'I don't think coming down hard will help. You know Millie.'

For all his violent words, still Nick stood irresolute. She felt a rush of compassion. This language wasn't like him.

She laid a hand on his arm, feeling the warm skin. 'Look. I'm as angry as you are. But we have to stand by her. Whether she's pregnant or not, something has happened we can't change. We have to love her through it.'

'You think I don't love her? That's what hurts so much. My little Millie.'

Yes, she thought, with a flash of knowledge. Your little daughter. Millie was right. Fathers can't help thinking they own their daughters. And now, Millie belongs to another man. Or at least a boy. That hurts you.

'What I don't understand,' she said, 'is who it could be. She doesn't have a boyfriend. She said as much herself. I find it hard to believe she'd risk a one-night stand with a boy she didn't care much about. Unless . . . Do you think it was someone older? Someone who could exert some kind of hold over her? One of Tom's friends from the sixth form, perhaps. She might have had a crush on him. Or even . . .'

'A teacher?'

They contemplated the dark possibilities.

Nick drew himself together. 'I'm going to see her.'

'Tread carefully. I tried, and I got nowhere. I can't understand why she wouldn't tell me. What it was she wasn't telling me.'

'I'm not sure we ever have understood Millie.'

She watched his tall form walk towards the house and found herself praying he'd find the right words. It was just possible Millie might soften for her father in a way she hadn't done for Suzie.

As he disappeared indoors, Prudence's words came back to her. '*Guess she'll keep you awake a few nights, worrying about a girl who looks like that.*' She hadn't expected it to happen so soon.

She sat on the bench by the pond, watching the sinuous flickering of goldfish and shubunkins. Their underwater dance did not relax her as it usually did.

When Nick came out of the patio doors, she read the answer in his hunched shoulders and the hands clenched at his sides. She wanted to hug him, but she was afraid to touch his tensely-strung body.

'She's still not saying, is she?'

'No. But I'll find out who he is, if it's the last thing I do.'

FIVE

I t had been Suzie who insisted they continue the search together. On the phone, she had brushed aside Prudence's tactful assurance that she'd be fine researching on her own. 'You're right. We do have a problem at home. But I'll be better filling up the time while Millie's at school than brooding. And we never did get to see that lease for Hole.'

'You don't think we'll get that snooty guy who thinks we should stick to microfiche?'

'If they've filmed it, fair enough. But I doubt it. We won't know if there's more information to find than there was on the abstract until we see the document.'

Now, as they walked down the road from the bus stop through the industrial estate to the Record Office, Suzie felt the motherly sympathy of the woman beside her. She was grateful that Prudence hadn't prodded her to say what was troubling her, yet had made it clear she knew something was wrong and was concerned for her new friend.

'It's Millie,' Suzie said suddenly, before she could stop herself. 'She bought a pregnancy testing kit, but she won't say why. She says she hasn't used it. And she won't even tell us whether she's pregnant or not. Or who the boy was . . . Or the man.'

It made her feel sick to put that dark thought into words.

'So you guessed she'd been having sex?'

'Well, of course! Why else would she buy that kit? That's what makes it even more upsetting. We didn't even know she had a boyfriend.'

'And does she?'

'She says no.'

Prudence was silent for a long while. She looked at Suzie thoughtfully as they walked. As they turned into the car park she said, 'You're right. There's something going on here. You want to pray about it?'

Suzie was startled. No one had ever made that sort of suggestion to her, outside a church. 'Well, I . . .'

'Sure. I forgot. You folks over here are more buttoned-up about that sort of thing. Don't worry. I can do it for both of us.' She sat down on a bench outside the entrance and folded her hands in her lap.

After a hesitation, Suzie joined her.

Prudence's tone was almost chatty. 'Dear Lord, it seems like Millie's gotten herself into some kind of situation that could lead to trouble. Love her like the Father you are. Guide her in the way she needs to go. And put your arms round Suzie here, and Nick, because they're hurting for her. Give them the wisdom to say and do the right things for Millie.'

Suzie murmured an embarrassed Amen.

Yet, as she got to her feet, she felt more supported. Someone was helping her shoulder this burden. She couldn't imagine any of her other friends making the same response, if she'd shared this confidence over a cup of coffee. But perhaps she underestimated them.

Inside, they walked up to the enquiry desk. They exchanged conspiratorial glances. Would they really be allowed to see the original lease?

This time, it was a younger woman who turned a helpful smile on them. Once again, Suzie passed across the paper on which she had written the catalogue number of the document.

'Yes, it pays to see the original, if you can,' the archivist agreed. 'We can't possibly put all the details in the catalogue. That's just there to whet your appetite.'

The lease, when it appeared, had been folded for so many years that the ink was wearing away on the creases. The archivist brought them weights to hold it flat.

The handwriting was hard to read. Not only because of the fading ink, but because the letters were formed in an archaic way.

Suzie frowned as she laboured to decipher it. 'I can get the first bit. *Sir George Salter of Haddon, knight.* He must be the landowner. *And Adam Clayson, husbandman.* Well, we already knew their names from the abstract on the website.

'What's this "husbandman"? Does it mean he's got a wife?'

'No, that was the name for a small-scale farmer, less than a yeoman. The lease is for *Hole, in the parish of Corley* and the . . . I think that says *watercourse* . . . running through it. Well, that makes sense. If Hole is in a hollow, there'd be a stream down there, wouldn't there?'

She tried to read on, but it became more difficult, now that she had got past the words she already knew from the Internet catalogue. 'Something something *lawful English money*, something *two capons* – that's castrated cocks – *or three shillings.* So he had alternative ways of paying his rent.'

She was suddenly desperate to get home. 'Look, why don't I ask if I can photocopy it? Then we can wrestle with it in our own time.'

'Sure.'

If Prudence was disappointed, she was trying not to show it.

Nick slid an arm round Suzie's waist as she chopped parsley in the kitchen.

'I see you're still doing your bit for Anglo-American relations.'

Suzie pushed back a lock of falling hair. 'I'm not sure I really meant to. I invited her back here for a meal, but I didn't think she'd come. I didn't press her. I was just being polite. I'd already told her why I was upset about Millie. I thought she'd do the tactful thing and leave us to ourselves tonight.'

'At least Millie's not giving her the cold shoulder.'

Beyond the kitchen, they could see Prudence and Millie in the conservatory. Prudence had her back to them. Only her brown waves showed over the back of the sofa. They had a sideways view of Millie, curled in a cane armchair. The television was on, but the two were talking. At least, Millie occasionally turned her head and said something, if briefly.

'I'm glad she's making an effort to be polite.'

'Millie cares about people, you know.'

'I was afraid . . . I didn't tell you. Prudence suggested we pray about Millie. On a bench, outside the Record Office. Wouldn't it be too embarrassing if she tried to pray over Millie?'

'Who knows?' Nick's grin warmed his eyes for her. 'You never know with Millie. She might not be as negative about it as you might think.'

'That's what gets to me. I don't really know my own daughter, do I?' She chopped fiercely. 'You might like to tell them that tea will be ready in five minutes.'

'Will do.'

They made polite conversation over the meal. Prudence told them something more of how she had traced Adam Clayson back to south-west England.

'It was my son who got me on to it. He's the one who's hot on this computer business. He looked up the passenger lists of immigrant ships in the eighteenth century and got no joy. But then he hit pay dirt. He tracked down a crew list. And there Adam was.'

'A crew list? So he worked his passage to the New World? Good for him.'

'Adam Clayson, twenty-five, from Corley, Devonshire England. Deckhand on the good ship *Tavy* out of Plymouth, 1764. And the date checked out with the immigrant records.'

'So he jumped ship when he got to America?'

Prudence bridled. 'He'd worked his passage. So, of course, when I knew what part of this country he'd come from, I had to come and investigate.'

'We can take you to Corley on Saturday,' Nick volunteered.

'No, really. You guys have lives of your own to lead. I can get the bus.'

'I'm not sure that you can. Buses can be pretty thin on the ground to some of those outlying villages.'

'I thought you Brits had got this public transport thing wrapped up?'

'The lure of the motor car has got to us, too. Buses are an endangered species.'

'And we usually do go out on Saturdays on the family history trail,' Suzie added. 'We'd love to take you.' She did her best to sound enthusiastic. Her eyes kept straying to Millie, across the table. Millie's eyes were on her plate. She was not joining in the conversation. Would it be right to leave her on her own, the way things were?

Common sense told her that Millie probably wouldn't stay home, anyway. She'd be off into town with Tamara, looking round the shops, having milkshakes with their friends.

As soon as the meal was over, Millie slipped away to do homework.

Prudence settled back in her chair and gave them a broad beam. 'Guess I can set your minds at rest about a couple of things. Your Millie's not expecting. And she's never been with a boy.'

Suzie felt her jaw drop. 'She *told* you?'

'Maybe it's easier that I'm not family. I didn't come carrying any baggage. But I did let her know that her folks are concerned. Talked to her like a Dutch uncle. Can I say that? I've never heard of a Dutch aunt.'

'And she didn't clam up? Or stalk out of the room?'

'I guess she's feeling just a little bit guilty. Glad to have someone put the record straight.'

'But why wouldn't she tell *me*?' Suzie protested.

Prudence's colour heightened. 'You guys have been so kind to me, I feel bad about saying this. But I kinda think Millie wasn't levelling with you because she was angry.'

'Angry? About what?

'We–ell, maybe you jumped to conclusions about what was going on. I mean, it's only natural. Most parents would.'

'What was I supposed to think? What else could it have been?'

'Did you ever think that kit might be for somebody else?'

Suzie and Nick stared at her. A sudden joy was flaring in Suzie's heart.

'*Not* Millie?'

'I think she was kinda hurt that you thought it might be her. Plus, she's protecting someone.'

Nick buried his head in his hands. 'I thought . . . I was afraid . . . someone had forced her into it. Someone older.'

'It's not that bad,' Prudence consoled him. 'Or not for Millie. But I'd better warn you. Millie wasn't telling me everything by a long shot. There's something else going on here. And whatever it is, it's got Millie scared.'

SIX

When Nick had taken Prudence back to her hotel, he and Suzie found Millie back downstairs in the conservatory. They took up positions on either side of her. It felt, Suzie realized, shamefaced, as if they were guilty teenagers and she the adult.

'I'm sorry,' Suzie began. 'I jumped to conclusions. I shouldn't have done.'

'It's because we love you so much,' Nick put in. 'We couldn't bear to think someone had taken advantage of you. We weren't blaming you.'

Millie eyed them warily. She said nothing.

'Look, you can tell us,' Suzie said. 'Whatever it is that's going on, you can share it with us. I know it's confidential. But you can trust us. We won't spread it all over the place. Only, it's a big responsibility for a fourteen-year-old to carry alone. We can help.'

'Is that what you think? Adults know best? Trust me, I'm a parent?'

Suzie felt the shock of rejection and knew that Nick shared it.

'It's what parents are for, Millie,' Nick said.

'*Some* parents.'

'Not us?'

Suzie watched the struggle in Millie's face. She decided to move forward. 'It's one of your friends, isn't it? You were trying to help her. Not *Tamara*?'

She saw the sudden flinch in Millie's expression and knew that she had struck home. She had a sudden vision of Tamara rushing past her in the hall, the first time she had brought Prudence back with her. The flushed face, half hidden behind a fall of brown hair. The over-brightness of her eyes. '*Is* she pregnant?'

No answer.

'It is her, isn't it? Two days ago, when I brought Prudence home, Tamara ran past us. I was too taken up with Prudence to wonder why. Is this what she was upset about?'

Millie's mouth set in an obstinate line.

'Millie, if Tamara's expecting a baby, she needs help. Does her mother know?'

Millie stared at her knees. At last she burst out, 'It's not that simple. You just don't know!'

Suzie racked her mind, trying to think what could be so bad that Tamara couldn't confess it to her mother. A boy they wouldn't approve of, for some reason? Race, religion? Though their daughters had been friends for years, she didn't know Lisa Gamble all that well. They met at school functions and on the occasional Sundays Suzie went to the Methodist church. Sometimes they rang each other to decide who should transport the girls. She seemed a sympathetic enough woman. It would be a difficult confession for any schoolgirl, but sooner or later it had to be done. Most mothers stood by their daughters, in the end.

And Tamara's father? A flash of memory pulled her up short. Tamara's parents had been separated for years. But recently . . .

'Her mother's remarried, hasn't she? There's a stepfather. I think I met him at the last parents' evening.'

A large imposing man, she recalled. Rather pompous.

Millie's grey eyes flew to her, suddenly alert. 'At Easter.' There was an edge to her voice.

'Is he the problem? Would he come down hard on Tamara?'

Millie's already slight form seemed to shrink into itself. 'It's Tamara's secret,' she muttered. 'It's not my business to tell anyone else.'

'Millie.' Nick's voice hardened, in spite of his efforts. 'Tamara's under age. If she doesn't want to have the baby, it should be easy to arrange an abortion. Nobody wants to saddle her with a problem she can't cope with. But it has to be done properly, safely. People have to know.'

Again, that grey stare which gave so little away. 'Do they? Have to know?'

'Well –' Suzie backtracked for Nick – 'there are confidential advice services. I don't know if it covers an actual abortion, for someone her age. But, at the most, I think it would only be Tamara's mother who needs to know.'

A little voice in her head wondered about that. Would they have to get hold of her birth father, too, for permission? She decided not to ask aloud.

A slight relief softened Millie's features. Then she seemed to recollect something that made her defensive again. 'What if she doesn't want an abortion? What if she doesn't believe in killing babies?'

'That's her decision. If it were you, we'd support you, whatever you chose. Wouldn't Tamara's family?'

Millie got up and stalked to the door. 'You don't know anything, do you?'

Next day, Millie went off to school in an obstinate silence.

Suzie was still uneasy, though her worst fears had been allayed. There was that puzzling observation Prudence had made, that Millie had seemed scared about her friend's situation. Shock, pity, concern, these would be normal reactions. But fear?

She tried to shake off these troubling thoughts and invited Prudence to abandon the Record Office for an afternoon raiding the Fewings' bookshelves. Soon the table, and even the carpet, were covered with open volumes and maps. It gave Suzie a feeling of smug satisfaction to be able to turn up an eighteenth-century engraving of Corley, the village where Johan had given birth to Adam. It showed an expansive green, bordered by a rather grand house, with humbler cottages crouching in the corners. In front of the wrought-iron gates of the house paraded a gentleman and lady. The latter wore the spreading skirts of the period and carried a parasol. A little boy in a smart suit bowled a hoop, and a tiny dog frolicked beside him.

'That's not really how I thought an English village would look,' Prudence commented.

'These would be the local gentry. Possibly real ones, who lived in that big house – they may have commissioned the picture. Or just ones the artist made up. It doesn't look as though he thought real country folk like the Claysons were interesting.'

'Do we know what that big house is?'

Suzie thumbed through a book which gave a potted description of all the parishes in the county. 'Corley. Let's see. Yes, here it is. *Corley Barton was built in 1721, beside the village green. It replaced a medieval farmhouse. It was the home of the Marsdon family until the mid-twentieth century.* They must have been the local squirearchy. Country gentlemen.'

'Squirearchy. I love that word. You said something, the first time I met you, about those kind of folks. How they might take advantage of a servant girl.'

'Oh, yes. It's a common story, I'm afraid. Droit de seigneur, sort of. The lord's right. Difficult for a girl to say no to her employer. Or his son. You can't usually tell. If the girl got pregnant, the decent ones might pay a local man to marry her. Give him a sum of money to set the couple up. If the first baby was born rather soon, you wouldn't know if the father was her husband or somebody else who'd rather not be named. Well, there was probably gossip in the village, but it doesn't go down in the parish register. Other times, I'm afraid, they just threw the girl out.'

'And you think that happened to my Johan?'

'Who knows? It's a possibility. It would explain why she didn't get a husband.'

There were even darker scenarios. Should she mention to Prudence the possibility of incest? There were families then, as now, who nursed uncomfortable secrets. If Johan *had* grown up in Hole, hidden away in its hollow, who knows what might have gone on in secret? If the girl's mother was still living, when Johan fell pregnant, she would probably have put it out that the child was her own.

Suzie decided not to venture down that road. Prudence had gamely come to terms with bastardy. Incest might be a step too far.

She switched the subject of paternity hurriedly. 'People were pretty two-faced about sex before marriage in those days. If the girl managed to tie the knot soon enough, nobody thought anything of it. In fact, there's a local tradition that says if the banns of a marriage aren't called on three consecutive Sundays, the child in the bride's womb will be born deformed or mentally handicapped. You see? It was almost taken for granted that the bride would be pregnant at the altar. But if she failed to secure a husband in time, it was a very different story.'

She rummaged among the books to find one on church life in the eighteenth century. 'Listen to this: *Seventh of March 1761. Anne Luscombe of the said parish shall present herself before the Minister in the Parish Church aforesaid upon the next Sunday forenoon, with her head bare and a white sheet upon her, her feet and legs bare, and shall openly confess and acknowledge that she has born a male child unlawfully begotten on her and shall show hearty repentance, beseeching God to forgive her and the Minister and People to pray for her amendment.*

'Sometimes they had to do penance in the church porch, but it might be in the marketplace. Either way, she'd have to walk there wrapped in her sheet, with everyone watching and half the men hoping it would slip off.'

Prudence's jaw dropped. 'They really did that? Drove a half-naked woman through the streets?'

'It was the law. I don't know how long they went on doing it. I thought morals were pretty slack by the late eighteenth century. I expect it varied from parish to parish. I bet there were some that didn't have the heart for it. But I can imagine others where the rector and churchwardens were upright Puritans, who carried out the ruling to the letter.'

'Well, darn it. Haven't they read what our Lord said when they brought him a woman caught in adultery? "He that is without sin among you, let him first cast a stone at her." And they all went sneaking away.'

'In my experience, people who are keen on punishment use the bible selectively. They choose the verses that suit them, and they're usually not from the Gospels.'

Prudence was quiet for a moment. 'I guess I was raised a lot like that. Like we were the holy people, and everybody else was a sinner. Poor Johan. Do you think they did that to her?'

Suzie shrugged. 'There might be a record about her in the

archdeaconry court, but it's a long shot. But they'll certainly have put pressure on her to name the baby's father. It was important, you see, to get money out of him, so that the child didn't become a burden on the Poor Rate.'

Prudence stared at the engraving of the village. 'It's the queerest feeling. I could be looking at the man who fathered Adam. Another ancestor of our Claysons. But I can't tell. There he is, with his smart clothes, his fine house, and his wife on his arm. And no one knows what he might have done to Johan.'

'Or it may just have been a tumble in the hay with one of the grooms.'

Prudence let out a long sigh. 'Don't you just wish you could have a spyglass into the past? Not just questions with no answers.' Then she brightened. 'Say, do you think I could take copies of some of these? That map? The engraving? The book which says what they did to unmarried mothers?'

'No problem. I'll scan them on my printer.'

For a while they were busy collecting all the relevant material and copying it.

'Gee, I'm so grateful. I guess I'll be buying another suitcase by the time I'm finished.'

'There's something else you could try. There are lots of one-name societies researching a particular surname. There might be one for the Claysons.'

But Prudence stood staring down at the page in her hand, with the punishment for a single mother. 'This friend of Millie's. Tamara. There's something there Millie's not telling us. Is there anything we should know about the girl? What would her family do if they found she was pregnant?'

'I know her mother, sort of. She seems normal. I'd expect her to react the same way I would, if it were Millie. I'd be upset at first – well, I was, wasn't I? – but I'd stand by her, whether she wanted to keep it or not.'

'And the girl's father?'

'Her real father left them several years ago. He's a famous children's author. He writes under the name of Reynard Woodman. Rather attractive, actually. I liked him, or I did until he walked out on Lisa. I think he's somewhere in the Midlands now. Tamara goes to stay with him occasionally.'

'But you said there was a stepfather.'

'Her mother remarried this Easter. Leonard Dawson's a headmaster. Not at Millie's school, but another one in the city. I only know him by sight. But he has the reputation of being a bit of a disciplinarian.'

'So? Do you think Tamara might be scared to tell him?'

'You mean she'd be afraid of the modern equivalent of flogging her naked through the streets?'

'Well, maybe not in public. I guess he might think it would reflect badly on him, if he's been laying down the law to his students. That could be pretty important to a disciplinarian. Can't even control his own stepdaughter.'

A shiver ran through Suzie. 'Control. That's a nasty word. She's not his possession.'

'Oh, believe me, I know plenty of men who would tell you a daughter is.'

SEVEN

Millie stood in the garden with her back to the house, tearing a glossy camellia leaf to shreds. Suzie watched her. Presently, she got up and strolled towards her daughter. For a while she stood, saying nothing.

At last Millie broke the silence. 'Tamara wasn't in school today.'

'Is that important? If she's expecting a baby, there are probably some mornings when she doesn't feel very well.'

'I rang her mobile, but it was switched off. So I tried ringing her house after school. And when her mother answered, it was, like, weird. As though she didn't know Tamara wasn't at school. She covered up pretty quick. Said she'd been feeling off colour. But she didn't sound *normal*. Like she was making it up off the top of her head. And, like . . . frightened. Said I shouldn't come round to the house because Tamara was in bed.'

'Frightened?'

'She was talking too fast and jumpy.'

'And you didn't go round?'

'I keep trying her mobile. Nothing. I've texted her, like, dozens of times. She never answers.'

'If her mother says she's in bed, Tamara may have switched her phone off to get some sleep.'

'If she wasn't well, she'd have rung me.'

'Women do funny things when they're pregnant. It takes people different ways. I'm sure she'll be in touch tomorrow.'

'She was scared.'

'Yes, you said that. Talking strangely on the phone.'

'Not her mother. *Tamara*. Ever since she told me she thought she was pregnant. I mean, we'd all be scared, if it was us. But she wasn't just scared about having the baby. It was as though there was something else she didn't dare tell anybody. Not even me.'

Suzie ran over all the nightmare scenarios she and Nick had envisaged when they thought it was Millie who was pregnant. 'Is it something to do with the father? Not a schoolboy date? Something worse than that?'

'I've no idea. She wouldn't tell me *anything*.'

Suzie watched a goldfish shimmer under the lily leaves of the pond. 'Her stepfather. He's a bit of a disciplinarian, isn't he? At least, he is at school, by all accounts. Is she frightened about what he'll do when he finds out?'

'I don't know. He does give me the shudders, though. He's so big and jolly when you first meet him, but he can change like *that –*' she snapped her fingers – 'if he thinks you've said something out of turn.'

'So Tamara would have reason to be scared of him.'

'Yes. But it's not just that. She'd tell me if it was. So it's got to be something worse.'

'Don't let your imagination run away with you, love. Tamara's got herself into a mess, but it's not the end of the world. It happens to other girls. It changes their lives, of course, but they adjust.'

'Why doesn't she *ring* me? Or text?'

'Stop worrying. She'll be at school tomorrow, or she'll get in touch.'

'There's something else about her stepfather—' Millie stopped.

'What?'

'Oh, nothing.'

But Suzie had seen the shudder that ran through her daughter before she turned and walked into the house.

But Tamara was not in school the next day. Millie called round at her house, but there was no answer. Her mobile stayed silent.

'Are you sure you'll be all right?' Suzie asked on Saturday. 'I don't like leaving you alone. I could stay home.'

'No, you couldn't. You said you'd take Pru to Corley.'

'She'll understand.'

'I can go into town and meet the rest of the crowd. I don't need you to hold my hand.'

But her face had a hurt, disappointed look.

Suzie hesitated. But she had promised Prudence.

When Nick and Suzie picked Prudence up at the Angel in the cathedral close, her face was bright with expectation.

Suzie insisted that she take the front seat. 'I can enjoy the views any day.'

'I'm so excited,' Prudence said as she climbed into the car. 'This is going to be such a wonderful day out before I have to leave you folks.'

'You're going?' Suzie exclaimed. 'But I thought your plane wasn't till next week?'

'Yes. I was planning on asking what church you folks go to, and if I could come along with you tomorrow. But I've had a phone call. You remember you put me on to that one-name group? The Clayson Society? Well, guess what? When I let them know who I was, and that I was looking for Adam Clayson in the 1700s, this William Clayson got in touch with me. Would you know, he's invited me to visit with him and his wife for a couple of days. Says he has a mountain of stuff on the early family. My Claysons of Corley might be related to them. Well, I couldn't pass up an opportunity like that, could I? Plus, they'll take me to Stratford-upon-Avon while I'm there. He sounded so helpful. So I'm off tomorrow. But I'll be back, and I plan to take you folks for a fine dinner before I go home. As a thank you.'

'That's terrific. He's probably got all sorts of stuff on the family that we haven't.'

'But he hasn't got all this. This is the real thing. Sort of my home country now.' She gestured at the view through the windscreen.

They were leaving the city. The wooded valleys and climbing fields of the countryside were opening up before them. Hay-making was in full swing. Green fields were turning golden where the crop had been shorn and the bales lay ready for the tractor.

They treated Prudence to lunch at one of their favourite country pubs and enjoyed her delight at the date of 1654 carved in the oak beam over the enormous fireplace.

'I'm so jealous of you, living amongst all this,' Prudence said.

'The irony is that Nick designs houses for the future. Lovely ones. Eco-friendly and energy-efficient.'

Nick grinned modestly. 'I can still learn a lot from the people who built these. They understood their environment and their local materials better than most of us do nowadays. I'd be proud if anything I designed was still being lived in four centuries later.'

After lunch they plunged deeper into the narrow lanes, then tackled a winding hill. Nick eased the car round the last bend. Cob-walled farmhouses turned their curved backs to the road, sheltering age-old farmyards. Chimneys rose high above thatch.

'This is just so English,' breathed Prudence. 'How old would these be? A couple of hundred years?'

'Maybe five, six hundred.' Suzie was enjoying her friend's amazement.

'You're kidding me?' Prudence peered through the car windows as though she couldn't get enough of the rural scenery. 'Not just one building, like that pub where we ate. A whole village.'

One last corner brought them to the village green. At the
far end, the church's crenellated tower reared up. Cobbled
paths led to rows of cottages, with rainbow-flowered gardens.
And there was the big house, hardly changed from the
eighteenth-century engraving. Corley Barton.

'This would have been quite new when Adam was born.
Seventeen twenty-one, wasn't it?' Suzie asked. 'Personally,
I'd rather have had the medieval farmhouse. Look at that stone
barn. That's probably older than the house. Stop here, Nick.'

Prudence was out of the car and taking photographs, almost
before Nick had parked. Then she stood, looking up at the
house, with its Georgian frontage. 'So that's where she
worked?'

Suzie joined her. 'It was just a guess. We don't know that.
They'll have employed a lot of local girls as servants. Johan
might have been one of them.'

Prudence looked around her at the quiet green, the cobbled
paths. 'However it happened, I can't help seeing her, going
about this village. People turning a cold shoulder to her,
gossiping behind her back.'

Nick spoke from behind them. 'Didn't you say something
about your ancestor being a Dissenter?'

'Presbyterian. Right from the time he landed in Pennsylvania.
That's what I've read.'

'Then, if your Johan was one, maybe her boyfriend's family
didn't approve. Wouldn't let them marry.'

'Yes, but . . .' Prudence turned to Suzie. 'She got Adam
baptized in the parish church. And you told me about unmarried mothers having to confess there.'

'Until the Toleration Act of 1689, everyone had to go to
the parish church on Sunday. You got fined if you didn't. Even
when the Dissenters were allowed to build their own chapels
they had to leave the door open during services, to make
sure they weren't preaching treason. In Johan's time, a lot of
people still thought you had to be baptized in the church to
get the right of settlement in that parish. Being legally settled
in the parish entitled you to poor relief. You'd got your proof
of entitlement in the baptismal register. She may have been
taking out insurance. So she could have been a Dissenter and

still used the parish church. Besides, I couldn't find any evidence of a Presbyterian chapel in Corley. She'd have had to go to South Farwood, the nearest market town. Maybe she had friends who would support her there . . . Or perhaps not.'

'You think the Presbyterians might have thrown her out when they heard about her baby?' Nick asked.

'Lord knows,' Prudence sighed. 'Folk can be mighty cruel.'

Suzie was tempted to remind Prudence of her own shock at the discovery of illegitimacy in her family, but decided it was better to say nothing. Prudence had come a long way on her voyage of discovery. Johan Clayson had become real to her.

As they turned away from the house, Suzie's thoughts flew back to another girl, another shock of illegitimacy. A strait-laced stepfather.

Tamara was only fourteen.

'I wonder how old Johan was when she fell pregnant?' she wondered aloud.

They moved up the yew-lined path into the church. Suzie's eyes were drawn to the finely carved screen at the head of the nave. But Prudence had halted in the porch.

'So she might have knelt here.' Her voice was tinged with incredulity. 'Bare-legged, in just a sheet. With the whole congregation staring at her. And had to confess her sin and ask forgiveness, before they'd let her in. And do you know, a week ago, I might have approved of that. Now, it makes my stomach curl up to think of it.'

They stood silent. But Suzie was thinking of that other girl. Tamara. Too frightened to tell even Millie exactly what had happened. The stern stepfather, who might indeed flog her, if only in private.

She shook the black thought away and said more brightly, 'Look. That's the font where Adam was baptized.'

Nick called from the aisle where he was examining the carved bench-ends. 'It says in the booklet that the font's probably Norman.'

'What does that mean?' Prudence asked.

'Eleventh or twelfth century.'

Prudence's mouth fell open. All she could manage was:

'My!' But soon she was busy with her camera. 'Is it all right to take photographs inside the church?'

'Go ahead. There's nothing that says you can't.'

When she had finished, Suzie asked, 'Well, have you seen enough here?'

'It's been wonderful. I just love to touch these things. Feel the connection.'

It was Nick who suggested: 'Do you still want to find that farm? The one where your Adam was apprenticed?'

'Could we do that?' Prudence's face was filled with delight again.

'Of course we can. Got the map, Suzie?'

'Yes. It's up on the high ground, on the edge of the parish.' She swivelled round to survey the surrounding hills. 'That one, I think, with the patch of moorland on top.'

'Right. All aboard.'

Suzie leaned forward from the back seat. 'You have to imagine Adam walking this way into the village every Sunday. I imagine all the farm apprentices were expected to attend the service. The farmer's family might have travelled in a cart or trap, or ridden horses. But my bet is that the apprentices had to walk.'

It was a long winding road down over a narrow ford and then up the steep hillside. At first the view was barred by high earth banks with hedges growing on top.

'Looks like they dug this road deep down. Why would they do that?'

'I don't suppose they did. It's just the passage of feet and hooves over all those centuries, carving it down into the earth.'

Prudence shook her head. 'It's hard to imagine all those hundreds of years, all those travellers. And you folks live with this history all around you.'

'Yes. It didn't really come home to me until I started tracing my family history. It makes me look at everything from a different angle. Through other people's eyes. I've found out so much about English history I didn't know before. Not just the kings and battles, but the way ordinary people lived.'

'I guess I ought to be getting out and walking this. Just to live my Adam's experience.'

'Hang on,' said Nick. 'We'll let you out at the top.'

They crossed a cattle grid, and suddenly the day was bright around them. Hedged fields gave way to open moorland of bracken and heather on the top of the hill.

Suzie consulted the map. 'Norworthy's not far from here. I make it the second farm after this cattle grid.'

Nick drove on, skirting sheep that sauntered across the road.

'This is Lower Norworthy.' Suzie read the board at a farm gate. 'Next one.'

The road climbed gently now. The moors and valleys of half the county lay spread around them. Another farm came into view.

Nick stopped the car. 'This seems to be it.'

The three of them got out. Suzie felt the moorland breeze fresh on her face. The song of a skylark cascaded down to them.

'Will you look at that,' Prudence marvelled. 'How did they ever shift such stones?'

The barn nearest to the road was made of massive granite blocks. No two were the same size, yet they bonded together to make an outbuilding strong enough to resist any onslaughts of weather or time.

'Who knows?' said Suzie. 'That hayloft may be where the apprentices slept.'

The yard was quiet.

'Do you think we dare knock on the door and ask if we can see inside that farmhouse?'

'You could try,' said Nick. 'But from the look of it, it's been rebuilt since Adam was here in the eighteenth century. Not much of its history left, I'm afraid.'

Prudence still looked wistful.

'No harm in trying,' Suzie said.

They walked up to the closed front door. Nick was right. The house was modern. It did not have that thrill of history that the stone barn did.

Suzie rang the bell. There was no answer.

'Gone into town for their Saturday shopping,' Nick said. 'Probably get their food from Sainsbury's nowadays.'

Prudence swivelled slowly, taking in the surroundings. She got out her camera again. 'The house may be new, but I guess that view hasn't changed in centuries.' She snapped the four quarters of the horizon, then the stonework of the barn.

'You're right about the weight,' Nick commented. 'It gives me a hernia just looking at some of those stones.'

Prudence shook herself slowly, as if trying to convince herself of the reality of what she saw. She reached out a hand and stroked the masonry. 'I'm here. Where he lived. From the time he was eight years old.'

Suzie wandered back to the gate, giving the other woman space to form her memories.

Nick looked at his watch. 'Did you want to go to this other place?'

'Hole? It's the other side of the parish. Time's getting on. And I haven't found a definite link to it with this younger Adam. Maybe we should leave it for today. Pru's in England for another week. If we find her family did live at Hole, I can bring her back when she returns from William Clayson's.'

Nick drove them home.

Millie met them, pale and distraught. 'I've been over to her house. She's not there. Her mother's trying to cover up, but I don't think she knows where Tamara is either.'

EIGHT

Nick put his arm around Millie's shoulders. 'Hey, love. Calm down. There's bound to be a simple explanation.'

'I know this is the twenty-first century,' Suzie said. 'But they may be hoping to keep her pregnancy a secret. With her stepfather being a headmaster of the old type, he'll be thinking of his own reputation, as well as hers. I expect they've sent Tamara off for a few days to have it dealt with.'

'You mean an abortion? But she wouldn't. She absolutely *wouldn't*. We talked about it. She thinks it's a real person, from the moment it was conceived. She said she felt responsible for it. Another life.'

'She's only fourteen. Her parents may have talked her into it.'

'Her mother wouldn't.'

'But her stepfather might. By all accounts, he's a pretty forceful man. She may not have been able to say no to him.'

'Pig! He couldn't make her, could he? He was there all the time I was talking to her mother, sort of glaring at me. At her too.'

'Legally, no, he couldn't,' Nick said. 'But emotional pressure can be hard to stand up to, particularly from a man used to exercising authority on teenage girls.'

An idea was growing in Suzie's mind. 'Unless . . .' She hesitated. She didn't want to worry Millie further. 'If Tamara couldn't say no to him, might she have run away?'

All this time, Prudence had been hanging back tactfully, pretending to admire the roses along the garden path. Now she spoke for the first time. 'I'm with Tamara about the baby. In my book, it's a living human being. Question is, if Tamara's run off to save it, where would she run to?'

The adults were looking at Millie for help.

She thought for a while, then shook her head. 'I can't think of anywhere. No one she talked about. Unless . . . What about her father? Her real father? You remember? Reynard Woodman.'

'Kevin Gamble, before he got famous.' Suzie's eyes questioned the others. 'Would she?'

Nick shrugged. 'Depends how close they still are.'

'She used to go and see him once a fortnight,' Millie said. 'Stay the weekend. Lucky cow. Reynard's a bundle of fun. Or he used to be when he lived here.'

'Don't they get on now?'

'She doesn't talk about him so much nowadays. If I ask her how her weekend was, she just sort of mutters "OK". There was one good day. Her aunt came over and took her shopping in Selfridges in Birmingham. But otherwise . . . I told her, if she doesn't want to go any more, she could let me go instead. I think he's fabulous.'

'Why don't you try ringing his number? In case she *has* gone there.'

Millie's eyes widened. 'Could I? Speak to Reynard

Woodman?' Her tone was almost reverential. 'Thanks, Mum! That's a brilliant idea.' She made for the door. 'But I still can't understand why she's not answering her mobile. It's been switched off since I saw her on Wednesday. She hasn't even sent me a single text.'

'That's little short of a miracle,' said Nick. 'Girls your age seem to spend half their lives on the phone. Sounds as if she's going out of her way not to let anyone find out where she is.'

'Why would she do that to *me*?'

'I don't know, love,' Suzie comforted her. 'She's obviously upset. She probably wants some time to think about it. Sort herself out. She'll get back to you, I'm sure.'

'That man!' Millie burst out. 'Mr bloody Dawson. All the time I was talking to Tamara's mum he was there. Sort of looming in the background. He didn't say anything. But he was listening, all right. And Mrs Dawson kept looking round at him. Like she was frightened of saying the wrong thing.'

'Hey, easy,' Nick put in. 'If Tamara's really disappeared, they'll be as upset as you are. I don't think I'd be behaving normally if you'd done a runner.'

'If she has run away,' Prudence said, 'they'd tell your police, wouldn't they? Don't you worry, Millie. They'll find her.'

'Well, I'm going to ring Reynard Woodman,' Millie said. 'What's the number for directory enquiries?'

They were drinking tea on the patio when she came back. Millie's face was sullen, her anger only just under control.

'He's ex-directory.' She threw herself into an empty chair. 'Why? It's like walking up to a building and all the doors slam shut and the lights go out. *Why* can't I reach her?'

'I'm sure her mother will have his number.'

'I don't fancy going back to ask. She practically threw me off the doorstep last time. I mean, I've been going round to Tamara's house for years, and it was like she didn't want to know me.'

'Look, he's bound to have a website. That'll tell us how to contact him. I'll check it out.'

She went to her computer and came back a few minutes later. 'No joy, I'm afraid. It says all enquiries should be addressed to his agent. I'm not sure this is the sort of query I'd want to do through a third party.'

'What's her father like?' Prudence asked.

'Do you mean her real father?' Suzie asked. 'Kevin?'

'Mum!' Millie protested. 'Nobody else calls him Kevin Gamble any more. He's Reynard Woodman now. Author of *The Secret of Humbledown Forest*, and all that series.'

Prudence looked apologetically blank. 'I'm sorry?'

'He writes children's books. I used to love them when I was younger. I've still got most of them up in my bedroom.'

'That's right,' Suzie remembered. 'You were so excited the day you found out. You came running home from primary school to tell me you'd sat next to this new girl and she was his daughter. But that was years ago. He'd only just written his first best-seller. We still knew him as Kevin Gamble round here. How long is it since he and Tamara's mother broke up?'

'Four years. It was our last year at Blackhills, before we went to Bishop's High. I stopped reading his books for a bit, because I was mad at him for leaving them.'

'It's a shame. I remember him as a fun person. He used to take you with them for picnics and boating on the river.'

'Well, he doesn't seem much fun now. He doesn't want anybody to know his phone number.'

'He's famous. I expect he'd get inundated with calls if he was in the directory. Maybe we can find out how to reach him through his agent. It'll have to be after the weekend.'

'If he's ex-directory, I don't suppose they're giving his phone number away.' She flounced from her chair, every line of her slender body evincing frustration.

Prudence followed her with her eyes. Then she bent to retrieve her handbag. 'You guys have been so wonderful to me. I can't tell you how much I've enjoyed today. Just to stand in the actual village where Adam and Johan lived. To touch the font where he was baptized. It's a dark story in places, but at least it's real to me now.'

'Won't you stay for supper?'

'No, thank you kindly. I've imposed myself enough on you. And Millie's not going to want to make polite conversation with someone she still hardly knows, the way she's feeling.

Besides, I have to be off early in the morning. I'll be back in two or three days. And I sure hope Millie will have found her friend before that.'

Suzie and Nick were startled awake as the bedroom door flew open. Nick snapped on the light.

Millie hurled herself at the bed, a spectral figure in a long white T-shirt. Her face was haggard. 'Mum, Dad! I've just thought of something terrible. I've been lying awake, worrying about Tamara, and I suddenly thought: what if she's dead?'

Nick swung his legs out of bed and put an arm around her. 'Millie. Don't give yourself nightmares. Tamara's got herself into trouble. It's been a shock for her. But she'll get over it. It's not like a Dickens novel, where young women throw themselves into the Thames. This is the twenty-first century. It happens all the time.'

'I don't mean *she'd* do it. Commit suicide. She wouldn't. But what if someone wanted to shut her up? What if whoever it was doesn't want her to tell whose baby it is?'

Suzie hoisted herself up and draped a fold of duvet around Millie's cold legs. 'You've been giving yourself nightmares. It can't be as bad as all that. It's easy to start imagining terrible things in the middle of the night. Then it all seems silly next morning. You'll see.'

'But why won't she answer her phone? It's been *days*. She'd have rung me if she'd gone away. I know she would. And her mum couldn't wait to get me out of the house. She was scared of Mr Dawson. I'm sure she was. What if *he's* done it? And Mrs Gamble – I mean Mrs Dawson – knows about it and is terrified of him?'

'Millie, Millie!' Nick laughed. 'This is real life, not a TV thriller. Mr Dawson may have his reasons for wanting to hush up her under-age pregnancy. But I hardly think he'd resort to murder.'

'Not even if he was the father of her baby?'

A stillness fell over the bedroom.

At last Suzie found her voice. 'Do you have any reason to think that?'

Millie bent her head and began to twist the edge of the

duvet. 'She wouldn't tell me who the father was. And I'm her best friend. If it had been one of the boys at school, I'd have known about it. I'm sure I would. And she was really scared of her stepfather.' She raised an accusing face to them. 'Don't tell me it doesn't happen. Men having it off with their daughters. You see it on the news. He doesn't have to shut her up in a cellar for it to happen.'

'Like those servant girls in the big house,' Suzie murmured. 'They can't say no to him.'

'And he wouldn't just be ashamed if *that* got out,' Nick mused. 'A headmaster? It would finish him. He'd not only go to prison; he'd never work with children again.' Then he shook himself and stood up. 'Look, Mum's right. It's the middle of the night. Everything seems much worse then. We're letting our imaginations run away with us. You go and snuggle under the bedclothes, and I'm going to make you a hot chocolate. Deal?'

'Deal,' said Millie, reluctantly. 'But you're not denying it could have happened?'

'There's a one in a million chance, yes. But there'll be a simpler explanation. You'll see.'

When they were gone, Suzie lay in bed, wondering. Nick was right. It was a preposterous suggestion. But what if they'd been too concerned with the guilty young woman in church, naked except for a white sheet, before the accusing eyes of the congregation? *She* had to confess the name of the father.

They hadn't thought enough about the man involved.

NINE

Suzie came to with the realization that it was Sunday. She stretched luxuriously and settled herself more comfortably on the pillows. No rush to get to the office, after seeing Millie off to school. No need to head for the supermarket for her Saturday shopping. It was a day to do what she liked.

She was just snuggling down again when a memory struck

her. Prudence Clayson saying: 'I was planning on asking what church you folks go to.' That confident assumption which contained no 'if'.

Suzie would have answered, with only a twinge of guilt: *Springbrook Methodist*. It was partly true. Christmas, Easter, occasional Sundays in-between. But it was not a regular habit. She would, of course, have offered to take Prudence there this morning. But Prudence was off to the Midlands instead.

She was halfway out of bed before she realized she had made a decision.

Nick propped himself up on an elbow. 'You're up bright and early.'

'Prudence said something about going to church with us this morning. I know she's gone off to make contact with her living Claysons instead, but I thought I might go.'

She walked over to the window and pulled the curtains back. A fine drizzle was beading the summer foliage with moisture. She stood looking out for a while. Then she said, without turning, 'I know Millie gets melodramatic, but this stuff about Tamara. It *is* worrying.'

'And you think praying might help?'

'I don't know if it does, but I feel I need to.'

Nick sat up in bed, only half reluctantly. 'I'll come with you, if you like.'

'You don't have to.'

'It looks like it's raining, anyway. I wouldn't get much done in the garden.'

There was a shyness between them. Neither of them was openly religious. They had taken the children to Sunday School when they were younger, but other things had intervened as Millie and Tom approached their teens. Football leagues, gardening, Suzie writing up the results of family history expeditions the day before, Millie's teenage lethargy. Yet still there was the pull that drew them back from time to time.

Now it seemed more important than usual.

They left Millie in bed.

The doors swung open on a foyer filled with chatter. Coffee cups were being lined up on the counter. Small children dodged around the adults' legs. A mixture of nationalities was streaming towards the worship centre, exchanging greetings as they went.

'Nick, Suzie, good to see you. How are you?'

Alan Taylor, Springbrook's minister, looked younger than his fifty years. His brown eyes glowed with enthusiasm and his broad grin was genuine.

Suzie felt herself enfolded in friendship. The great thing about Springbrook was that nobody censured you for the times you didn't appear. They just seemed really glad when you did. Alan hadn't been there long, but he had lifted the spirits of the place.

'We're fine, thank you.'

It was silly, really, this English habit of insisting that everything was well. But she could hardly have blurted out at the church door: 'I'm worried stiff that Tamara Gamble may be in danger.'

And yet, as Alan Taylor released her hand and turned to greet the next arrivals, something in her wished that she had.

She and Nick found themselves seats towards the back. Suzie let the organ voluntary soothe her worried thoughts. She had been right to come. It would help to get things into perspective. She'd been almost as foolish as Millie, letting lurid imagination run away with her. As Nick kept saying, there would be a simple explanation for Tamara's disappearance and subsequent silence.

She leafed through the service sheet and the week's notices. As she lifted her head she saw a couple moving along the side aisle to seats nearer the front. She stiffened with surprise. Of course, she should have known they would be here.

The woman was small and slender, with short dark hair elegantly arranged across her forehead. The man was large, with a fleshy pink face. Little curls of pale hair covered the back and sides of his head, leaving a bald crown.

She nudged Nick urgently. 'There's Lisa Gamble. Sorry, Dawson. Tamara's mother. And that's Leonard Dawson with her.'

'The dreaded stepfather. I've seen him here before. He looks a decent enough guy. A bit pompous, but amiable.'

'That's not his reputation with his pupils. Tom knows a boy who goes to his school. He says he scares the daylight out of them.'

'Well, at least they don't look as though they're sick with worry because Tamara's missing. Whether she's at home or not, I'd put money on their knowing where she is. I knew Millie had got it all wrong.'

'We can't see their faces from behind.'

'Well, here's your opportunity. You can go and talk to them after the service.'

There was no time for more. The minister announced the first hymn. The congregation rose.

'*O Lord our help in ages past.*'

The old familiar words comforted Suzie. Nick was right. Everything was fine. Well, not everything. Fourteen-year-old Tamara was still pregnant. Unless her stepfather had forced her to do what she didn't want to and get rid of it. How? The black thoughts were crowding back.

She joined in the prayers with more heartfelt intensity than ever before.

The service was over. People were heading for the coffee bar or stopping to talk with friends and welcome newcomers. Suzie saw the Dawsons making straight for the exit. She wriggled past the people between her and the aisle and hurried after them.

'Lisa!'

It was Mr Dawson who turned first. That broad pink face should have looked genial, but, close to, there was something about the smallness of his eyes and the hardness of their look that sent a different message.

Then Tamara's mother turned too. Suzie stopped in shock. It had been a month or two since she had seen the new Mrs Dawson. In that time the other woman seemed to have aged years. Her cheeks were sunken. There were black rings under her eyes. The eyes themselves had a look which Suzie could only describe as haunted.

Suzie struggled to find the words of casual greeting she had been going to say. Instead, she blurted out, without preliminaries, 'I'm sorry to hear Tamara's not well. Millie's been missing her.'

Lisa Dawson's eyes flew to her husband, as if seeking permission to speak. Her voice took on a forced cheerfulness. 'Tamara's fine. Nothing to worry about.'

The imposing figure of Mr Dawson stepped forward, almost shouldering his wife out of the way. A smile Suzie would have described as 'professional' creased his fleshy jowls. His voice was higher than she expected.

'I'm afraid she's been overworking. Girls that age live on their nerves, don't they? We decided she needed a break. Peace and quiet. I'd be grateful if your daughter would leave her alone for a bit. School's not what she needs to be reminded of, just now.'

Nick's voice came from behind Suzie, firm, with a hard edge. 'I should have thought we all need friends, especially when life's not going too well. I'm surprised she didn't tell Millie she was going away.'

The smile vanished. 'Are you trying to teach me my job, Mr . . .?'

'Fewings.'

'And are you a child psychologist? No? I thought not. In case you are unaware of the fact, let me inform you that I have the care of nearly a thousand children. I think my judgement about Tamara's state of mind might be worth something. Now, if you'll excuse us . . .' He took his wife's elbow, forcing her round.

'Give Tamara my love, and Millie's,' Suzie said hastily as they turned away. 'I'm fond of her. Tell her I hope it's . . . I hope everything works out well for her.'

Is it true? And do they know? she thought frantically. Do they know Tamara's pregnant? Has she told them? Or did she just . . . disappear?

Mr Dawson's small eyes stared back at her coldly. 'What could you possibly mean by that, Mrs Fewings?' Before she could answer, he steered his small wife towards the door.

'Well,' said Nick when they had gone. 'Did you see that bruise on her temple under the hair? I may not be a child psychologist, but I can recognize a battered wife when I see one. I'll bet good money she didn't walk into a door.'

Suzie stared back at him, her thoughts churning. Nick had seen more than she had, but Lisa's expression had been enough.

TEN

The drizzle had stopped. Sunshine lit the flower beds with vibrant summer colour. Nick dried the patio chairs, while Millie laid the table outside for lunch.

They were halfway through their lasagne and salad when the conservatory doors burst open. A tall eighteen-year-old erupted on to the patio, glowing with health and laughter and a Mediterranean tan. The waving black hair and deep-blue eyes were the mirror image of Nick's.

'Tom!' Suzie flew from her chair to hug him, ridiculously glad of her son's strong embrace, of his almost mature height. He had only been gone ten days, but she realized suddenly how still and colourless the house had been without him. 'What happened? We weren't expecting you back till Tuesday. But it's lovely to see you.'

'Thunderstorms in the South of France, would you believe? For weeks, we've been sweating in that exam hall in a heatwave, and then we get flooded out of our campsite in the Camargue. There's no justice. Our gear was so sodden, we reckoned we might as well pack up and head back for the Channel ferry. Hi, Dad. Cheers, Millie. How's things?'

Their laughter faded. It had been a casual question, not expecting a serious answer.

'Tamara's missing.' Millie delivered the news with genuine solemnity, but relishing, Suzie sensed, being able to position herself at the centre of the drama, upstaging her elder brother.

'Seriously? Since when?'

'She wasn't at school on Thursday, and nobody's heard from her since.'

'Have they got the police on to it?'

The others exchanged glances. Suzie said carefully, 'It's a bit odd. We're not quite sure about the position. Her parents – well, her mother and stepfather – are acting as though everything's under control. They haven't admitted she's missing. They say she just needs a rest. But they won't let Millie see her, and Tamara isn't answering her phone.'

'She's pregnant,' Millie burst out. 'We're afraid they've sent her away for an abortion. But she doesn't want one. What if she's run away to avoid it and they're afraid to tell anyone?' She clapped her hand over her mouth. 'You're not to say anything about that. It's a secret. Nobody knows but me. At least, not till I told Mum and Dad.'

'Trust me. My lips are sealed.'

'To be honest,' Suzie said, 'we don't even know if she's told her family she's pregnant. She could have run away because she's too scared to face them.'

'Because she's scared of Mr Dawson. Or what if he's the father, and she's terrified of what he'll do?' Millie's face was avid with the darkest possibilities.

'As you can see,' Nick said over Millie's head, 'there's been no shortage of wild theories. All the same . . . We met Mr Dawson this morning, and I can see why Tamara might be afraid of him. He certainly terrorizes his wife.'

'That wouldn't be *the* Mr Dawson, would it? The Head of Briars Hill?'

'That's the one.'

Tom whistled. 'Poor kid. I certainly wouldn't want to come home to him every evening, from what I've heard. But you don't seriously think he'd, well, put her in the club?'

'It happens,' argued Millie. 'Just because he looks respectable. Headmaster, going to church, and all that. You can find paedophiles anywhere. If it had been one of the boys at school, I'd have known they were going together.'

'Mm. You sure? Why don't I ask around? See if any of the gang have heard anything?'

'You mustn't tell them!' Millie cried. 'It's a secret. Tamara wants to keep the baby, but nobody else knows yet.'

Tom grinned, his blue eyes crinkling in the way that made Suzie's heart turn over. 'I'll employ my famous diplomatic skills. Promise. I could make out that I quite fancy her myself. See if there's word of any competition.'

'Would you?' Suzie felt a rush of relief. 'We've all been worrying ourselves silly, thinking up dark scenarios. It's bad enough anyway, because she's under age. But it would be a relief to know it was just a boyfriend, after all. We've been letting ourselves think of things much worse than that.'

'Well, yes. I get your point. Incest's not very pretty, when it's a middle-aged man with a reputation for bullying and a fourteen-year-old kid.'

'We're not kids!' Millie protested.

'Strictly speaking,' Nick said, 'it wouldn't be incest. They're not blood relations. But it would certainly be an abuse of a position of trust and authority. He'd go to prison.'

'I think there are quite a few kids at Briars Hill who wouldn't be too sorry about that. Sorry. That's no help to Tamara, is it? Look, leave it with me. I'll do the rounds this afternoon. Let the world know I'm back. I'll start to put the word out casually and see what I can turn up . . . Hey, that lasagne looks good. Is there any more?'

Suzie was occupied, but in a lazy, Sunday afternoon sort of way. She was skimming fallen petals from the garden pond. Nick, more energetically, was hoeing the first signs of weeds from his cherished flower beds.

Suzie smiled as she netted the white and pink flotsam. It was amazing the difference it made having Tom back. The sun seemed to shine more vividly. The worries of this week shrank. Tom would come back with a simple explanation.

She was aware of movement behind her. She turned to find Millie leading someone across the lawn.

It was Lisa Dawson. Even without her husband, she looked scared.

Nick was right. There was a dark-red bruise behind that fall of hair.

Suzie dropped the net she was using and rubbed her wet hands on her jeans. 'Lisa. How nice to see you.'

It felt the wrong thing to say. There had been that uncomfortable encounter at church this morning. Lisa's husband had closed down the shutters on further contact.

Tamara and Millie were best friends. The families lived only a few streets apart. But Lisa and Suzie only met occasionally. They were not in the habit of visiting each other.

And it was evident that this was no social call. Lisa's face was flushed and her breathing hurried.

'I shouldn't be here. Leonard's playing tennis at the country club. But if he knows I've talked to you, he'll be furious.'

'Sit down.' Suzie steered her towards the garden chairs. 'Millie, get us some drinks, will you? Tea? Coffee? Fruit juice?'

'Oh . . . I don't know . . . Tea?' Lisa looked distracted, as though such a simple question was beyond her agitated mind. 'It's Tamara. What we told you this morning isn't true. She's gone.'

'We were afraid of that.' Suzie put her hand over the other woman's. 'Why? Millie's upset that Tamara didn't tell her she was going. And their form tutor doesn't seem to know why she's absent.'

Lisa hung her head, letting her sharply-cut hair hang over her bruised face. 'Not even Leonard knows this. But Tamara said goodbye to me. Sort of. She hugged me and said she loved me. She didn't actually say she was running away; only, when she didn't come home that day, I realized that was what she meant.'

'Why would she do that?' Suzie asked, but another question was burning in her mind. *Does she know Tamara is pregnant?*

'I know she's frightened of Leonard. He can be a bit strict, sometimes.'

An understatement.

'Does he beat her too?'

Lisa lifted a scared face. 'I don't know. Sometimes he calls her into his study. I don't know what he does there. She looks sort of white and upset when she comes out.'

Incredulity almost silenced Suzie. 'Haven't you asked her?'

Lisa shook her head.

She doesn't want to know, Suzie thought. Whatever Leonard Dawson does to her daughter, she wants to pretend it doesn't happen.

How frightened did you have to be of someone, not to want to protect your daughter from him?

Protect her from what? Physical abuse? Or something worse?

'Where would Tamara go? Are there friends? Relations? Where have you tried?'

Again Lisa Dawson hid her face. 'I thought she might have gone to Kevin. But Leonard won't let me ring anyone.'

Millie was walking across the patio, carefully carrying a tray with mugs of tea.

Lisa threw an appealing look at her. 'I thought Millie might have some idea.'

'That's what really gets me,' Millie said, setting down the tray so sharply that the tea slopped. 'I mean, I've been her best friend for years. And suddenly she's gone, without saying a word to me. I've haven't the faintest where she is.'

'Why won't your husband let you ring people?' Suzie asked. 'Surely he's as keen to find her as you are?'

'He says he has his reputation to think of. Can't you imagine it? Tamara's picture in the papers. *Headmaster's daughter on the run.* Leonard's a proud man. I think he's afraid people would laugh at him.'

'But it wouldn't have to be in the papers, would it? Unless you were afraid something had happened to her.'

'I didn't like to argue.'

I can see that, Suzie thought, looking at the apprehensive woman. She handed her a mug and offered sugar. 'Can't you phone your ex without telling Leonard?'

The frightened glance Lisa gave her shocked Suzie. The mug rattled back on the table. Lisa jumped to her feet. 'Look, I really shouldn't be here. It was only . . . Seeing you in church this morning, I thought perhaps you could help.'

'*We* could ring him,' Suzie said. 'Millie would, if you gave us his number. But if she's gone there, surely he'd have let you know she was safe?'

'I'm not sure if I ought.' Her face was wracked with indecision.

There's something else, Suzie thought. Something she's afraid to tell me. Does she really think something worse has happened to Tamara? That she didn't manage to get away?

She was frightening herself now.

She was aware that Nick was standing behind her, quietly listening.

'Finish your tea,' he said to Lisa. 'It's only a few minutes' walk back. If Dawson's out for the afternoon, you're quite safe.'

Lisa subsided again and took up her mug with trembling hands.

'How has Tamara seemed lately? Before she ran away?' Suzie nudged closer to the crucial question.

'Edgy. I think there was something on her mind.'

'Did you ask her?'

Lisa shook her head.

Suzie tried to imagine what it must be like to be so dominated by your husband that you didn't dare ask your child what was wrong, because you feared the answer.

The whisper came. 'She was sick the other morning, before she went to school.'

'And you still didn't ask her?'

'No.' It was barely audible.

Suzie looked up at Nick. So Lisa Dawson had thought the unthinkable too.

There was a painful silence. Then Lisa's whisper came again. 'I told Leonard.'

'*And*?'

Lisa raised her frightened eyes to Suzie's. But she seemed unable to speak.

ELEVEN

'Y ou could have offered to run her home.'

'I thought it better not,' Nick said. 'If Dawson *did* decide to come home early, she'd probably have found it hard enough to explain why she'd suddenly decided to go for a stroll. But imagine if she turned up in another man's car.'

'It must be terrible to live like that,' Suzie said slowly, tracing a dribble of tea across the table. 'Completely under his thumb. She wasn't a bit like that before. She and Tamara seemed to be doing fine on their own, after Kevin left. She's changed so fast.'

'It wasn't as good as you think,' Millie said. 'I mean, it couldn't be, could it? He was fun enough when he was just Kevin Gamble. But Reynard Woodman was, like, extra special. Sort of magical. Like, he was the wizard, and there were those creatures in his books. Half deer, half human. It was fantastic. You couldn't just forget you'd lived with him. Tamara couldn't.'

'Do you know why they split up?'

'No prizes for guessing,' Nick said. 'He'll have been playing the field. I think I get the picture. Youngish man, starting to become famous, adoring fan club. That sort of thing breeds its own charisma. Nothing succeeds like success. It's like an aphrodisiac. I'll bet there weren't just kids queuing up for his autograph.'

'Dad! He was *fun*. He took us picnicking in the woods, and we'd play these games. He could make it so that it really *was* Humbledown Forest, like in the books. He made you believe in it.'

'You see what I mean?'

'I suppose she must have missed that magic,' Suzie said. 'Lisa, I mean. And she'd be sore because another woman had taken away what she had. And then along comes this other man. Just the opposite sort from a philandering fantasy writer. Someone reliable. Pillar of the establishment, chapel-going. I suppose it must have seemed like a sort of security. Someone who was never going to two-time her.'

'Don't be so sure of that,' Nick said, caressing her cheek. 'Churches get their share of the other sort, too. They're not all saints.'

'So it seems. I don't suppose Springbrook Methodist knows what goes on behind the Dawsons' door. And Lisa isn't going to tell them.'

'Fat pig.' Millie slammed the empty mugs back on the tray. 'Preaching to the kids at school assembly. Swanning around at his posh country club at the weekends. He made Tamara go there, to play tennis. She didn't want to. I mean, she's good at tennis. Streets better than I am. But she says they're all

terribly competitive there. You can't just go and play for fun.
Mr Dawson wanted her to go in for all sorts of tournaments.
He wasn't going to be happy till she brought back a shelf full
of cups. She has to go for coaching, every Sunday, and after
school some days. She said the only good thing about it was
the coach. Dan something. She really fancies him. She has
this picture of him she carries around with her. I have to say,
he's a bit tasty. Blond curls, square jaw. That sort of thing.'

'She carried his photo around with her?' Suzie felt the
sudden prickle of awareness.

'Yeah. Like, she was really smitten. You don't get that sort
of talent at school.'

Suzie looked up at Nick, wanting him to share the same
understanding. Something worrying enough, but that would
be better than the sour taste of the scenario they had been
imagining, behind the closed door of Leonard Dawson's study.

'You're sure about this, love? How long has it been going
on? This coaching?'

'I didn't say anything was *going on*. She just fancied him.'
Millie bridled with indignation.

'If the Dawsons married at Easter . . .' Suzie was calculating
rapidly. 'And Tamara started having coaching at the start of
the summer term?'

'Pretty much.'

'And we're well into June now. So there would have been
time . . .'

Millie let the tray fall back to the table with a crash. 'You
mean this Dan something-or-other? The tennis coach? You're
suggesting he and Tamara were having it off? That *he's* the
father?'

'It would fit. And if she liked him . . . Well, wouldn't that
be better than . . . what you were thinking? About her
stepfather?'

Millie looked stricken. 'But if it had got that far, she would
have *said*. Like, we're best friends.'

'Chances are he'll be at the country club right now.' Nick
was already looking down at his gardening clothes and heading
for the house.

'What are you going to do?' Suzie called after him.

'Confront him on the tennis court and tell him what a rotter he is? That's more Mr Dawson's style. He's hardly going to confess to you, is he? If it's true, he'd lose his job, wouldn't he? Having sex with a member's daughter who's a minor. The only thing that's better about that theory is that he's young and good-looking.'

'And not middle-aged, fat and bald. And a pompous hypocrite,' Millie said bitterly. 'And anyway, where's Tamara?'

'Too true,' Suzie sighed. 'That's the real worry, isn't it? There must be somebody who knows. But who?'

'It won't do any harm to ask.' Nick's face was grim. Suzie knew he was imagining Millie in Tamara's situation.

'How will you get in?' Millie asked. 'You're not a member.'

'I don't imagine you have to show a pass to guards at the gate. If I keep away from the clubhouse and head straight for the courts, nobody's going to stop me.'

'We'll come.' Suzie rose as she reached a sudden decision. 'You can say you want to discuss coaching for Millie. Say Tamara recommended him. That should produce an interesting reaction, if we're right.'

Excitement raced through her veins. At last there was something she could do, other than sit at home and worry about the possibilities. Her mind was in a turmoil for Tamara. A predatory young tennis coach was not such a loathsome prospect as a domineering stepfather, but it was only a matter of degree. Where did either leave Tamara's future? What had been in her mind when she ran away?

Had she only fled because she feared Leonard Dawson's punishment?

Nick was right, of course. It was easy to drive into the grounds of the country club, whether you were a member or not. They swept up the long drive, through shrubberies, past sloping lawns, towards the clubhouse.

Nick looked keenly from side to side. 'Any idea where the tennis courts are?'

'Stop the car,' Millie ordered. 'Switch off the engine.'

She lowered the window. Sure enough, there was the distant clunk of balls on racquets, high voices calling.

'There are parking signs pointing round the back of the house,' Suzie said. 'Or the overflow car park's that way, nearer the courts.'

'I'd rather keep as far away from the clubhouse as possible.' He turned the wheel towards the distant sounds.

A fork in the drive took them over the brow of the hill to a hollow with a handful of cars.

'Good enough. There aren't too many people to question what we're doing here.'

'Stop worrying,' Suzie said, getting out of the car into the heat of the afternoon. 'This was your idea. I shouldn't imagine anyone knows all the members by sight.'

'I'm having second thoughts. It's OK for you. Some of these people will be my clients.'

'Is that a problem?' Suzie thought of Nick's architectural practice in the city, with its reputation for futuristic, eco-friendly buildings. Would it really matter that they were trespassing on his clients' playground?

'Maybe not. But since the story we're spinning is not entirely honest, the fewer people who know I'm here the better.'

The three of them began to walk across the grass to where the sounds of tennis were becoming louder.

Behind a screen of azaleas, still dazzling with blooms of purple, orange and magenta, the courts came into view. The players, Suzie observed, were all carefully attired for their Sunday afternoon game. No scruffy trainers, or jogging pants. No inappropriately coloured shorts, such as you might see on the municipal courts in the park. She glanced at Millie and realized with surprise that she did not look out of place here. She had put on one of her smarter dresses: sleeveless, peppermint green. With her cropped blonde hair, she looked a picture of cool elegance. Not for the first time in recent weeks, Suzie had to adjust the mental image of her fourteen-year-old daughter.

Then she was struck with a sudden chill. Had Millie dressed up like this to catch the handsome tennis coach's eye?

'That's got to be him.'

Nick had been scanning the players. He pointed to one of the further courts, where a good-looking man in his twenties was adjusting the grip of a rather fat boy, who looked several years younger than Millie.

'Blond curls. Yep, that's the one,' Millie agreed. 'Nice.'

'He's a bit old for Tamara, isn't he?' Suzie said.

'Mature,' said Millie.

They worked their way around the wire-mesh enclosure until they stood at one end of the coach's court. He came back to the side of the net to watch his pupils resume their game. After a while, his eyes went to the Fewings. He waited until the boys changed ends, then he strolled towards them. Suzie noticed how his eyes raked appreciatively over Millie, and not just, she thought indignantly, her daughter's face. The square-jawed features Millie had commented on lit up with a smile.

'Can I help you?'

Did he ask that of every spectator? Suzie was already beginning to regret her idea of bringing Millie along to provide the excuse to get into conversation.

'Yes,' said Nick. 'You're Dan . . .?'

'Curtis.'

'That's right. Is it possible to have a word?'

The coach looked at his watch. 'Give me a few minutes. These brats' hour is nearly up. And I've had a cancellation for the next session. Is that all right?'

'Fine.'

His appraising eyes went back to Millie, before he turned his attention to the boys slugging it out with much panting and perspiration.

'Mm. I see what Tamara means,' Millie said.

Alarm bells rang louder in Suzie's head.

The session ended. The young man came through the gate and strolled towards them. Sunlight on his blond curls. He glowed with health. Suzie felt her nerves tightening. This is not about Millie, she scolded herself. We're here because of Tamara. It was all too easy to see how a teenage girl might have fallen for this sporting Adonis. But even if it had ended in pregnancy, why would that make her leave home? The two of them clearly hadn't run away together.

'Now.' His smile embraced the three of them. 'I'm all yours.'

Nick held out a hand. 'James Peters. This is my wife Anne. And my daughter Sally.'

Suzie threw him a startled glance. But Millie, she saw, was grinning. Nick really was covering his tracks, not wanting to risk his real name coming up in clubhouse gossip.

'And what can I do for you?'

'We're new here,' Nick said. 'And we were wondering if it was possible to arrange for Sally to have some coaching.'

The smile positively shone from Dan Curtis's face. His eyes were fully on Millie now. 'I'd be delighted.' This time the smile was for her alone.

Millie blushed.

I bet you would, Suzie thought. Instead, she said, wrestling his attention away, 'You were recommended to us. By one of your pupils. Tamara Gamble? She's a friend of Mi— Of Sally's.'

A momentary cloud obscured the smile. Then it was gone, replaced by professional courtesy. 'Of course. The charming Tamara. How kind of her. As a matter of fact, she's let me down today. It's my session with her that was cancelled. I heard she was unwell. I hope there's nothing seriously wrong?' He turned his inquiring eyes back to Millie.

'I . . . I don't know,' she gulped. 'She's gone.'

'Gone?' A frown of what looked like genuine concern crossed Dan Curtis's face. 'Gone where? Her father just said she was feeling off colour.'

'We don't know. Do you?'

The sudden aggression in her voice broke through her shyness. The question knocked the young man's confident charm away. 'Why should I?'

Millie shrugged, her blush returning. 'I just wondered.'

'Look, I don't know what you're suggesting. I only saw her a couple of times a week. On the tennis court. With witnesses.'

It was the coach's turn to sound aggressive now.

Nick took hold of Millie's arm and turned her away. 'I'm sorry, Mr Curtis. Sally's a bit upset about this. Perhaps we'd better talk about coaching another time.'

'Suit yourselves. If Tamara's really has left, I'll have a vacancy on Sunday afternoons. But you'd better make up your minds quickly. My services are in considerable demand, you know.'

His eyes followed Millie with a heightened mixture of admiration and curiosity. Millie, Suzie was disturbed to see, turned her head to gaze back at him over her shoulder.

When they were out of earshot, Suzie rounded on her daughter. 'Well, that didn't exactly go to plan. You practically accused him of being involved in her disappearance.'

'And whatever story Dawson has been putting about,' Nick added, 'the word will be out now that she's missing.'

Millie shook off Suzie's rebuke. Her eyes were sparkling. 'So what? Did you see? When you said Tamara's name, his face changed. He was all smiles before, then, poof! He went all serious. He covered it up fast. But there was something.'

'He might just have been cross because she'd stood him up at short notice,' Nick reasoned.

'I bet he wasn't. He knows something.'

'I think we were expecting too much,' Suzie said as the car came in sight. 'He was hardly going to put his hands up and say, "It's a fair cop, guv. I got her in the club."'

'You can imagine it, though.' Millie's voice took on a dreamier tone. 'Tamara wasn't exaggerating, was she? He's better than the photograph. I can see why she fell for him.' She shook her head, as if to clear it. 'He's a beast, though. If he did it. There he is, playing tennis as if nothing had happened. While Tamara's . . . nowhere.'

The word fell chilly on the heated air.

'Stop exactly where you are!'

A yell from behind made them spin round. Cresting the ridge at speed was a very large man in white shirt and flannels. His face and the crown of his head were pink and perspiring. He was brandishing a tennis racquet.

It was Leonard Dawson.

The Fewings flinched. Suzie had a desperate desire to run for the car.

Nick recovered faster than any of them. 'Can we help you?'

Dawson came striding down to tower over them. Suzie eyed

his racquet nervously. The pudgy hands were clenched so hard that the knuckles showed yellow through the flesh.

'You!' he exploded. 'What do you mean, calling yourself Peters? You're the bloody Fewings.'

'I'm sorry . . .'

'I thought I told you to stay out of our affairs. What do you mean by telling Dan Curtis lies about Tamara? What the hell are you suggesting?'

'We came to talk about tennis coaching.'

'And I'm a Dutchman. You gave that young man a false name. That shows you've got a guilty conscience. I warned you this morning, when you were bothering my wife. Can you not understand plain English?'

He was shouting at them now from point-blank range. Suzie retreated from the flying spittle. Alarmed, she saw the fist with the racquet begin to rise. She pulled Nick back.

For a moment, Dawson's face flared purple. Then he swallowed and gained control of himself. To Suzie's relief, the racquet fell to his side.

She did not trust the cold smile he now gave them.

'You may be reassured to know that Tamara's gone away for a rest. On medical advice. From what Curtis has just told me, you'd have thought sick leave was a matter for a police enquiry. Have you any idea who I am?'

'Of course. Leonard Dawson. Headmaster of Briars Hill College.'

'That should speak for itself. And I'm also a member of the management committee of this club. As is the Chief Constable, by the way. So I recommend that you get yourselves off these private premises double quick. And should you ever have the temerity to apply for membership, I'll have you blackballed. And as for you –' he glared venom at Millie – 'you say one word more against the good name of my stepdaughter, and I'll have you in court for slander.'

'Sorry,' Millie said in a small voice.

They turned, feeling like cowed dogs, and found their car. They slipped into the seats in silence.

'Well,' Suzie said, with an attempt at humour, 'that's us told.' She found she was shaking.

'Imagine living with that,' Millie said. 'Poor Tamara. No wonder she went. I don't believe that stuff about a rest cure for one moment. But why on earth didn't she ask me for help?'

'I wish I thought that all he did was shout at her,' Suzie said as the car slipped down the drive. 'I really thought he was going to brain you with that racquet, Nick.'

'I'm not surprised she preferred the coach,' Millie said. 'He was a dream, wasn't he? You don't get talent like that in our year group. But if it was him, why would he let her down?'

'You're forgetting the important thing,' Nick said. 'It's not just the baby. She's still fourteen.'

'So?'

'Whoever did it, he's committed a criminal offence.'

TWELVE

'Y ou have to go to the police.' Millie turned abruptly from the window, where she had been staring moodily at the garden. 'Something bad's happened to Tamara. I'm sure it has. It's been five days now, and I haven't heard a word from her.'

'Be reasonable,' Nick told her. 'I know you're upset. We're worried too. But the police are hardly going to listen to us, are they? We're not her parents. You heard Mr Dawson. He's a very well-respected man in this city. If he says they've sent her away for some sort of rest cure, the police are going to believe him, not us.'

'That's not what her mother said. She thinks Tamara's run away.'

Suzie sighed and sank into an easy chair. 'I know, love. I believe Lisa. But can we get her to say that in front of Dawson?'

'I'm not sure I do believe her,' Millie said stubbornly. 'She only *thought* Tamara must have been saying goodbye to her. Tamara didn't actually say that. She just disappeared.'

'And your point is?' Nick asked. 'It's not unheard of for teenagers to run away. Especially in her condition. I'd suggest

getting the Salvation Army to trace her. They're supposed to
be great at that. But it would be the same as the police. They'd
trust her parents, not us.'

'And think what would happen to Lisa if Mr Dawson found
out what she'd told us. It doesn't bear thinking about. It would
blow his story to shreds.'

'That's what I mean!' Millie cried. 'You saw the way he
was waving that tennis racquet at Dad. I was scared he was
going to kill you. Tamara was really frightened of him, even
before the baby. What if he found out about it and . . . and . . .
hit her. It could have been in a temper. But he might have
done it deliberately. Get her out of the way, so nobody could
talk about it behind his back. What if he's *killed* her?'

'Millie!' Suzie's cry of protest was joined by Nick's.

'Well, you saw what he's like.' Her voice was harsh with
defiance. 'He could have lost it. And then covered up what
he'd done. Buried her somewhere.'

'But even supposing for a moment that was true, he
couldn't keep it secret for long,' Suzie protested. 'People
would want to know what had happened to her. Your school,
for instance.'

'He's a headmaster, isn't he? He'd know how to do it. What
you need to say. He'd make up some story about sending her
somewhere else. You heard him. He's started to do it already,
hasn't he?'

'I'm not sure.'

Suzie tried to order her troubled thoughts. Could Dawson
do that and get away with it? Permanently? Was it so easy for
a girl to drop out of existence and nobody realize?

She was horribly afraid that it might be. There had been
too many stories about children slipping through safety nets.

'What about Lisa?' she tried. 'She'd know it wasn't true.'

'She's terrified of him,' Nick said, weighing the idea. 'And
with good reason. She's got the bruises to prove it. And abused
wives can fool themselves. They can't let go of the idea that
he's still the man they fell in love with, and if they hang on
to him, it will all come right. I'm rather afraid she'd *want* to
believe whatever he told her. The alternative doesn't bear
thinking about.'

'She'd just let Tamara go, and never hear from her again?' Millie was incredulous.

'Even if she suspected, he'd probably terrorize her into believing she was guilty too . . . Look here!' He slammed his hand on the coffee table. 'You've got us doing it now. Talking as if Tamara's dead. Have you forgotten your theory about the glamorous tennis coach? There's not the slightest evidence that anything's happened to her since she got pregnant, except that she's done a runner.'

'There is,' Millie said. 'She hasn't phoned me for five days.'

As she spoke, the house phone rang. Suzie sprang to answer it. The familiar voice came, it seemed, from a lifetime away. Could it really only have been yesterday that they were showing Prudence Clayson round the peaceful English village of Corley? There was something comforting about the warm Pennsylvanian accent.

'Gee! I'm having the greatest time. You folks over here are so kind. This guy I'm staying with seems to know just about everything there is to know about the English Claysons. Apparently, there's only a small pocket of them in your neck of the woods. But he told me something else. It might be really important . . . No, I think I'll hang on to that till I see you. But I guess we might get that computer of yours working again.'

Suzie let the gush of words wash over her. She was still too stunned by Millie's conviction to think clearly. Certainly not about anything as removed from it as family history.

It didn't matter. Prudence's enthusiasm swept on. 'And tomorrow, they're taking me to see Stratford-upon-Avon. Would you believe, one of his Claysons actually went to the same grammar school as William Shakespeare? He says I really couldn't be this close and not go see it. I'm so excited. Shakespeare was such a big thing for me at high school. I was Rosalind in *As You Like It*. Can you imagine that?'

Suzie murmured polite responses, hardly knowing what she said.

'Well, I'll see you guys in a couple of days, then. God bless.'

The phone went silent. Suzie tried to reorder her thoughts. 'That was Prudence. She seems to be having a great time.'

'I'm glad somebody is,' Millie retorted.

*   *   *

It was nearly six before Tom swung his bike into the drive and breezed into the house. Once again, Suzie felt the shock of altered perception. The world seemed suddenly sunnier for having her tall, energetic son back home. His arms crushed her in an enthusiastic hug. He ruffled her hair and threw himself on to a kitchen chair with dangerous abandon.

But the sparkle in his eyes cooled. 'No luck, I'm afraid. I must have cycled half round the city, catching up with guys. Dropped the odd question about Tamara. Got the answer you'd expect. A couple of them knew she'd been out of school last week. Most of them looked blank. Sorry, Millie,' he added as he saw her standing in the doorway of the conservatory, listening avidly. 'She doesn't seem to have scored with the sixth form. There was a bit of a word about Justin Soames in Year Eleven being keen on her, but nothing definite. Of course . . .' He grinned ruefully up at Suzie. 'They all think I've got the hots for her now. I tried to make it sound casual, but I guess they were bound to wonder why I was asking about her, my first day back.'

'Just as long as nobody thinks *you're* the reason she's disappeared.' Nick's voice came from the sofa behind Millie.

'Hey, leave me out of this. It's the big, bad Dawson she's running away from, isn't it?'

'But the kid's father could be someone else,' Nick warned. 'We don't have to believe the worst.'

'We don't know she *has* run,' Millie said. 'What if she hasn't? Mum and Dad don't want me to go to the police. But if Tamara's dead, the sooner someone starts looking for evidence, the better.'

THIRTEEN

S uzie twisted restlessly in the hot summer night. Could Tamara really be dead? By daylight, it was easy to dismiss Millie's wilder imaginings. She was at that age when the most ordinary event could become a melodrama. But lying in the dark, with Nick heavily asleep, it was not so easy to shake off the idea. Millie and Tamara were such close friends. In vain she puzzled to think of some explanation for Tamara going off without telling Millie, and still not getting in touch.

Yet was it really possible to think that Leonard Dawson had killed her?

In the hot darkness she saw him looming over her, as he had at the country club. The fleshy bulk of him. The face reddened with exertion and rage. Those small, glaring eyes. Even now, her throat constricted as she saw the metal-framed racquet swing above his head. For an awful second, she had thought he was about to bring it smashing down on Nick.

She sat up, pushing her side of the bedclothes back. It hadn't happened. Whatever the anger he had felt, he had made himself behave like a member of the civilized establishment.

They had been in a public place. Mr Dawson was a member of the management committee. He had a reputation to uphold.

But in private?

She recalled the bruise on Lisa Dawson's temple, only half-hidden by her fringe. So dark red, it was almost black. Ugly. The evidence of an uglier scene.

She wished Nick was awake, so that she could talk to him. He was better at pouring common sense on Millie's ideas. But he slumbered on.

She padded downstairs and took a glass of cold milk through to the conservatory. She rested her hot forehead against the window pane.

Nick would have designed a better house than this. Summer heat rose to the bedrooms and beat down through the tiles. It was cooler down here. She felt less feverish now.

But the black thoughts would not go away. It was not melodrama now, but cold reality that told her such things were possible. A violent man could strike one blow too many. She pictured Tamara going down before him. Not rising. A trickle of blood on her white face. And the head of one of the most respected schools in the city knowing he had committed murder.

She almost felt compassion for him as she imagined his panic. This could not have happened to him. It must not have happened. He had to do something, fast. Wipe out the evidence. Get rid of Tamara. Permanently. Bury the body where no one would find it. Concoct a story about her moving away. A temporary arrangement at first, not to arouse suspicion. Lengthening into permanency.

At what stage had Lisa known? Had she witnessed it? Had he told her later? Got her to help dispose of the body, so that she was an accessory? Or had she only guessed?

She must know, mustn't she?

Suzie struggled to imagine how she herself could ever have kept silent if someone had committed such a crime against Millie. She would want to scream it to the sky. But then, she was not the cowed and frightened person Tamara's mother had become.

She seized on a sudden shred of hope. Lisa had told them Tamara had run away. That she had as good as said goodbye. Millie had doubted it, but what if it was true after all?

But Tamara had said nothing to Millie. Her best friend.

Her hopes fell. She swallowed the milk and felt its chill course through her body.

Lisa had *wanted* to believe that. Because the alternative she feared was too unbearable to live with.

She hadn't reported Tamara missing. No one had gone to the police. The school must have been given a plausible reason for Tamara's absence. Millie was right. A headmaster would know what to say.

There was only one person who could not be so easily satisfied.

Millie. Like a piece of grit in a shoe.

Millie, who had bombarded Tamara's phone with unanswered messages.

Millie, who was not going to stop asking awkward questions.

Millie was the obstacle which stood between Leonard Dawson and the successful silencing of what he had done.

And now the image of that furious bull of a man came rushing back. This was how it happened, wasn't it? The first murder, almost an accident. But then the next, made inevitable to cover up the first. Anything to stop Millie going to the police.

She wrenched herself away from the window, suddenly cold.
They *had* to tell the police now. It was not just Tamara they
should be afraid for. As long as only they knew, Millie wasn't
safe. They had to act before Leonard Dawson decided that
Millie's insistent questions had to be silenced.

She crept back to bed, shivering. Even the duvet wasn't
enough to warm her.

Rational doubt returned with daylight. When Suzie came back
from the bathroom, she sat brushing her hair. She felt oddly
ashamed of raising the subject. Nick had his back to her,
dressing.

'You know, I think Millie may be right. We ought to tell
the police. Even though we're not her family.'

Nick stopped, in the act of hoisting his trousers. 'Tell them
what? That Tamara's gone away, but her parents don't seem
to have noticed there's a problem? Don't you think I've made
enough of a fool of myself at the country club yesterday?'

'Lisa knows Tamara's not away on sick leave. She thinks
she's run away. Or she says she does.'

Nick's face sobered as he fastened his belt. 'Whatever Lisa
Dawson believes or doesn't believe, she's not going to stand
up in court and say it, is she? She's too scared.'

'So you *do* think there's something which could end up in
court?'

He kissed her head. 'Let's say, I don't think Leonard Dawson
is the pillar of rectitude he'd like the town to believe.'

'Nick! It came to me in the middle of the night. If something
has happened to Tamara . . . If he lost his temper and hit
her . . . too hard. Then he's doing a pretty good job of covering
up. Presently, we'll hear that Tamara has moved to another
school. A boarding school, even an international one. No one
will ask any questions. Except Millie.'

Nick's silence was expectant. Clearly, the wires of his mind
had not connected with the same explosive force which she
had experienced. Putting it into words was bringing it back to
her.

'So?'

She swung away from the mirror to face him. 'So don't

you see? Millie is in danger, too. She has to tell the police before he . . . shuts her up too.'

She saw the storm of emotions pass over Nick's face. Shock, incredulity, the desperate struggle to hold on to normality.

'Steady on, love! It's one thing to guess he might have lost control and killed Tamara. That's pretty far out in itself. It's far more likely she was scared of what he would do to her when he found out she was pregnant, and ran away. But even supposing he did, that would be manslaughter. To deliberately go after Millie . . . You're talking about murder.'

'You've seen what he's like. He came within a millimetre of hitting you with his racquet, because you interfered. He'd have done you serious damage. Tom says he terrorizes the kids at Briars Hill. If he thought that only a fourteen-year-old girl was standing between him and freedom, respectability . . . He'll know he'll go to prison if she doesn't keep quiet . . . Is it really so fanciful to think he'd silence her too? Nick, it's our keeping quiet which is putting Millie in danger. Once she's told the police, it'll be too late for him to do anything to her.'

Nick was thinking, frantically. 'But . . . If this whole idea weren't totally ridiculous . . . If, for the sake of argument, he did . . . silence Millie, there'd still be us. We've been asking questions about Tamara. Remember? And I'd sure as hell go after him if anything happened to Millie.'

'Anything we say is second-hand. It all comes down to her. The evidence about Tamara being pregnant. She's probably the only one who knew. The absence of a credible boyfriend. Tamara's fear of her stepfather. How she didn't want to have an abortion. From us, it's just hearsay. Millie's the key witness.'

Nick checked himself in the mirror. Short sleeves, because of the heat already building. Cool, but smart. But behind the appraising glance, his mind was working fast. 'OK, then. I've got a couple of meetings with clients today. Suppose we pick Millie up after school and take her to the police HQ?'

Suzie felt alarms beginning to sound. The long day stretched in front of them. Another day of silence, until late afternoon. Another day when Millie would not have told anyone else what she knew.

She'd be safe at school, wouldn't she? Mr Dawson would

be at Briars Hill. They'd be waiting for her in the car at the school gate.

'All right,' she said reluctantly. 'Pick me up here first. About half past three?'

FOURTEEN

The Monday morning breakfast table had a purposeful feel. Nick and Suzie were dressed for work. Only Tom, A-levels over, had the luxury of lingering in bed.

Millie came into the kitchen. Since her new haircut, she seemed to carry herself taller, and she wore her school uniform with a more businesslike air. Suzie felt an unexpected nostalgia for the sloppily-fastened tie, the world-weary, mid-teen slouch she had grown used to. Millie looked almost grown-up.

She gave her daughter an encouraging smile. 'Your father and I have decided you're right. We ought to tell the police.'

There was a stab of guilt when she saw the smile of joy and relief that flooded Millie's face. They should have done this sooner.

'You're a star, Mum! Thanks, Dad!' She hugged them both.

'We'll pick you up after school, if that's all right,' Nick said.

Millie's face fell. 'What's wrong with this morning?'

'Dad has people to see. She's been gone since Wednesday. A few hours more won't really make any difference.'

'And some rich guy who wants Dad to design him an office is more important than Tamara? She may be *dead*! Don't you have any sense of priorities?' Millie flung herself into a chair.

Nick and Suzie knew better than to reason with her.

They ate in a silence that was resentful on Millie's part. Nick and Suzie were not hurrying, but aware of the clock.

Unexpectedly, they heard Tom's bounding step on the stairs. Suzie realized how much she had missed it in the days he had been away.

'I should have thought he'd have stayed in bed till lunch-time,' Millie muttered. 'I would.'

The letter box rattled. Tom appeared in the doorway, with the day's post in his hand. He made a performance of reading out the recipients' names and handing the letters round, like Father Christmas.

'Oh, ho, ho! And here's one for Miss Millie Fewings.'

Millie snatched it from his hand. Suzie looked across the table in curiosity. It was unusual for the children to get letters. Mobiles and emails took care of their social contacts. Nor did this look like a formal, computer-printed address. She caught the uneven handwriting as Millie ripped the envelope open.

'It's from her!' she almost screamed.

The morning grew suddenly brighter.

'Tamara?' Suzie breathed.

A wary expression came over Millie's face, as if she was afraid she had already said too much. She scanned the contents swiftly and silently. All Suzie could see was the front of the notelet on which it was written. A drawing of a half-timbered, thatched cottage.

'At least we know she's alive,' Nick said, with evident relief. 'Where is she?'

Millie read to the end and raised troubled grey eyes. 'She doesn't say.'

Tom reached for the envelope, to read the postmark. 'London, W1A.'

Millie shook her head. Reluctantly, she passed the card to Nick. Suzie read it over his shoulder.

TOP SECRET!!! DON'T LET ANYONE ELSE SEE THIS!!!

Dearest Millie,

I'm <u>really, really</u> sorry! You must hate me. I couldn't tell you I was going because I didn't know myself until I'd walked out of the house. I put a change of clothes in my school bag, just in case, but I had to screw myself up to do it. I couldn't stay. Not now he knows. He said he'd kill me if I told anybody. He wants me to get rid of it, but I'm not going to do it. I probably won't tell the kid anyway, even when it grows up. I mean, who'd want to know <u>that</u> about how they came into the world? It's not because I'm worried about his precious career.

I was going to ring you as soon as I got here. Honest! Only, then I remembered this guy who told us they can trace where your mobile is, even when it's switched off. So I got scared and threw it in the river. And I forgot to write down your number before I did. I've been afraid to ring your home phone in case somebody recognizes my voice. I know your parents are really decent, but I can't trust <u>anyone</u>. And don't think you can find out where I am from the postcode because I'm getting someone else to post this in London. I daren't even go into the village, in case someone sees me. I keep expecting my face will be in the papers, but nothing so far.

I'm scared, Millie. I'm scared he'll find me. You have to burn this letter as soon as you've read it. Don't tell anyone about it. I'm taking a risk even writing to you. ~~My~~ The person I'm staying with didn't want me to, but I couldn't bear thinking about my best mate wondering why I'd do a thing like this and not tell you. I wish you could write back, or ring me, but I daren't give <u>anything</u> away.

Pray for me, Millie. I don't know what I'm going to do. She says I have to see a doctor soon, because of the baby. But they're not allowed to tell your parents, are they, if you don't want them to?

No more space.

Love and kisses,

XXXXXXX

Suzie cast a worried glance up at her daughter. 'She hasn't even signed her name. She asks you to burn this and not tell anyone about it.'

'Yeah, well. I'm not sure I can handle this on my own. And you –' with an accusing glare at Tom – 'are not to say *anything*, or I'll murder you. Don't even breathe a hint to your mates that you know something they don't.'

'As if! Cross my heart and hope to die.'

She scowled at him suspiciously.

'Well,' said Nick, rising from the table, 'the good news is she's still alive. The bad news is that he's threatened to kill her.'

'Oh, come on, Dad,' Tom protested. 'People say that sort of thing. Doesn't mean they'll follow through.'

'Tamara's scared enough that he means it to go into hiding,' Suzie said. 'Where would she go, Millie?'

'I wish I knew. All this says is that you can rule out London.'

'Unless she's bluffing,' Tom countered. 'Put us off the scent.'

'What about her father? Her real father, I mean. Reynard Woodman. We never did get through to him.'

Millie frowned. 'I'm not so sure about that now. I kind of feel they don't get on like they used to.'

'Still –' Suzie pointed to a word that had been crossed out – 'she started to write "My", then changed her mind and put "The person I'm staying with". Somebody's sheltering her. Somebody she knows.'

'Ah, the family history detective at work. Studying the fine print of the documents.' Nick forced a grin. 'Still, it's good to know she's staying with someone she can trust. Anyway, she could hardly book in at a B and B at her age, without someone asking questions. And she wouldn't have the money . . . Look, folks, I really do have an appointment at nine. I've got to go. We'll talk about this later.'

'You're picking me up after school, remember,' Millie called after him. 'To go to the police.'

'I'm not sure that's necessary now. I'll ring your mother this afternoon. Bye.'

Millie rose from her seat, slopping milk from her cereal bowl. 'He can't mean it! He's backing out? Just when we got him to agree it's important. If he won't, I'll flipping well go on my own.'

'Calm down, love. We need to think this out. Tamara believes she's in danger. But suppose the police start asking questions of Mr Dawson? I'm sure he can be very plausible. Just a hysterical teenager. They'd probably help him find her. And then what? Do you really want Tamara back in that house with him?'

Millie shuddered. 'That's awful. That means that people like him can get away with whatever they like. A pillar of the community. Butter wouldn't melt in his mouth. You think they really wouldn't believe Tamara?'

'Would she testify against him? Supposing he *is* the father. She wouldn't even tell you who it was.'

'I hate to break up the party,' Tom said. 'But don't you two usually go to work and school on Monday mornings?'

Suzie glanced at the clock in dismay. 'Come on, Millie. We have to run.'

Millie picked up the notelet and looked at it doubtfully. Then she set it defiantly on the kitchen shelf, like a birthday card. 'Exhibit Number One,' she declared. 'No, Tamara, I'm not going to burn this.'

FIFTEEN

At one o'clock Suzie closed down her computer in the office at the back of the charity shop. Normally, she would have gone straight home. But there were some bits of shopping she wanted to do in town, and she needed to change her library book.

She collected her handbag and walked out through the shop.

'All done?' Margery, the manager, gave her a warm smile, which faded into a look of concern. 'Is everything all right?'

'Yes. Why?'

'I don't know. You were looking a bit . . . bothered when you came in this morning.'

Suzie hesitated. It was tempting to pour out her worries on to Margery's always sympathetic shoulder. But Tamara's secret was not hers to share. And she knew that Janet, one of the volunteer helpers, was in the cloakroom. She could come back at any moment. Margery, she knew, would be discreet, but Janet's ears flapped at the slightest hint of gossip.

Reluctantly, she lied. 'No, I'm fine. I was sitting up too late talking. Tom came home yesterday. They were washed out of their campsite in France.'

'Oh, that's good news. I don't mean about his holiday being spoilt!' Margery laughed. 'But you'll enjoy having him back. I expect you missed him.'

'Yes, I did.'

Soon, Suzie thought, I'm going to lose him for longer than ten days. He'll be going to university at the end of summer. It will never be the same without him.

She smiled gallantly for Margery. 'Still, that's what happens, isn't it? They grow up. Leave home. We wouldn't want to stop them, would we?'

Too late, she remembered that Margery, so eminently motherly, was childless.

But Margery was more concerned for her. She held Suzie's eyes. 'Still, if there *is* anything . . . You won't mind if I pray for you.'

Suzie found herself envying the ease with which Margery, like Prudence, could say things that like. It wasn't a Bible-thumping assertion of her faith, just that it really was natural to her to say it. She felt a stab of guilt. She should have been praying for Tamara herself.

'Thanks, Margery.' It was the nearest she could get to admitting that Margery had been right.

Please, look after Tamara. Be with her, wherever she is. I mean, I know you already are. But help her feel it.

She left the shop for the midday heat of the streets. There was a baker's next door which sold sandwiches. Suzie settled for prawn and cucumber and crossed the road to eat them in the cathedral close, among the tourists and pigeons.

She glanced across at the Angel Hotel in the far corner. Tomorrow, Prudence would be coming back. She found herself unexpectedly looking forward to meeting the plump American again. At least there was no reason why she shouldn't talk to Prudence about Tamara. After all, it had been Prudence who had made the breakthrough with Millie and got her to confess the truth about that pregnancy test. It would be unfair not to update her on this latest development. Prudence, she felt sure, could be trusted to keep the information to herself.

Her mobile rang. She fished it out of her handbag. It was Nick.

'Look, I've been thinking it over. I'm not sure it's such a terribly good idea to go to the police. Not since Millie got that letter. Tamara's safe where she is at the moment. Since Dawson evidently hasn't disposed of her, we can forget the threat to Millie. But if we get the police on to it . . . The worst thing might be if they found her and brought her back.'

'That's just what we told Millie. I mean, who are they going to believe? A well-known headmaster, who's already warned us he's on first-name terms with the Chief Constable, or a teenager? Unless Tamara's willing to report he abused her, if that's what happened. Even if it did, I'm not sure she's ready to talk about it.'

'So. It's a big responsibility, either way. I'm beginning to feel like she's my own daughter. But my hunch is that we should let it ride. I don't see Dawson getting to Tamara any time soon. He has less idea where she is than we do.'

'Yes, I know what you mean. I'm dying to do something to help her, but I can't think what.'

'I'll text Millie, shall I? Tell her to come home from school as usual.'

'She isn't going to be pleased. Though we did try to explain why.'

'You don't think she'd go to the police station on her own, do you?'

'You can never tell what Millie will do.'

There was a pause. 'Should I ring Tom? Get him to meet her at the gates. Make sure she comes straight home.'

'Are you joking? Her big brother? I really don't think that would be a good idea.'

She brushed the crumbs of her sandwich from her lap, attracting the swoop of a predatory seagull.

Half an hour later, she had finished her shopping. A new library book was in her bag. But instead of heading for the bus stop, she found her steps turning towards the Local Studies Library next door.

It wasn't her usual afternoon for family history research. She recognized the symptoms immediately. Avoidance strategy.

She didn't want to go home and face the thoughts that waited for her there. Tom would probably be out. There would just be the silent house and Tamara's card, sitting accusingly on the kitchen shelf. A girl apparently frightened for her life.

She shook the unsettling thought away. Besides, she told herself, she did feel a little guilty. She had really meant to do some more research while Prudence was away, so that she would have some fresh discoveries to give her when she came back. The dramas of Lisa and Leonard Dawson yesterday, and Tamara's letter today, had driven it out of her mind.

She felt the studied peace of the search room fold around her. The walls were lined with books, all crammed with local information. Researchers sat at the microfiche readers and computers. Two librarians at the desk were ready to help.

Suzie's first thought was to try to trace Prudence's Clayson family further back. Fiches of the registers were available here too. Then she remembered that they had already gone past the point where the Corley parish registers began. Too late a date for Johan's baptism. But at least she could find out more about Corley. There was always a chance that the Clayson name might crop up in parish histories. There were books which wouldn't show up on Internet searches. And even if not, she could paint a more vivid picture for Prudence of the life of the village in the seventeenth century and earlier. Bring to life the background against which Prudence's ancestors would have lived.

She checked the computer catalogue for Corley. There were three possibilities. One was the booklet about the parish church which they had already picked up on their Saturday visit. Another seemed to be a fuller account of the parish by the same author, a previous rector. The third was a type-written manuscript by a member of the Marsdon family of Corley Barton. Suzie felt a prickle of indignation. She could not get out of her mind her first conviction that Johan Clayson had been a servant in that grand house and that baby Adam was the result of abuse she had suffered from one of the Marsdons.

Of course, she had no proof of that. It could just as well

have been any of the young men in the village, with Johan a willing partner.

But then, why had it not ended in marriage?

A thought crept up on her. Was she projecting her theories about Johan Clayson on to Tamara?

She ordered both the second and third documents and waited for the librarian to bring them from the storeroom.

As she let her gaze roam over the book titles around her, she caught the eye of a fellow researcher further down the table. There was a start of recognition between them. It was Alan Taylor, the minister of Springbrook Methodist. She gave him a slightly guilty smile. Every time she went to Springbrook she wondered why she didn't go more often. He always made her feel so welcome.

They were too far apart to talk, or she would have told Alan how much she enjoyed his service yesterday . . .

She felt the smile leave her face. It had been a good sermon, full of modern relevance, and the full-throated singing was a joy. But that was not what she remembered most about yesterday. There had been that confrontation when the service ended. Her attempts to talk to a nervous Lisa Dawson, and then Leonard Dawson seizing her arm, warning them off.

It cast a long shadow. The wound under Lisa's fringe had been more than a bruise.

The librarian was at her elbow, with the books she had ordered. She found some paper in her handbag and settled down to make notes.

Where to begin? The ancient geology of the hilltop village and the valley below? The Palaeolithic flints? No trace of the Iron Age or Romans here. The story picked up again with the Saxon settlement. Frustratingly, this was too early for common people to have surnames yet. Walter of Sheepdown might or might not be related to the Claysons. She made a few notes and moved swiftly on to later medieval times.

Hole. Her eye was arrested by the name of the little farm-stead in the valley. The name they had found on the lease, rented out to an older Adam Clayson in the early 1700s, and later to his son Robert. No proof that these were Johan's direct forebears, but it was a reasonable presumption.

Now here it was again. From the manorial court records, 1462. *Robert of Hole was distrained to answer to the lord because on Tuesday, in the feast of St Katharine the Virgin, he broke and entered a close of Simon Marsdon lord of this manor called Corley and then and there killed and took away 12 gooseanders without the leave of the said lord to the prejudice of the said lord.*

The lord of the manor, sitting in judgement on a case in which he himself was the plaintiff. What chance did Robert of Hole stand?

Was there a possibility that this Robert was related to the Robert Clayson who had been named in the lease of Hole in 1716? Did tenant farmers have that sort of continuity? She suspected not. But Prudence would like this story.

She wished now they had made the time to visit Hole as well when they went to Corley.

She looked at her watch and closed the book. She hadn't even started on the typewritten manuscript. But she ought to go. Millie would be back from school soon, probably full of indignation.

Her spirits lifted. Tom might be home.

She was crossing the room towards the desk, to hand in her documents, when there was a light touch on her elbow. Alan Taylor had turned from his book as she passed his chair.

'Hi, Suzie. Don't tell me you're a family history nut too?'

She smiled. 'I'm afraid so. Is that why you're here?'

He threw back his head and laughed uproariously, making other researchers turn to stare at them. 'Some chance! Being a Methodist minister is a twenty-four seven job.' He turned over his book to show her the cover. *Methodism in a Cathedral City: 1757–1900.* 'Mugging up for next Sunday's sermon, would you believe? But my wife's been bitten by the bug. Who hasn't, these days? Her problem is that most of her family are from round Barnsley, and I've dragged her down here to the rural south-west.'

'I'm lucky,' Suzie said. 'Pretty well all my father's family were born in this county. So I've got the resources on my doorstep.'

'Good for you.' He pushed his chair back and stood up.

'Look, Suzie, I'm glad I've got the chance to talk to you. Is it OK if we have a word?'

'Yes.' She raked her mind to think what he wanted to say to her. Was he going to ask her to get more deeply involved in church activities?

'Maybe outside, so we don't disturb these good people.'

He steered her across the gardens behind the library to the Arts Centre café, bright with posters of shows. He set down a cup of tea in front of her and frowned thoughtfully over his. After a few moments, he raised his brown eyes to meet hers. 'I'm sorry about yesterday.'

'Why? I thought it was a great service. I meant to thank you afterwards.'

'But you got waylaid. I saw.'

Suzie felt a flutter of nervousness in her throat. He was treading on delicate ground. How much was it safe for her to say? 'I was talking to Lisa Gamble . . . sorry, Dawson. Our daughters are friends.'

'Tamara, yes. Nice girl. She's been coming to Young Church lately. She's a real asset.' His eyes crinkled with appreciation.

'Yes. I'm sorry. Millie stopped going when she was younger. Perhaps I ought to have . . .'

'Don't worry. She's not the only one, by a long way. There are a lot of things competing for teenagers' time and interest. But at least you've given her a good grounding. Something to hold on to when she's older. No, that wasn't what I was getting at. I was just sorry that you were on the receiving end of Leonard Dawson's attentions. Look, he's a great guy. He pretty much masterminds our finance committee at Springbrook. And they say he runs a tight ship at Briars Hill. They get great results. It's not easy being a headmaster these days. So don't get me wrong, I'm not running the guy down. But he's under a lot of pressure. He can be a bit . . . forceful.'

'I know.'

'I wouldn't want that to put you off coming again.'

'It's all right.' But she could visualize the trepidation she would feel, going there next time. She studied her saucer for a while. When she looked up, Alan Taylor still had those brown eyes fixed on her face.

'Do you want to talk about it? If I'm putting my big foot in it, just tell me to shut up. But it was something about Tamara, wasn't it? Is she all right? Since Len and Lisa married, he's been making her come to church with them. She's a joy to have, though I don't think she was any more keen at first than your Millie. But she wasn't there today. Is something wrong with her?'

Suzie met his eyes. The friendly humour had died. It was replaced by a look that was deeper, more compelling. She felt something tug at her guts. He was a minister. Someone people turned to when they were in trouble. She could trust him, couldn't she?

As if he had read her thoughts he said quietly, 'We don't do confessions in the Methodist Church, but we understand about confidentiality.'

'Yes,' she said. 'It was about Tamara. And no, she's not all right. For days, Millie had no idea what had happened to her. Now Leonard Dawson says she's been overworking and they've sent her away for a rest. He won't say where. But her mother thinks she's run away. And then this morning, Millie got a card. Tamara's in hiding. She says he threatened to kill her.'

Concern furrowed Alan's face. Then he smiled. 'Why? Look, Suzie, you've got teenage kids. You know the score. They say that sort of thing all the time: "He'll kill me!" It's not meant literally.'

'Because – look, I don't want this to go any further – she's pregnant.'

This time the look was consternation. He ran his hand through his hair. 'Poor old Tamara. That's tough. But it's still not the end of the world, is it? It isn't a hanging offence, thank God.'

'She's fourteen.'

He winced. 'Point taken. Still, that happens oftener than it should, more's the pity. I doubt if they'd send the boy to prison, even if is a criminal offence. But I wouldn't like to be in his shoes when Leonard finds out.'

'If it is a boy.'

His eyes narrowed. 'There's something you're not telling me, isn't there? Go on.'

'Do you think it could have been serious? The threat to Tamara? After all, Mr Dawson has his reputation to think of. He might think she'd made a fool of all his moral lectures to his pupils. But . . .' She played nervously with her teaspoon. 'What if it's worse than that?' He waited. She was unwilling to meet his eyes. 'What if Leonard Dawson is the baby's father?'

She heard the intake of breath. There was a moment's silence.

'That really would throw us in the deep end, wouldn't it? Have you any evidence of this?'

'N–no. But it's beginning to be the only answer that makes sense. Tamara practically implied it.'

'You say she's run away, but he hasn't reported her missing? Well, no. Come to think of it, he was behaving normally in the vestry yesterday. Not a word about Tamara being ill, let alone missing. That does sound odd, on the face of it. I'm usually one of the first to hear if someone's in trouble.'

'You don't think I'm being hysterical? Like Millie?'

He swirled his teacup slowly between his hands. 'I wish I did. In my line of business you learn a lot about what goes on under the surface. Even in a church like Springbrook. Salt of the earth, most of them. They'll go the extra mile to help other people. But some of them have stories to tell of what they've suffered that would make your hair curl. It's not all tea and jumble sales. You'd be surprised what goes on behind some very respectable doors.'

'So you do believe me? You think Tamara really is in danger?'

'Let's say, there are some serious questions to be answered.'

'We're desperate to help Tamara. But we don't know how. We've no idea where she is.'

'You said there was a letter. Wasn't there an address, a contact number?'

'Nothing. She was too afraid to tell Millie where she is. And she's thrown away her mobile, in case it's traced.'

'A postmark, then?'

'She said she was getting someone to post it in London. It sounds as if she's somewhere out in the country. She talked about "going into the village". But it could be anywhere. And we're afraid to go to the police, in case they find her, and Mr Dawson rubbishes her story and they bring her back.'

Alan Taylor thought about this. 'As I said, Len can be a pretty forceful character. Her word against his? I see what you mean. Listen, what about the Salvation Army? They have a Family Tracing Service.'

'We thought about that.' Suzie sighed. 'But they're not going to take her case up on our say-so, are they? If her parents haven't reported her missing? We're not even related.'

'I see your point. I suppose the same might apply to the Missing Persons Helpline.' His grave face relaxed into a grin. 'This might just be one time when a dog collar comes in handy. Leave it with me. I think I can sweet-talk the Sally Army into doing their stuff. They're very good at it. They have an amazing success rate with finding runaway teenagers.'

'And when they find her? If they do?'

'Yes. That's the million-dollar question, isn't it? How do we make sure what the truth is, and that it's safe for her to come home?'

The grin had gone. His eyes were troubled.

SIXTEEN

S uzie walked from the bus along the avenue towards home. There was a spring in her step which had been missing for days. She had not expected that talking to Alan Taylor would lift such a weight from her. It was probably something ministers were trained to do.

It was, surely, only a small hope though. He might persuade the Salvation Army to search for Tamara, without her parents' knowledge, but would they succeed? Yet he had seemed so confident.

And then what? Suppose they found her. They'd preserve her confidentiality, wouldn't they? If she was safe where she was, they would leave it to her to decide whether she wanted to get back in contact with family and friends. And, from her letter, Tamara certainly wouldn't want to come home.

Would she risk telling the Fewings where she was? When she had been so careful to keep this information even from Millie?

Her spirits were sinking again, the nearer she got to home. Nothing had changed. Tamara was still on the run from an intolerable situation. Still afraid.

There was a turning ahead. Maple Lane. The road where Tamara lived . . . had lived. Suzie's gaze went along the first detached houses in their mature gardens. Tamara's father's royalties had made sure they could continue to live there after the marriage broke up.

Where had Leonard Dawson been living before he moved in? Suzie hadn't given much thought to that before. Was he divorced, a widower, a middle-age bachelor, when he married Lisa?

If the police shared the Fewings' suspicions about Tamara's baby, they'd be interested in Leonard Dawson's first family, wouldn't they, if there was one? What other children might he have been preying on?

She was crossing the junction now. From here, she could see Tamara's house.

Her heart quickened. There was someone walking up to the gate. A girl in a grey school uniform.

For a crazy moment, she thought it must be Tamara.

But the figure was too slight. The sunlight fell on a crop of white-blonde hair.

Millie.

Suzie halted in the middle of the road. Then she shook herself. The moment of panic subsided in a shiver. There was an obvious reason why Millie should call on her friend's mother. In fact, that was just what she *would* do. Suzie scolded herself for not thinking of it herself. Millie must be going to tell Lisa Dawson the news that Tamara was safe. That she had had a letter from wherever she was hiding.

Suzie could imagine what a weight that would be off a mother's mind.

Millie was through the garden gate, starting to walk up the path, when a large silver car swung round the junction behind Suzie. The brakes squealed. The horn blasted. Belatedly realizing where she was standing, Suzie sprang out of the way.

As the car completed its turn, she saw the irate face of the driver turned to her through the side window.

Leonard Dawson.

Terror froze her.

It was too far to call out to warn Millie. Too late, anyway. The car was sweeping along Maple Lane. She saw the brake lights snap red as it started to turn into the drive.

The car stopped, its rear still half in the road. The door flew open and the burly figure of Mr Dawson leaped out. His roar rang down the road.

'AND WHERE DO YOU THINK YOU'RE GOING?'

Caught on the garden path, Millie twisted her pale face towards him. He was covering the ground between them, still shouting. His forceful strides were shattering the flowers in the beds. Suzie was too far away to distinguish more words.

She started to run towards them. She cursed the fact that she had worn heels today, instead of her usual flat pumps.

When she reached the gate, Leonard Dawson was berating Millie. His face was the same ugly red she remembered from yesterday, its usual baby pink verging towards purple.

'Get off my land, you two-faced little slut! Do you not understand plain English? I made it abundantly clear that I will not have you poking your nose into my affairs and upsetting Tamara. Do you want to make her more ill than she is already? And I won't have you badgering my wife. *Do you hear?*'

Suzie saw the fear in Millie's face. It was not that there was anything in Mr Dawson's words which was explicitly threatening. It was the venom with which he said them. He loomed over her. The overbearing force of his personality and physique, crashing down on a fourteen-year-old.

The pressure Tamara must have felt on her. Daily.

'Mr Dawson!' It was hard not to let her own voice sound like an inadequate squeak.

He swung round, fresh fury in his eyes.

Suzie made herself look past him and speak directly to Millie. 'Oh, there you are! I think you should come home now. It's obviously not a convenient time to call on Tamara's mum.'

Her eyes called her daughter, willing her not to argue. To her relief, Millie accepted the summons gratefully. She edged her way back down the path. She had to step aside on to the wrecked flower bed to avoid Mr Dawson's implacable bulk. She scuttled along the pavement to Suzie.

He was shouting after both of them now, though the volume was lowering. Suzie blotted out the words. She took hold of Millie's arm and turned her away. With what dignity they could manage, they headed back to the avenue and turned the corner towards home.

Millie was shaking. 'That *man*! I thought it would be safe. Tamara said he never came straight home from school. He always had meetings or something. It was her best time, with her mum. How could she *live* with him?'

'She couldn't,' Suzie pointed out. 'Not for more than a couple of months.'

'Long enough, though.' Millie scowled. 'Long enough for him to ruin her life. I could kill him.'

'What did you think you were playing at, going round there without telling us?'

Suzie's knife halted over the cucumber she was slicing for a salad. Tom was out with friends. Nick was standing over Millie, his voice loud with anger. Suzie winced. She knew he was only giving voice to his fears for Millie, what might have happened to her. But the hectoring tone was too like Leonard Dawson's for comfort.

Millie was hidden from view, hunched up on the conservatory sofa. She had just finished an indignant account of their encounter outside Tamara's house. Clearly, she had been expecting sympathy.

'But he's a headmaster. He has meetings. He's *never* home straight after school. And I know Tamara's mum gets in from work around five. I had to tell her, didn't I? I mean, wouldn't you be worried stiff if it was me? She'd love to know I've heard from Tamara. That she's . . . well, sort of all right.'

'You could have asked one of us to go with you. You knew what he was like yesterday. Waving that racquet about, as if for tuppence he'd have knocked my brains out. Stay away from that house in future. One girl in danger's enough. I don't want you caught up in it too.'

'But she's my friend, Dad. I can't not be.'

Nick turned away and walked swiftly out into the garden. Watching him through the kitchen window, Suzie felt how he was wrestling with protective anger.

She called softly to Millie. 'Don't take it to heart. He's only cross because he's worried about you. What might have happened.'

'I know *that*.'

Suzie was just setting the meal on the table when Nick came in. He took his usual chair, but sat staring down at his plate, as though he was not really seeing the food.

Then he raised his head. 'It doesn't fit. It's too obvious.'

'What is?' Suzie encouraged him.

'Leonard Dawson. The big bad bully. Shouting at everyone who questions where Tamara is. Drawing attention to himself. At church, at the tennis club. Don't you think if he really had a guilty conscience about Tamara, he'd keep quiet? Play the suave, everything-under-control stepfather?'

'Surely that's what he meant to do, with that story that Tamara was unwell and they'd sent her away for a bit? Cover it up until people had stopped asking questions.'

'Mmm. But he's in danger of blowing his cover, then. He's not being clever enough. And he *is* a clever man.'

'But that's how he *always* is,' Millie said. 'Shouting at people. You ask anyone from Briars Hill. He has them wetting their pants.'

'Using anger as a weapon to browbeat children is one thing. Losing your temper at the country club is another. Anyone could have come along and seen him. That sort of behaviour is generally frowned on.'

'Even if we were genuinely at fault?' Suzie queried. 'I mean, we were there on false pretences. He had a reason to bawl us out.'

'He's worried somebody will find Tamara. That she'll tell

the police what he did to her. That's why he's scared as hell.' Millie stared belligerently at her father.

'Maybe. I'm not denying he's a dangerous man if he's crossed. That's why you should keep away from him. I just feel that the more he has to hide, the more careful he'd be.'

'You think he's *not* the baby's father?'

Suzie frowned. 'He's just too proud to let people know she's missing? That's a bit extreme, isn't it? Anything could have happened to her. As far as he knows, she might not have run away. She could have been murdered by a stranger.'

'Who's being extreme now?' Millie exclaimed. 'Aren't most murders committed by someone close to the victim?'

'I didn't tell you, did I? I met Alan Taylor in the library today. You know, the minister at Springbrook.'

'Yeah, Tamara told me about him. He sounds a good laugh. She says he gets on great with the youth group at church. Better than the old one used to.'

'I . . . Well, I found myself telling him about Tamara.'

'Mum!'

'I know, but you can say things to ministers you wouldn't tell anybody else, even your best friend. And you're right.' She turned to Nick. 'He did notice that we were having a bit of a set-to with Leonard Dawson. And he's not unaware that there's a personality problem there. *Forceful* was the word he used. Anyway, the upshot is that he's going to ask the Salvation Army to see if they can trace Tamara. They might not do it for us, because we're not her parents, but he thinks he can persuade them to do it for him.'

Millie's eyes lit up. 'You really think they could find her?'

'There's a good chance. Unless she's covered her tracks extremely well. But don't get your hopes up too high. Even if they do find her, they won't tell anyone where she is unless she wants them to. So we might not be much better off than we are now.'

'Maybe we should just drop it,' Nick said. 'We know she's safe. At least, for the moment. Somebody seems to be looking after her. She probably wants to stay there until the baby's born.'

'Dad!' Millie cried suddenly. 'There was something in her

letter about seeing a doctor.' She jumped up and grabbed the notelet. 'Look! You don't think someone's making her have an abortion, after all?'

Suzie and Nick studied the words. Suzie read them aloud. *'She says I have to see a doctor soon because of the baby.'* Suzie's head shot up. 'She? I never noticed that before. She's staying with a woman? Who could that be, Millie?'

Millie shrugged. 'I haven't a clue.'

'Seeing the doctor could mean anything. Antenatal care. An abortion. She doesn't say.'

'I'm sure she wouldn't. Agree to an abortion, I mean.'

'Makes sense,' Nick said. 'If she had wanted that, it could all have been taken care of by now. She wouldn't need to be in hiding. But she might be so that Dawson can't put pressure on her to get rid of it.'

'Dad! What if *he* finds out where she is?'

'He knows less than we do. I doubt he can find her if he won't go to the police or the Sally Army.'

'We have to get there first,' Suzie said slowly. 'We need to find out what really happened and persuade her to go to the police. Even if it's only physical abuse, and not something worse.'

'Or *we* go to the police,' Millie insisted.

The phone rang. Millie sped to answer it. They heard her breathless query turn to laughter. Then: 'It's for you, Mum. It's that nice American lady.'

Suzie hurried to take the call. 'Hi, Pru. How are you?'

'I'm doing great. I've had the best time. And I'm dying to share my news with you. It just might open a few more doors than we thought. Look, I'm coming back tomorrow afternoon. How about if I come round to your place about eight? Fill you in on the details?'

'That would be great.' Suzie stifled the voice of conscience that told her she should invite Prudence for a meal. 'Eight would be fine. But can't you tell me over the phone?'

'Wait till tomorrow. I want to see your face when I tell you.'

Suzie came back to the table with a mixture of feelings. It was comforting to be reminded again about Prudence's family history. Safe. Its dramas securely in the past. But it was hard to sound enthusiastic about the unmarried Johan Clayson of Corley when a real, living girl was hiding from her parents, waiting to have a baby whose existence might be the result of rape or, at the least, coercion.

SEVENTEEN

S uzie was surprised by the rush of affection she felt when she saw Prudence Clayson on the doorstep, in her crisp green dress and white jacket. She had only known this dark-haired, carefully-coutured American woman for a week, yet it felt like welcoming a much-loved member of her own family.

It was laughable to think of that moment of hostility in their first encounter, when Prudence had found it difficult to accept the evidence of bastardy.

The women embraced warmly.

'Come in. I'm dying to know what you've found.'

It was not strictly true, but she couldn't help responding to Prudence's enthusiasm.

Prudence unwound her white chiffon scarf and settled herself on the sitting-room sofa. She beamed, with the delighted confidence of one who believes she has a treat to give. 'I sure struck gold with William Clayson. He's just a mine of information about the family. Around Birmingham, the south-west, the south-east, you name it. He's got 'em all covered.'

'And?' In spite of her other worries, Suzie was warming to the excitement she could see in Prudence's eyes.

'He told me one handy little bit of information you and I never suspected.'

'Which is?'

'Well, we've been chasing up the name Clayson. And, thanks to you, we did pretty well. Adam's baptism. Poor little Johan. That apprenticeship at Norworthy. The lease on the farm down in the valley you said we could go look at one day. I'd be excited enough to take all that back to the family. But that's only the half of it. Of course, I knew all along that people weren't too particular about the way they spelt their names in those days. Back when most folks couldn't read and write.'

Suzie laughed. 'They pull schoolchildren up for getting the spelling of Shakespeare wrong. But even Shakespeare couldn't spell Shakespeare. He wrote it about fourteen different ways.'

'Is that so? Well, that sure makes me feel better about my own spelling. But this William Clayson's pretty sure that, early on, the Clayson name was Clarkson; in some parts, anyways.'

'Clarkson? Are you sure? When you look for someone on the IGI Family Search, they throw in all the variant spellings for you. But when I searched for Clayson, Clarkson never came up once. I'm sure of it.'

'Guess the IGI don't know there's a connection.'

Suzie was thinking rapidly. 'When I get on the A2A website, looking for documents, I usually put in asterisks to cover variant spellings. With Clayson, I probably typed in Cla*son. That would cover things like Clason, without the y. But once the list of hits comes up, I run my eye down it and pick out just the ones that look possible.' She felt the jolt as she grasped the point. 'So, if I saw there was a document about someone called Clarkson, I wouldn't have bothered to click on that and get the details. In fact, I remember now that's what we did. There were lots for John Clarkson which I didn't bother to open.'

'But that's just what *we* did. Follow up the Clarksons. Well, Will did it for me. He got to this – what do you call it?'

'The National Archives, A2A. That's Access to Archives, from all over the country.'

'That's the one. And he picked out one of those Clarkson documents, from right here in your County Record Office.'

'And? Don't keep me on tenterhooks any longer.'

'It was a bastardy bond.'

There was a beam of huge pride on Prudence's face. She looked for Suzie's reaction. An expression of doubt at what she saw dimmed her expectant delight.

'That's what you call it, isn't it? A bastardy bond? I'm pretty sure that's what Will said.'

Suzie could contain herself no longer. She burst into peals

of laughter. 'I'm sorry,' she said, when she could speak at last. 'That's really rude of me. But when I first met you . . . Do you remember, at the Record Office? You spat that word at me as if it were just about the worst thing you could imagine. And now, here you are, looking as if Father Christmas has called in the middle of June, because you've found a bastardy bond.'

Prudence looked startled. She seemed to be casting her mind back. Then a rueful grin spread over her face. 'You've got me there. I guess I was a little put out.'

'Put out? You were shocked.'

'Well, yes. And I'm still planning how I'm going to tell the good folks back home that their story's not what they think it is. Those good old God-fearing Dissenters.'

'Johan might have been godly,' Suzie said more seriously. 'We still don't know what happened to her, to make her pregnant. We probably never will.' Her grin grew again, to match Prudence's. 'But join the club. You're a real family historian now, if you're putting the flags out because you've discovered a bastardy bond for your family. Lucky you. I'm green with envy.'

'You're *jealous*?'

'Well, yes. It's not often you turn up the details of such a human story from 260 years ago.'

'I'm still not sure I'd call it lucky. It was a pretty sad affair, from what you've told me, being an unwed mother in the 1700s.'

'I said lucky because most of us would give our eye teeth for one of those documents. We've all got them on our family trees. Unmarried mothers. It nearly always means the trail goes cold. You've only got the mother. Occasionally, the child is given a second baptismal name that's the father's surname. But otherwise, you're never going to know who he was. It's the ultimate brick wall. But if you've got a bastardy bond, that's your breakthrough. You've found yours. Who was he?'

'The catalogue says "Michael Atkins the younger, mainte-nance of Joane Clarkson's male bastard". It's Joane without the h. J. O. A. N. E. But you told me that didn't matter.'

'Of course! What an idiot I've been. I remember that entry

now. We saw it on the Record Office computer, and I said how lucky someone else was. I never thought it might be your Johan. Look, we're definitely going back to the Record Office tomorrow to see this bond.'

'You really think it's the same person? Joane Clarkson, Johan Clayson?'

'Was there a date for this bond?'

'Seventeen thirty-nine.'

'That fits exactly with Adam's baptism. And the place?'

'Corley parish.'

'It's got be her, hasn't it? An unmarried mother, in the right place and at the right time. Corley's not a very big village. I think William Clayson's cracked it.'

Prudence sat back, glowing with success. 'Now, my dear, you tell me what's been happening to you.'

And then the present came rushing back.

How much could she tell Prudence, this newcomer she had known for such a short time? 'Foreigner' didn't sound right. This woman felt almost like her own family, as though their shared search had made them relations. And it had been Prudence, not Suzie, in whom Millie had chosen to confide the fact that the pregnancy test was not for her.

Hesitantly, selecting her words with care, she began to tell Prudence something of the events of the weekend. The differing stories of the Dawsons in church. The Fewings' doubts about the tennis coach. The furious confrontation with the racquet-wielding stepfather. One thing she kept back.

Tamara's secret wasn't hers to share.

A movement of air behind her told her that the door had opened. Millie was standing there, listening.

'We know he hasn't killed Tamara. She's run away from him.'

The girl turned and went back to the kitchen. When she returned, Suzie was startled to see she had Tamara's notelet in her hand.

'That's all we have. She's hiding in this village, or country house, or something. Out in the sticks. Could be anywhere.'

Prudence studied the contents carefully. 'I'd say she was with someone she knows. Someone she trusts.'

'It's a woman,' Suzie said. 'She talks about *she*.'

'And you can't think who that could be?' Prudence's bespectacled eyes gazed at Millie thoughtfully.

Millie shook her head. 'Nope.'

'It could be a couple,' Suzie suggested. 'It would be the woman who'd put her in touch with the antenatal stuff.'

Prudence closed the card. Her ringed hand rested on the picture on the front. She drew it aside, revealing the drawing. A half-timbered, thatched house. She gave a little start. Her head bent to examine it more closely. 'You know where this is?'

'No,' Suzie said. 'I thought the name might be printed on the back, but it's not. It's just a drawing of a cottage.'

'I was there. Just yesterday. That's Anne Hathaway's cottage in Stratford-upon-Avon.'

Millie and Suzie stared back in silence. Then Millie started forward. 'You mean, you think she's there? Well, near it?'

'I guess they could sell these cards all over. But most gift shops sell ones of local places. If the person she's staying with has a packet of these, well, it's the best clue yet.'

'Somewhere near Stratford-upon-Avon?' Millie was thinking rapidly. 'It looks like I was wrong. I didn't really think she would have, but maybe Tamara's gone to her father, after all. Her real father.'

'Reynard Woodman?' Suzie asked. 'Why? Where does he live?'

'In a little village six miles from Stratford-upon-Avon.'

'And is there a woman there?'

Millie pulled a face. 'Her stepmother. I don't think they get on. That's why I thought she wouldn't go there.'

Suzie was aware of a commotion outside in the gathering twilight. She turned her head to find Tom storming up the drive, wheeling his bike somewhat awkwardly with one hand, while the other appeared to be dragging a boy scarcely half his size.

The bike clattered against the garage wall, the front door flew open and the boy was propelled into the hall. Millie dashed to see what was happening. Suzie hurried after her. Nick and Prudence were still getting to their feet.

'Justin Soames!' she heard Millie cry.

'That's the one.' Tom pushed the boy into the sitting room. 'This is the nerd who's been boasting about having it off with Tamara Gamble.'

'Liar!' Millie shouted.

'I never! I didn't actually *say* that.'

The boy's thin, sharp-featured face looked scared. He hunched his shoulders as he looked round in fright at the assembled adults. Tom's face, on the other hand, was alight with triumph.

'But you've been hinting at it. Putting the word around.'

'As if she would! You pathetic little slug!' Millie stormed. 'Tamara's never even been out with you. Has she?'

'N–not exactly.'

'What's that supposed to mean?'

The boy lowered his eyes. 'We met up a few times,' he muttered. 'She fancies me.'

'In your dreams!'

'Look.' Tom had hold of Justin's collar. 'Tamara's off school at the moment.' Suzie shot him an alarmed warning, but he went on, choosing his words carefully. 'Apparently, she's not well. Her stepfather says she's been overworking and they've sent her away for a rest until she's better. Do you know anything about that?'

'I heard she was off school,' he muttered. 'Didn't know why.'

Tom pulled the boy round and leaned over him. 'I'm asking you what you *did* know. Because I'm not sure that Tamara *has* been overworking. I think she may have been upset. And I'd very much like to know who's responsible. So if there's anything between you two you haven't told me about, you'd better cough it up fast.'

'It wasn't me!'

'But you boasted you've been out with her. When was that?'

'He didn't,' Millie insisted. 'She'd have told me.'

Justin wriggled uncomfortably. 'I *did* meet her. But we didn't exactly go out. I see her sometimes when I'm swimming at that country club. You know. Out on the West Road. My mum goes to their gym. We had a bit of a lark round the pool. I don't care what you say,' he rounded on Millie. 'I could see she fancied me.'

'And?'

'I asked her to go to the Year Eleven disco, when we'd finished exams. But she turned me down.'

'She told me about *that*. We had a good laugh.'

The boy shrank visibly.

Tom let him go. 'And that's really all? You two have never been on a date? You haven't tried any funny business behind the swimming pool? That's all lies you've been telling your mates?'

The boy shuffled his feet. 'Yeah. I guess so.'

'Get out. And if I hear one word more about you and Tamara having a thing, I'll break your neck.'

'Yes, Tom. Sorry, Tom.'

Tom pulled the door wide open. Justin Soames fled through it.

Tom turned to them, his blue eyes ablaze. He brushed his hands together, as though to rid them of dirt. 'There! I wanted you to hear that. I think I believe the little snot-nosed runt. She splashed him a couple of times in the swimming pool, and he thinks he's God's gift to women.'

'You don't think you've made things worse, do you?' Nick asked. 'Drawing attention to the fact that she's been sent away?'

'She hasn't,' Millie objected.

Nick checked himself. 'No, of course not. That's just the story the Dawsons are putting about. What I mean is, won't it start people asking questions?'

'They *should* be asking questions,' Millie said.

'We needed to know,' Tom defended himself. 'Think about it. In real life, the most obvious reason for a girl getting herself in the club is that she's been having it off with her boyfriend. Or a one-night stand with some boy, anyway.'

'Tom! I'll kill you for that! Tamara's not *like* that. Do you think I wouldn't know?'

He held up his hands. 'Kid, she's human. It happens. But the only name on the street is Justin, because he's been talking big about her. I had to check it out. And if it's *not* him . . .' He looked at Millie under lowered brows. 'If there's someone else we haven't heard about, well, maybe if Justin spreads the word I did him over because of her, something else may come out of the woodwork.'

'You don't believe it was that Dawson beast?'

Tom shrugged. 'I'm keeping an open mind. Wouldn't you rather it was someone her age? Even a nerd like Justin?'

There was silence in the room.

Then Millie said in a small voice, 'Then why would she run away? Supposing it *was* him, and he's lying to us?'

EIGHTEEN

'I know what you're thinking.' Nick lay in the darkness with his back to her.

'What?'

'That we ought to follow it up. Pru's hunch. Get in touch with this author guy. Find out for certain if Tamara's there.'

'Would he tell us? She didn't want even Millie to find her.'

'It's worth a try.'

'Millie tried to get his number. He's ex-directory.'

'He's bound to have a website, isn't he? They always have a "Contact Me" button.'

'I tried that last week, remember? It said all enquiries should be directed to his agent.'

'Well, then. We ring the agent up and ask him for Gamble's number.'

'Her. His agent. Josephine something.'

'Whatever.'

'If Reynard's become as cagey as that, she probably won't give it. He probably gets thousands of fans trying to contact him.'

Nick struggled up on his elbows and turned to look down at her in the thick greyness of the summer night. 'I thought you *wanted* to find out about Tamara. Make sure that she's safe.'

'I do. But don't pretend that you don't too. Why else are

you interrogating me in the middle of the night? You're worried stiff about her, aren't you?'

He slipped down in bed and put his arms around her. 'I keep thinking, suppose it was Millie? Running away, and too scared even to tell her mother where she was going. Can you imagine Millie not telling you? And then so frightened he'd find her that she can't tell her best friend how to contact her.'

'Lisa Dawson's bound to have her ex's number. They must be in touch to arrange Tamara's visits. But I'm not sure I'd have the nerve to go and ask her, after what happened when Millie showed up there.'

'I don't know. Millie's right. She was just unlucky. Head teachers are busy people. It'll only be once in a blue moon he gets straight home after school.'

Suzie lay in the cradle of his arms, trying to imagine braving that house again. 'You were the one who spotted the bruise on her forehead, under her hair. If she's too terrified to tell the police Tamara's missing, she's hardly going to be brave enough to help us find her. Dawson's obviously ordered her to keep quiet. And we're the last people he wants her to talk to.'

'I'd come with you, but after the country club, that might only make things worse. It'll have to be girl talk.'

'I'll ring the agent in the morning. If she won't give me his number, she might at least pass on a message.'

'Mm.' Nick's hold was relaxing as he drifted back towards sleep. 'And what message would that be?'

'That we want to know if Tamara's with him . . . Ah! I see what you mean. It's not going to work, is it? He'd keep her secret. Well, how about if I just ask him to contact me? Say it has to do with Tamara's safety. That might scare him into breaking cover, if he cares about her.'

'You don't think we'll be making things worse for her? Putting her into more danger? More people knowing where she is? Even if it's us?'

'I don't see how. I thought you wanted to find her.'

'All right, all right. Only, I'm beginning to feel this whole thing is like a keg of dynamite. I don't know what would be the match that sets it off.'

* * *

Suzie walked up the steps of the Record Office with a sense of heightened anticipation. She felt more optimistic than she had for a week. Surely it was more than a happy coincidence that the breakthrough in Pru's family search had led them directly to identifying Tamara's hiding place? Equating Johan Clayson with the Joane Clarkson of the bastardy bond, giving the revelation of Adam's father. And the notelet with Anne Hathaway's cottage, pointing so plainly to the Stratford area. In the past and the present, the pieces were falling into place.

She and Pru deposited all but the essentials in the lockers and entered the search room.

'A bastardy bond? Great stuff!' Enthusiasm lit up the archivist's face. 'Yes, you really do need to see the original. We only put the names of the principal characters on A2A. With luck, you should find out a whole lot more.'

As she turned away towards the stockroom, Suzie and Prudence exchanged triumphant grins. They settled down at their table to wait. It was not long before the archivist hurried over with a cardboard folder.

At first sight, the bastardy bond looked not unlike the apprenticeship indenture. Much of it was preprinted in eighteenth-century type. Their eyes were drawn to the handwritten entries which gave the details particular to this case.

'Here!' Prudence's voice was rising in excitement. '*Michael Atkins the Younger and Michael Atkins the Elder and Robert Clarkson. Bond for Maintaining Michael Atkins the Younger's Bastard Child.* So his father gets in on the act too.'

'And Robert Clarkson,' Suzie chimed in. 'He must be Joane's father, mustn't he? Do you think he's the Robert Clayson whose name we found on that lease? Son of the older Adam Clayson?'

'Gee. I can see why it gets to you. When the pieces of the puzzle all start to come together.'

'There's more. You've really struck gold. *Mr Michael Atkins the Younger and Michael Atkins the Elder of Corley Helliers and Masons, and Robert Clarkson of the same place Woolcomber.* You've got all their occupations.'

'Hellier? What's that?'

'A roofer or tiler, I think. Anyway, they've all bound themselves to the churchwardens and Overseers of the Poor of

Corley for forty pounds, to make sure the baby doesn't become a charge on the parish. That'll be so much for the lying-in, and then a weekly payment. And here!' She gave a cry that turned the heads of other researchers. 'Do you see where they've signed their names at the bottom? The younger Michael Atkins signs his name. All Robert Clarkson can make is a rough letter C. But look at the older Michael's mark. See those half moons and that triangle? It's much more elaborate than a single letter. I wouldn't mind betting that's his mason's mark. He'll have left that on every bit of stonework he built.'

Prudence was only half listening. 'Will you look at this?' Her finger was pointing to a long, unpunctuated sentence halfway down the page, which Suzie had skipped over. 'Say, they didn't believe in much punctuation, did they? *Joane Clarkson of Corley aforesaid single woman did in her life time and by her voluntary examination in writing and upon oath before George Thorne Esquire one of his Majestie's Justices of the peace declare that she was with child and that the said Child was likely to be born a bastard and Chargeable to the said Parish of Corley and that the above bounden Michael Atkins the Younger was the father of the said Child which said Joane was about six weeks since delivered of a male Bastard Infant according to said her Examination which said Male Bastard Child is now living the mother thereof the said Joane Clarkson being since dead.'*

Her voice broke off.

Suzie followed her finger. A chill ran through her.

'Poor soul,' whispered Prudence. 'She may have brought little Adam into the world. But she paid the price with her life.'

The thrill of the eighteenth-century drama faded. Suzie saw an illegitimate child. A teenage mother dying in childbirth.

Tamara, pregnant. In the twentieth century, but in fear of her life.

'And that's the guy's father. Adam's grandfather.' Prudence was staring down at the mason's mark. 'I have the strangest feeling. It's kind of beautiful, the way he does it. The guy couldn't even write, but he's a real craftsman. All over this little town, he'll be building walls, putting the roofs on. I get a feeling it's something I should be proud of. And yet his son's got this girl into trouble, and all *he* can do is sign his name to say he's going to pay for the kid. Why doesn't he marry her, for heaven's sake?'

'He might be married already,' Suzie suggested quietly. 'We could check it out.'

With a touch of regret, she returned the yellowed document to the folder and left it on the desk. 'Thanks, that was great.'

They turned back to the Corley registers on microfiche.

'Déjà vu. This is how we met.' Suzie smiled at Pru.

'Was that only last week? It seems like I've known you the longest time.'

It did not take long to find what she suspected.

1735 was baptized Thomas son of Michael Atkins 22 August.

1737 was baptized Sarah daughter of Mr Michael Atkins 3 April.

1739 was baptized Alice daughter of Michael Atkins 4 October . . .

'That last one's the same year as Adam!' Prudence exclaimed.

'There's your answer. He already has a family.'

Suzie took the microfiche out of the machine with a heavy heart. It was what she had been expecting – the older man exploiting a fresh young girl, even if it wasn't the local squire. But at the back of her mind she had been hoping for a more optimistic story. A young mason's apprentice would have been better. Someone closer to Johan's age. A teenage romance that went too far, and the boy unable to marry until he had finished his indenture.

'I wonder how it happened? If he's a mason, I suppose he might have been earning enough to employ a maid. Or he might just have come staggering out of the pub one night and caught her on her way home in the dark.' She paused. Her head bent closer over her notes. 'I missed that!' She slid the microfiche under the glass plate again and found the place in the register. 'Do you see? Seventeen thirty-seven, daughter of *Mr* Michael Atkins. Hang on.' She searched for her transcript of the bastardy bond. 'There it is again. Mr Michael Atkins the younger.'

Prudence looked at her, baffled.

'They didn't call just anyone Mr in those days. You had to be a bit of a gentleman. So your Michael Atkins wasn't just a horny-handed workman. He was someone with money and status. A substantial businessman. So we're getting back to something not unlike the squire in the big house abusing a female servant.'

'You don't think she was his willing lover?' Pru asked. 'She could have been flattered by his attentions.'

For a moment, Suzie didn't know how to answer. Prudence had been shocked by the idea of premarital relations when they first met. 'We'll never know.'

She gathered her notes together. This time, she was the one with a sour taste in her mouth.

She had wanted a different outcome for Tamara too. A love affair with someone her age. It was silly not to be able to shake off the conviction that the two girls were connected.

She braved a smile for Prudence. 'There. You've got your story. The outlines of it, anyway.'

'Not a pretty one, is it? Whichever way you look at it.'

'At least you know for certain who the father is. That's not what usually happens. And it opens up a whole new line. You can trace Michael Atkins back now . . .' She paused. 'No. I forgot. The Corley registers only start in 1729. This is nearly as far back as you can go.'

'I'm running out of time, anyway. I'm due back in the good old US of A the end of the week. I fly out on Sunday.'

'I can go on hunting for you. See if I can find who he married. It's so annoying when you get a rector like this one, who doesn't think it's worth recording the mother's name. Unless she was single, of course. There might be other documents about the Atkins family. Like that lease we guessed might be for Johan's father and grandfather.'

'Looks like you were right about her father. He could make his initial. That C. *The mark of Robert Clarkson.* It was a bit shaky, but it kind of touched me.'

'I wonder how he felt, putting his name to that bond? At least he'd got Atkins to own up to being the father of his grandchild, and to put his hand in his pocket to support him. That must have been some sort of satisfaction.'

On their way out, Prudence stopped at the enquiry desk. 'Is that really true that an unmarried mother had to parade through the streets in a white sheet?'

'Oh, that!' The archivist laughed. 'What date are we talking about?'

'Seventeen thirty-nine.'

'It was going out of fashion in the eighteenth century.'

'Well, that's a relief.' Prudence was turning away when the archivist's voice called her back.

'Unless she was a Dissenter. The Establishment would seize on any excuse to stigmatize someone who had stepped out of line.'

Prudence's face fell. 'Her child grew up a Dissenter.'

As they made their way back to the locker room, Suzie reflected, 'So Johan might still have been marked out in the village as a loose woman. Even after she was dead. Her father would have had to live with the shame on his family.'

The same shame the moralizing Leonard Dawson was feeling?

'I guess that's why those magistrates made him sign the bond too. So he couldn't just turn her out of house and home. He had to stay responsible for her.'

Suzie was aware of the double conversation going on. On the surface, they were talking about Johan Clayson in the eighteenth century. But neither of them could get out of their minds Tamara Gamble and the role her stepfather might or might not have played in her pregnancy and her flight from home.

Suzie threw open the door of the house to usher Prudence in. The women almost fell over Millie on the hall phone.

Her pointed face was animated. She was even blushing slightly. She flattened herself against the wall so that they could get past her. As Suzie brushed by, she saw that Millie was cradling the receiver against her face, so that her mother could not hear the conversation.

Suzie was halfway to the kitchen before she realized what was odd. Millie, like any other fourteen-year-old, was perpetually on her mobile. It was not often she used the landline. Yet the expression on her face clearly said that this was a personal conversation.

She'd been blushing. As Suzie ran the water into the kettle, she reflected that it was probably an unexpected call from a boy. Someone who didn't know her mobile number. A smile twitched at her lips. Some new romance? Someone from an older class, perhaps? If Justin Soames could nurse dreams of the curvaceous Tamara, someone else in his year might surely be stopped in his tracks by this newly-blonde and sophisticated Millie.

Too soon yet to start worrying.

They took their tea into the garden. Suzie was itching for an opportunity to do a little maternal detective work. But Millie was likely to retreat to her bedroom when she had finished the phone call. Curiosity would have to wait.

It was therefore a surprise when her daughter appeared through the patio doors. Her usually pale face was still flushed, and there was a glint of both pride and defiance in her eyes.

'You'll never guess who that was.'

'No,' Suzie said. 'But I expect you're going to tell us.'

'Only Dan Curtis!' The unfamiliar name fell into the silence. 'Oh, come on, Mum. You know. That gorgeous guy at the tennis club? They've got a dinner dance there on Saturday night. He found out my real name from Leonard Dawson, in spite of Dad's daft idea of pretending we were somebody different. He's invited me to go with him.' Her face blazed triumph. 'Just wait till I tell the girls!'

Suzie's teacup almost crashed on to the table. 'The coach? The one we thought Tamara might have . . . Millie, for heaven's sake! Besides, you're only fourteen. You're too young to be dating grown men. You don't even *know* him.'

Millie tossed her blonde crop. 'I've met him. Even if Dad was giving him the third degree. It's your fault for taking me there. And he's drop-dead gorgeous, isn't he? The girls will be so–o jealous.'

'You're not going.' Fear was coursing through Suzie. 'We still don't know whether . . . We may have been jumping to conclusions about Tamara and Mr Dawson. You said yourself, he's just the sort of young pin-up who could turn any girl's head. Yours, for instance. You don't know the first thing about him, but just because he looks like Leonardo de Caprio you want to spend the night with him.'

'*Mum*!'

Suzie gasped as she realized what she had said. 'I'm sorry, love. I didn't mean it like that. I just meant going out to a dance with that sort of man. Late hours. He'll offer you wine, probably, even though you're under age. Romantic music. I know his type.'

'You don't! *You're* the one who doesn't know the first thing about him. You've only met him once.'

'So have you.'

'But I know what Tamara told me about him.'

'You still have that card from Tamara?' Prudence's calm voice broke in.

'Yes, why?'

'Guess I thought you might be heading for that Stratford neighbourhood. Check out if she really is with her father, and if she's OK.'

A pause.

'Could we?' Millie's suddenly serious gaze swung back to her mother.

'I know your father will feel a lot easier if we find out for sure what's happened to her,' Suzie said. And so, she thought, will I.

'When can we go? Tomorrow?'

'It's a school day.'

'Mum, this is *important*.'

'Of course, if you've got other plans for the weekend . . .'

'Beast!' Tears started into Millie's eyes. She glared at her mother, then turned on her heel and stalked into the house.

'Thank you,' Suzie said, with a weak smile at Pru. 'We need to get our priorities straight.'

'I don't know about you, but I can't help getting their stories muddled up. Tamara and Johan. You haven't ruled that young coach out, have you? Just because that bastardy bond showed Adam's father was a married man? That was Johan's story. We're living in a different century.'

'You're right.' Suzie rubbed her hands over her cheeks. 'I'm confused. And anyway, Dan Curtis may be married, for all I know. I can't help feeling there *is* a connection. And I'm scared about the way Johan's story ended.'

NINETEEN

S uzie dialled the agent's number. A girlish voice answered. 'Hi. Bellacourt Literary Agency. How can I help you?'
'Could I speak to . . .' She checked the name in front of her. 'Josephine Tees?'

A pause. 'I'm sorry. She's in a meeting.'

'Well, perhaps you could help me. She's Reynard Woodman's agent. You know, the children's author? I need to get in touch with Mr Woodman. I wonder if you could tell me his address and telephone number.'

'Oh, sure, I know the answer to that one. We *never* give out Reynard Woodman's contact details to anyone. You can leave a message if you like. Josephine will pass it on.'

'I really need to see him urgently. It's a . . . confidential family matter. It's about his daughter.'

'Which one?'

The question rocked Suzie. Tamara was an only child, wasn't she? Then the truth sank in. It was years since the author had left Lisa and Tamara. There would be a new family now in his Warwickshire hideout. Always supposing Prudence had guessed right about the card.

The receptionist's voice gushed on. '. . . Persephone and Calliope. They're such sweeties! He brought them into the office once. I wouldn't be surprised if they grow up as cute as Bob Geldof's kids. Sorry. What did you say your name was?'

'Suzie Fewings. Mr Woodman may not remember me, but he knows my daughter Millie. She and Tamara have been best friends for years. Tamara's his daughter by his first wife.'

'Before my time, I'm afraid. Did you want to leave a message?'

'It's difficult to do over the phone.' She hesitated, then

plunged on. 'We're worried about Tamara. She's missing. She left without telling anyone where she was going. We wondered if her father knew where she was.'

'Gosh. It sounds like the plot for a children's book.'

'Will you get my message to him?' Suzie gave her phone number. 'But really, if I could talk to him that would be so much better.'

'I'll give your message to Josephine, and if she thinks it's important, she'll pass it on to Reynard Woodman.'

'It *is* important. I've just been telling you. She's been missing for days.'

'What about her mother?'

'Her mother doesn't know where she is, either.'

'Have you told the police?'

'Not yet. We . . . we were hoping to keep this private.'

'We–ell. I don't want to sound rude, Mrs Fewings, but you'd be surprised the stories people tell to get hold of Reynard Woodman's details. He'd have fans queuing up at his garden gate if we weren't discreet about it. Like I said, I'll tell Josephine Tees and leave it to her. I expect she'll get back to you if there's an answer.'

The phone went dead. Suzie stared at the sheet of paper in front of her, still blank except for the literary agent's name and phone number.

A cottage, maybe somewhere near Stratford? A different partner, younger than Lisa. A new family of cute little girls. How welcome would Tamara have been? An older daughter bringing reminders of a fractured past. Now carrying within her problems for the future.

'No luck,' she said, when Nick returned home. 'I couldn't even get through to his agent, let alone the great author himself. And she hasn't rung back.'

'But he'll get your message, won't he? If he's as great with kids as Millie says, he's bound to be scared out of his wits for Tamara. I would be, if it were Millie.'

Suzie's hand flew to her mouth. 'What if he rings Lisa? If Leonard Dawson finds out we're still asking questions about Tamara, he'll be livid. He'll take it out on Lisa, won't he? What have I done?'

Nick put his arm around her. 'I doubt if Reynard Woodman's any more enchanted with Dawson than we are. He'll only want to talk to Lisa.'

'You know what Dawson's like. He'll get it out of her. And make her pay for it.'

Tom's voice surprised them from the depths of the sofa. 'Why don't you get your retaliation in first? Tell Lisa Dawson yourself. Get *her* to ring this Reynard bloke.'

'Would she do it? And I'm not sure I have the nerve to go back to that house. Alan Taylor was right about him being forceful. You don't understand the power he has over people until you've experienced it. It's like being trapped in a thunderstorm. I don't like to think what he'll do if he catches me there again. Or what he'd do to Lisa.'

'This is getting beyond a joke,' Nick said. 'If the man's that abusive, it's time someone told the police.'

'I'm coming with you.'

Tom's determined assertion startled Suzie. Her usually sunny-tempered son was not smiling now. A dark wave of hair hung over his brow, shadowing his eyes.

'I'm the only one of the family he doesn't know. If he turns up at the wrong moment, Dad would be like a red rag to a bull, and he's already bawled Millie out. I could try the old blue-eyed charm on him.'

His grin did then break out, rocking her heart. So like Nick, and yet unlike. Tom knew only too well his ability to charm his way through life. He had left a swathe of lovelorn girls in his wake on his progress through school.

'I don't think Mr Dawson is susceptible to that sort of flattery.'

'Possibly not. But I'm probably bigger than he is.'

'Maybe a fraction taller, but he's at least twice your weight.'

'Bet I'm quicker, though. He'd think twice about roughing you up with me there.'

'I'm not expecting grievous bodily harm. Just a very angry man. And the whole point is to avoid him. I have to get to Lisa when he's not there.'

'So I'll case the joint and let you know when it's OK to

go in. I'm the only one he hasn't issued with an exclusion
order yet.'

Suzie had to admit that she did feel better, setting out in
the protective shadow of her tall son. They rounded the corner
into Maple Lane. Tom signalled her to stay back.

She watched him saunter along the avenue, casually flicking
at the sprays of flowering shrubs that overhung garden walls.
He came to the Dawson's house, and his steps slowed further.
His head turned sideways, studying the double-fronted, mock-
Tudor building. A few steps further on he turned and came
back to her.

'Only one car in the garage. A green Nissan Micra. What
did you say he drove?'

'Something big and silver. A Mercedes? The one with a
lion on the front.'

'Women! That's a Peugeot. Anyway, it's not there. Are you
up for it?'

'I think so. It's silly to be so afraid of someone. After all,
what can he do to me?'

'Quite a lot, by the sound of it. Beat his wife up. Terrify
his daughter so that she runs away. Even supposing he hasn't
done something worse to her. Watch yourself. I'll hang around
and whistle if I see him coming.'

'What am I supposed to do then? Walk straight out into his
arms?'

'Take cover. Then, when he comes in the front door, you
slip out by the side gate and leg it.' He grinned at her, a
mixture of concern and excitement. 'Go, girl.'

She hurried up the drive, feeling like a trespasser. The bell
trilled through the house. She felt a foolish hope that no one
would be in, even though she had seen Lisa's car in the garage.

A flicker of movement behind the glass panels. Lisa opened
the door. Suzie saw the startled look pass over her face.
Surprise, a spasm of hope, then consternation. Lisa's dark eyes
flew past Suzie, guiltily checking that her husband wasn't in
sight.

'What do you want?'

'Can I come in? It's about Tamara.'

It was painful to see how afraid Lisa was as she ushered

Suzie quickly into the dim hall. She stood there, like a bird trapped in the house, unable to decide which way to flee for safety.

'Why don't we go into the garden?' Suzie suggested, taking charge of the situation. 'If Leonard comes home, I'll slip out round the side.'

'He shouldn't be back before eight. But you never know. When he caught you and Millie . . .' Her arm strayed around her chest in a protective gesture, as if she was nursing painful ribs.

Suzie longed to tell her she needed help, that she shouldn't put up with this nightmare situation. But Tamara's safety was uppermost in her mind. 'Look, I won't stay long. We think we may know where Tamara is . . .'

Lisa's hand flew to her mouth. 'Don't tell me. Please!'

The panicked reaction shocked Suzie.

'He'll get it out of me,' Lisa went on. 'He's sure I know where she is and I'm not telling him. But I don't.'

'It's all right.' Suzie put a reassuring hand on the smaller woman's arm. She steered her towards the back of the house. 'Just tell me one thing. Have you rung your husband to ask if he knows anything about her? Sorry. I meant Tamara's father. Kevin . . . Reynard Woodman.'

Lisa shook her head dumbly. They had reached the spacious sitting room, where glass doors led out into a garden larger than the Fewings'. But whereas Nick had created a riot of colour and contrasting foliage in their own garden, with curves and unexpected vistas, someone had recently taken control here, uprooting flower beds and setting out annuals in regimented rows. Overhanging branches had been hacked back, shrubs disciplined into unnatural orderliness. Suzie felt a fresh pain as she surveyed it.

Still looking round her nervously, Lisa found her voice. 'I was afraid to ask him. Leonard has very strong opinions. When he found out Tamara was . . . expecting . . . he . . . was very upset.'

I bet that's an understatement, Suzie thought. 'So he knows? We wondered if she was afraid to tell him.'

'He didn't want anyone else to know. He wanted her to

have an abortion. When she said no, there was a terrible row. The next day, Tamara didn't come home.'

'And what have you done to try and find her?'

'Nothing.' The word came out in a whisper.

'*Nothing*?'

Your fourteen-year-old daughter's pregnant and she's run away, and you do *nothing* to find her?

'He wouldn't let me. He said she'd learn her lesson. She'd come back when she'd repented.'

'And you accepted that?'

'Leonard's had a lot more experience at dealing with teenagers than I have. I know some people think he's hard, but you have to be nowadays, don't you? There are some tough kids at Briars Hill. He couldn't make a success of that school if he was soft. He doesn't want to make Tamara's affair public. He thinks that if he sticks to his principles, she'll be sorry and come back of her own accord.'

'Do you?'

Lisa gazed back at her unhappily and said nothing.

'Look, it's not my business what happens between you and your husband. But I am concerned about Tamara. So is Millie. We all are. You may feel you can't disobey him, but there's nothing to stop *us* looking for her. Could you at least tell me how to get hold of Tamara's father? Just in case he knows anything about her. I couldn't get any joy out of his agent.'

Lisa turned away, back into the sitting room. She opened a drawer in a side table and took out her address book. Reluctantly, she opened it and handed it to Suzie.

'I don't think it will be any good. He used to adore Tamara when she was small. But lately I get the impression from her that he doesn't really care for teenagers. And of course, he's got *her* children.' There was a twist of bitterness in her voice.

Millie had said that Tamara hadn't been enjoying her visits to her father recently. It began to make sense now. The wicked stepmother? Perhaps they had been wrong about the Stratford notelet, after all.

She copied the entry in the address book. It was for a village in Warwickshire, as they'd guessed. She noted the telephone number.

She looked up to find Lisa's attention concentrated on the door. Suzie tensed, listening for the all-too-quiet hum of a car turning into the drive or Tom's urgent whistle. Even the silence seemed ominous.

'Thank you,' she said, turning a nervous smile on Lisa. 'I won't stay. Do you want me to tell you if we find her?'

Lisa gazed at her with longing. Then her face began to crumple, as though she would burst into tears. She mastered it. But she shook her head hopelessly.

What must it be like, Suzie wondered, to be so afraid of your husband that you daren't ask where your daughter is?

The walk through the wide hall and out of the front door into the sunshine was nerve-wracking.

The drive was empty. Tom was leaning against a wall on the opposite pavement. He straightened up when he saw her.

She had reached the gate, and he was coming across the road to meet her, when a large silver car swung into the road.

Suzie's gasp was almost a scream. In two strides, Tom was beside her. He seized her arm and began to propel her away from the house.

The car shot down the road towards them. For a horrified moment, Suzie wondered if it would mount the pavement and crush them against the wall.

It swept on past. They watched it turn into a drive at the far end of the avenue.

'Whew!' Tom mopped his brow in exaggerated relief. 'Amazing what a guilty conscience does for you. But did you get anything?'

Suzie showed him the precious paper with her notes.

'Well, guess that was worth a couple of heart attacks. Good stuff, Mum.'

'But she doesn't think Tamara will be there. She didn't get on with her stepmother.'

TWENTY

'Which of us is going to phone him?' Suzie looked round the assembled family, hoping that it wouldn't be her, but fearing that it would. Only Prudence was an interested but detached observer. 'And if his agent's set up the barricades around him, to protect him from his adoring fans, how's he going to react if one of us asks out of the blue for Reynard Woodman?'

'Now you've gotten me confused,' Prudence said. 'Her name is Tamara Gamble, right? And her mother married again, so she's Lisa Dawson? So how come this guy is Reynard Woodman? Why doesn't Tamara have *his* name?'

The Fewings looked at her, momentarily puzzled. Then Suzie slapped her hand down on her knee. 'Of course! We've been talking about his pen name. He's not going to be using that if he wants to keep a low profile in his country hideout. I bet he'll be known to the locals as Kevin Gamble, like he used to be when we first knew him.'

'No doubt a perfectly ordinary member of the local community,' Nick agreed. 'If a little secretive about his source of income.'

'I should have thought of that,' said Suzie. 'You gave me the clue yourself, Pru. Clayson, Clarkson. We didn't find Johan in the records at first, because we were looking for the wrong name. It's not Reynard Woodman but Kevin Gamble we need to ask for, so we don't sound like children's fantasy nuts.'

'I think Millie should ring,' Tom said. 'It would be a perfectly natural thing for her to do. She'd have done it days ago, if she'd had the number.'

'Me?' Millie turned pink as they all looked at her. She looked suddenly younger than her fourteen years.

'Why not?' Suzie asked. 'If one of us adults started asking questions, it would look a lot more suspicious.'

Nervously, Millie got out her mobile. Suzie passed her the telephone number.

'Hang on,' Nick said. 'Put that away.' He brought in the extension phone from the house line and switched on the loudspeaker. 'Now we can all hear.'

'What do I say?'

'Just ask if you can speak to Tamara,' Suzie suggested.

The four of them waited while she dialled and the ringing tone began.

It was interrupted by a girlish voice. 'Hello. Wood Cottage.'

'Not much of a disguise, if you've read his books,' Tom snorted.

'Can I speak to Tamara?'

'Who?'

'Tamara. Tamara Gamble.'

There was a surprised silence at the other end. Then a guarded: 'Who is this speaking?'

'Millie Fewings. Her friend.'

'And why would you assume Tamara Gamble is here?'

Millie looked helplessly at her parents. She improvised. 'That's her father's house, isn't it? Reynard . . . sorry, Kevin Gamble. Is she there?'

'If you're her friend, you ought to know Tamara doesn't live here.'

'I know where she *lives*. But she's not there now. I thought she might be with you. Are you Mrs Gamble?'

'Petronella Gibson. Not that it's any of your business.'

'Oh . . . But you're Mr Gamble's partner, right?'

'What's that to do with you? And I'm sure if Tamara wants to get in touch with you, she'll do that herself.'

The phone went dead.

Millie looked up at them, crestfallen. 'I'm sorry. I messed that up, didn't I?'

'No, you didn't, love,' Suzie soothed her. 'I don't think any of us would have done any better.'

'She didn't exactly say whether Tamara was there or not, did she?' Tom frowned. 'She could have been keeping it secret, but from her tone of voice, I'd say this Petronella Gibson isn't exactly enchanted with the idea of a teenage stepdaughter.'

'Tamara's father went off with some singer from a girl group,' Millie said. 'But that wasn't her name. From what Tamara said, he swapped her for a younger model. But you can understand why. *I'd* have run off with him.'

'Millie!' Nick exclaimed.

'But there are children,' Suzie reflected. 'So the receptionist at the agency said. Persephone and Calliope, poor things. I wonder if they're hers.'

'What now?' Tom said. 'Since the phone number didn't produce a result?'

'There's only one option, isn't there?' Nick said. 'Try the address.'

'You mean you really will go to Warwickshire?' Millie was suddenly half out of her chair. '*Can* we?'

'I'm not exactly sure about the "we", but I don't see any alternative. This has gone on long enough.'

'Tomorrow?'

'That's a school day,' Suzie pointed out. 'And your father and I have to work.'

'Saturday! Mum! You're only doing that to stop me going to that dance with Dan Curtis.'

'You're not still thinking of that?' Nick protested. 'We told you. He's twice your age. The fact that he even asked you says enough about him. Sorry, I'm putting my foot down. You go straight to that phone and tell him you're not coming.'

'You're just prejudiced. You're as bad as Mr Dawson. You won't let me do *anything*.' Millie made for the door, her eyes dangerously bright.

'I sure wish *I* could go back to Warwickshire with you guys.' Prudence's warm, level voice flowed across the tense room. 'I feel I'm missing out on the action. It's quite a story. I came looking for drama in my family history, and I've found it in the twenty-first century too. It'll be something to tell your kids, Millie.'

'I only hope this has a happy ending,' Nick said.

The past plucked at Suzie's memory. Johan Clayson, dead before the three men signed the bastardy bond for her child.

*   *   *

'Did you tell him?' Nick demanded, when Millie came back.

She nodded, though her expression was mutinous. 'I'm not going to forgive you for this, Dad. Anyone else in my class would kill for a date like that!'

'See sense, love. It's for Tamara's sake. We'll go up to Warwickshire on Saturday. You, Mum and me.'

'Hey, that's not fair!' Tom exploded. 'You can't leave me out.' He sounded like a mutinous small boy.

'I'm sorry, Tom,' Nick said. 'But this isn't a family day out. Millie has to come, to reassure Tamara, if we find her. And we obviously need a woman, so Mum's a given. And I'd rather be the one to drive them and deal with any awkward customers we may meet.'

'Are we expecting any?' Suzie asked. 'He's her father, for goodness' sake.'

'We're only guessing that she's there. I don't know where this trail may lead.'

'It's a five-seater car,' Tom insisted. 'Even if you bring Tamara back, there'd be room. And I need some practice in motorway driving.'

'Tom,' Nick said patiently, 'just imagine the scene. A whole family party marching up to the front door. Let's keep this low-key, shall we? Unthreatening.'

'I'm threatening?'

Suzie saw the disbelief in her son's bright blue eyes. Tom Fewings, who had teenage girls swooning in his path.

'It's just a question of numbers.'

'I know how you feel, Tom,' Prudence said quietly. 'I've gotten so caught up in this story, I'm dying to be there myself. But I certainly would be one too many. So I'm reckoning on spending my last few days in England in your wonderful old Library and Record Office. I guess I need to find all I can before I go.'

'I'm sorry, Pru.' Suzie felt a pang of a conscience. 'I wish I could stay and help.'

'No, girl. You've got more important things to do. My Johan's safely dead and buried, poor soul. It's young Adam I need to trace now. And his forebears, if I can. But you just *have* to find Tamara, and see she's OK until her baby is born.'

'Don't they have women's refuge thingies?' Millie turned from the window. 'Couldn't she be holed up in one of those?'

'Maybe. But I'm not sure whether they'd take in someone Tamara's age.'

A car drew up outside. Millie swung back to look as the door slammed. 'It's that Rev Taylor from church. The one Tamara said was a bundle of fun. What's he doing here?'

'I talked to him.' Suzie got swiftly to her feet. 'I told him about Tamara being missing. He was going to try the Sally Army, without telling the Dawsons. I expect he's got some news.'

She flew to the door and opened it before Alan Taylor could ring the bell.

'Hello!' he said, with a surprised grin. 'The clergy aren't always this welcome.'

'Come in. Have you got any news of Tamara?'

The minister checked as she ushered him into the room full of people. He looked at Suzie for guidance.

'It's all right. Everyone here knows about Tamara. Nick you know. And these are our children, Tom and Millie.'

'Hardly children.' Tom was taller than he was. 'Hello, Tom. Good to meet you. I gather you're celebrating the end of exams. Good luck with the results. And Millie. You must be worried about your friend.'

'I am.'

'And this is Prudence Clayson,' Suzie went on. 'She's over from Pennsylvania, researching her ancestors. But she knows all about Tamara.'

'It's been the strangest thing.' Prudence got up and held out a hand to the minister. 'Thanks to Suzie here, I've found this Johan Clayson, from Corley, very close to your city. She was in the same trouble as Tamara. A single mother. I guess it was a whole lot harder for a girl back then.'

'It was common enough,' Alan Taylor said, shaking her hand. 'But you're right. Society was a lot less forgiving. Premarital sex wasn't so bad, but you had to tie the knot once there was a baby on the way. You've heard all about having to do penance in a white sheet, I suppose?'

'Suzie's gotten me into all that. She and Nick even took me to see the church.'

'But Tamara?' Suzie begged. 'What have you found about her?'

'That's what I came to tell you.' Five expectant faces turned up to him. 'Nothing, I'm afraid. No word of her on the streets or in the hostels where a runaway teenager often turns up. She doesn't seem to have used her mobile.'

'She threw it away,' Millie burst in. 'She was afraid someone could trace it. That's why she had to write to me.'

A startled change came over Alan's face. He swung round on Suzie. 'She's written? You know where she is?'

'Not exactly,' Suzie said carefully. She paused, then made a decision. 'Tamara sent Millie a card. Presumably, she got it from the person she was staying with. It had a picture of Anne Hathaway's cottage.'

'And you think that's where she is? Stratford-upon-Avon?'

'Or somewhere close.'

'You don't know that,' Tom objected. 'Might have been a pack someone picked up on holiday.'

'True, but then, you see . . .' Suzie turned back to the minister. 'Tamara's father lives in that area. Her real father. Look, you won't say anything to the Dawsons about this, will you? I was going to tell Lisa, but she's terrified that Leonard would get it out of her. She acts as if she'd rather not find Tamara than have her brought back here.'

Alan's face looked oddly drained of colour. 'That's a terrible thing to think. Poor Tamara.'

'How well do you know her?' Nick asked.

'She's been coming to our youth group lately. I think Leonard Dawson insisted on it. Nice girl. But I don't know anything you don't, if that's what you mean. And where exactly does Mr Gamble live?'

Suzie shot a look at Nick. How much more should she tell him?

But there was something reassuring about Alan Taylor. He was a man whose daily work was sharing other people's problems. And if it gave the Salvation Army another clue to work with, it would do good, not harm.

'Burwood. It's a little village six miles from Stratford. We're going there on Saturday to see if we can find her.'

His eyes held hers. 'If you do find her, you'll let me know, won't you? I've been really worried since you told me.'

'Of course. Would you like some tea or coffee?'

'No, thanks. I've got a church council meeting.'

She saw him to the door.

When she returned to the sitting room, Millie turned a bright face to her. 'Tamara was right. He's not bad, for his age, is he? Not like the last one. And he sounded like he really cares about her.'

'But still no hard facts,' Nick said. 'We're on our own.'

TWENTY-ONE

'I wonder if we should have taken Millie out of school and gone to Warwickshire straight away. I have a sinking feeling that every day Tamara is missing, she's in greater danger.'

Suzie had borrowed the car from Nick. She was filling the time by driving Prudence to Corley again, but it was hard to concentrate on the troubled history of a teenage girl two and half centuries ago. Still, she owed it to Prudence to make the most of the few days remaining before she flew home.

The narrow lane was climbing, round tricky bends. They must be near the village now.

'You don't think she's safe where she is? Her father's evidently got money. If he's that famous, he'll have a full-on security system, where he is.'

A shiver ran through Suzie. 'I don't know exactly what it is I'm frightened of. It's just that Tamara is terrified. You could read it in her letter. But she's miles away from Dawson now, and he's tied up with his school.'

'But she seems to have found sanctuary somewhere. Maybe it's her father's house, maybe not. As long as she's safe, it might be better to leave well enough alone.'

Suzie was startled by a tractor appearing round the bend.

She hit the brakes. There was clearly no room to pass, and the tractor was still coming steadily towards them.

She racked her memory for passing places behind her. Nervously, she began to reverse. With relief she negotiated a bend and spotted a splay for a field gate. She pulled on to the grass. The tractor lumbered past, and the driver lifted a hand in acknowledgement.

Suzie steered back on to the lane. 'You think she might *not* be with her father? In spite of that card?'

'I'm afraid I don't know any more than you do. Just let's not jump to conclusions, is all.'

They reached the village green without further incident. The two women got out and looked at the imposing house that was Corley Barton.

Prudence gave it a grim smile. 'You know, I was really glad when we found that bastardy bond. I'd hated to think of Johan inside there, being abused by the master of the house. Just for a while, I could imagine it was a teenage romance with a young workman . . . until you found he was married. Then you spotted that *Mr* and suddenly it all seemed back to the same old story. Somebody with power was taking advantage of an innocent girl.'

'You don't think it could have been a romance?'

'She was either a partner in adultery or the victim of abuse. Either way, it's not a pretty picture. This is going to be a hard story to tell the folks back home.'

'I'd like to think that there was love in it somewhere.' Suzie sighed, scuffing at the cobbled pathway in front of the church. 'But that still wouldn't make it a happy story, would it?' She looked around at the huddle of cottages, the scattered farmhouses, the big house. 'Michael Atkins had to bring up his family here. Everybody would have known what happened. His wife, his children. Johan's family. You couldn't stop people talking.'

'But my Johan was spared all that, poor girl. After she confessed who it was, and the baby was born.'

'And little Adam was left an orphan.'

'What do you suppose happened to him? Would his father have taken him in, along with his other kids? Or did Johan's people give him a home?'

'He was apprenticed out at the age of eight. And not even to his father's trade. Farm work.'

'But he might have lived down at this Hole place. With his grandfather.'

'Shall we go there now?'

'That's why we've come.'

They got back into the car, and Suzie spread out the map. 'It's down at the bottom of the valley, as you'd expect. This looks like the road we need, round the back of the church.'

The lane plunged steeply through banks bright with red campions. At the bottom there was a brook shaded by trees. A narrow, humpbacked bridge led over it.

Suzie stopped the car. 'It should be on this side of the stream, but I can't see anything, can you?'

'Those are apple trees, aren't they? Do they grow wild here?'

'No. Or not in rows like that. You're right, it's an orchard.'

They got out and inspected the scene. Ancient fruit trees sprawled over the long grass. The half-formed apples were small and green.

Suzie lifted the rickety gate aside and walked in. 'I was wrong. You know, I do believe there is a house here, or was.'

The gable wall facing them was so smothered in ivy that it was hardly distinguishable from the foliage of the trees. There was no roof. Two chimneys rose above the gaping void, one at each end.

Suzie and Prudence walked round to the front of the ruined cottage. On the ground floor, window holes were still visible in the crumbling cob. Brambles and willowherb were all the furnishings inside.

'Must have been a pretty cottage once,' Prudence said.

'We call these cottages now, but really, the cottages the poor lived in have mostly vanished without trace. This may be a wreck now, but not long ago it was a snug little farmhouse. Do you see how it was twisted away from the road to face south? They wanted what sun there was, for the women to do their work by. Not that they'd get much sun, deep down here in the valley.'

'And my Johan lived here? Ran about among those apple trees?'

'Well, not those actual ones. It was nearly three hundred years ago. But the ancestors of these trees. Now we've seen that bastardy bond, I'm sure the Adam and Robert Clayson who held the lease to Hole have to be her grandfather and father.'

'So maybe she came back here. When she knew she was pregnant. Somewhere quiet, out of the way of gossiping tongues. If she had her parents here, she'd feel safe.'

'If they didn't throw her out,' Suzie said.

The two women fell silent.

Prudence looked at the deep shadows under the oak and hazel trees along the brook. The brown water caught only a hint of sunlight as it slipped past. Above them was the long climb to the village. The church and houses were hidden from view. She shivered. 'You're right. It's not exactly a homely place. I sure hope she was happy here. It's a long ways from any neighbours.'

Suzie was silent for a moment. This might once have been a bright and busy place: children tumbling in the orchard, women busy cutting vegetables or carding wool. And not just women.

'I've just remembered. Robert Clayson wasn't a farmer, was he? Not even a humble husbandman. According to the bastardy bond, he was a woolcomber.'

'What's that, for heaven's sake?'

'He'd have taken the fleeces from the sheep farmers and combed the wool out into hanks, ready for spinning. It was a skilled job, with special tools. This was great wool country once. There were serge-makers all over the county. They exported cloth to the continent. We were the richest county in England in Tudor times.' She pulled a face. 'But the cotton industry put an end to that.' She laughed. 'We can blame you American settlers for that. You shipped the cotton from your plantations to Lancashire and put us out of business.'

Prudence bridled. 'You won't find cotton plantations in Pennsylvania.'

'I'm sorry. I was only teasing. Shall we go?'

As they walked through the tangled grass to the gate, Suzie

turned and looked back. Had Johan been happy here as a child? Had she found comfort here when she needed it?

There was nothing in the records about Johan's mother.

An isolated house, far from the prying eyes of the village. There were stories about such lonely farms. Things that never surfaced in the parish registers. Incest between brother and sister. Fathers conceiving children on their own daughters.

Perhaps the stonemason was not the worst thing that could have happened to Johan.

'It's not fair.' Millie trailed a sweatshirt across the floor in her wake. 'What does it matter if I miss a day's school? Honestly, Mum? We could have been up to wherever it is her dad lives, found Tamara, and been back in time for the weekend. Sorted.'

Suzie looked up from her laptop. She scribbled a few notes of what she had just discovered, before she forgot. The registers for the Presbyterian chapel at South Farwood, the nearest town where Johan might have worshipped, were lodged at the Record Office.

'Mum!' Millie's hand crashed on the coffee table. 'You're not *listening*!'

'I am. You think we should have gone to this Burwood place today, and not waited till Saturday. Millie, she's been gone a week. She seems safe for the moment. Another day isn't going to make any difference.'

'It is to *me*!'

Suzie was suddenly aware that there were tears beading Millie's eyes. Knowledge dawned. 'You're not still thinking about that invitation from the tennis coach? What was his name . . . Dan Curtis? Millie, you have cancelled it, haven't you? You've told him you can't go?'

Millie's face showed mute, obstinate grief.

Suzie jumped up. 'Look, love. It's not just that we're going to Burwood. It would be just the same if Tamara was safe at home. He's way too old for you. He shouldn't even be asking a fourteen-year-old schoolgirl out. It shows what sort of man he is.'

Millie's lower lip pouted. 'You're just prejudiced. I'm quite old for my years. I wouldn't want to go out with any of the stupid nerds in our year. And he's *so* good-looking.' Her voice rose to a wail. 'I may never get a chance like this again. Just think what the girls at school would say if I could show them a photograph of us together at the dance. I'd have to get a new dress, of course.'

Suzie put her arms around her daughter. But a chill hand of fear moved down her spine. How long could she protect this fragile, lovely child?

No one had been there to protect Tamara.

'Look on the bright side. You'll be seeing Reynard Woodman again. You adored him when you were younger. That'll be something to tell your friends. I could take a camera and photograph the two of you.'

Millie sniffed. 'Don't be silly. He's married. He's got kids. It's not the same.'

When she had gone, Suzie went back to her computer, uneasy and unsettled. For a while she stared blankly at the screen. What was it she had found which seemed so important?

Oh, yes. The South Farwood Presbyterian records. Something else for Pru to follow up. The baptisms were available on the web, but not the burials. They had already discovered that Johan had not been buried at the parish church. Would that be where she was?

Her eye ran down the list of research sources for South Farwood.

Cemeteries. Presbyterian. Meeting Lane.

She grabbed her phone. 'Prudence? I've think I've got something for you to follow up while I'm away. You know we couldn't find Johan's burial in the Corley register? Well, if you can get to the Record Office tomorrow, they have the burial register for South Farwood Presbyterian Chapel. And if she's there, there's a Dissenters' burial ground in Meeting Lane. I'm sorry I can't take you, but there's a bus to South Farwood.'

An eager voice came from the other end of the line. 'That's fabulous. I'm so grateful to you. Let me check that out. This burial ground's in Meeting Lane?'

'Yes. You know, it's the oddest thing. I had a great-aunt in

South Farwood we used to visit. She told me Meeting Lane was the place where lovers met. It never occurred to me till today that it was called that because there used to be a Dissenters' meeting house there. With its own graveyard.'

'I'll surely follow that up. I wish you could come with me. But you've got more important things to do. I do hope you find your Tamara safely.'

'So do I. Though even if we do, I'm not sure that I can see how this will end. If she's as frightened as she seems, how can we put a stop to it?'

'I'll pray for you all.'

Suzie put down the phone. Currents of uneasiness swirled together in her mind. Tamara, running away from home, too scared to tell anyone where she was, or who had fathered her baby. Millie, flattered by a too-handsome older man, losing her sharpness of judgement.

It was not only Prudence who needed to pray.

TWENTY-TWO

They left the motorway for the quieter road of the rural Midlands. Gazing through the windscreen, Suzie thought it had changed less from Shakespeare's time than she might have expected. They passed orchards, their boughs beginning to bend with the swelling fruit. There were still a surprising number of half-timbered houses. It was a gentler landscape than the moors and sea-coasts, the steep wooded valleys of the south-west, but with its own charm.

'Left at the next crossroads.'

The road sloped down to a wide, shining stretch of the River Avon. They followed it through villages where modern wealth had built desirable residences by the waterside.

In the back seat, Millie sat up and began taking an interest. 'Is it far now?'

'Two or three miles. This looks like the Midlands version

of stockbroker country, in the days when the stock market was worth something. It's probably computer magnates now.'

'And best-selling authors,' Millie said.

'We think he's keeping that quiet.'

A few minutes later, Nick swung the car round a black-and-white pub with a hanging sign that announced the Bear and Staff. He glided to a halt and cut the engine. 'So this is Burwood.'

Suzie and Millie got out, into the summer sunshine. Further along, mature yew trees in the churchyard overshadowed the pavement. A yellow-and-red Post Office sign hung from the village shop. The street was quiet.

'Well?' Suzie looked questioningly at Nick. 'I suppose we could go to the shop and ask them where Kevin Gamble lives. All I've got from Lisa's address book is Wood Cottage, Burwood. They don't seem to bother with street names here.'

'I wonder if the locals know his pen name? I mean, there must be all sorts of stuff coming through the Post Office addressed to Reynard Woodman. From publishers and so on.'

'He may have them mail it to his agent. Then she could forward it to him as Kevin Gamble.'

'I bet they know. The question is whether the temptation to gossip about a celebrity wins out over local loyalty. Country people can be very close when they choose.'

'Always supposing it's still local people running the shop, and not some lifestyle refugee from London.'

'Are we going to stand here all day?' Millie enquired. 'I could murder a choc ice.'

They strolled to the village shop. A white-haired woman smiled politely as she gathered up her purchases and made room for them. They were left looking at a bony-faced young man behind the counter.

Suzie checked the range of ice creams on offer. 'Three Magnums, please.' She turned her brightest smile on the young man. 'Can you help us? We're looking for an address in the village. Wood Cottage. A Mr Gamble lives there.'

'Yeah, Kevin.' The freckled face showed no surprise or guarded hostility. 'He's a bit out of the village. Carry on past the end of the houses and turn right. The road swings back

on itself a bit, then takes a big bend and comes down to the
river again. The house is right in front of you. Lovely spot.
All right for some, eh?'

'Do you know what he does for a living?' She was pushing
her luck.

'Couldn't say.' There was a sudden abruptness in the shop-
keeper's manner. 'I thought you were friends of his.'

'It's been years since we saw him. He used to live near us,
but we lost touch. Millie went to school with his daughter.'

'Oh, right, then.'

His eyes followed them out of the shop.

'He knows,' said Nick. 'They're protecting his privacy.'

'Which would make it a good place for Tamara to come, if
she wanted to keep her pregnancy a secret until the baby was
born.'

'All the same,' Millie said, peeling the foil fastidiously from
her ice cream. 'I can't see her living with that stepmother for
months.'

'There are a lot of questions that need answering,' Suzie said.

The road swung round a bend. Shards of sunlight from the
river dazzled them again. It was dappled by a weeping willow
tree, so that it glinted like scales of dragon skin. To the left
of the tree stood a substantial Georgian house. Three storeys,
with, Suzie counted, six windows on each floor. A conservatory stretched its glistening length across the riverside lawn.
It could, she thought, accommodate a wedding reception.
Beyond it, the wood, from which the house took its name,
flowed down to the water, heavy with summer foliage.

'He calls that a cottage?' Millie exclaimed. 'I was expecting
one of those dinky black-and-white beam things. You know,
with hollyhocks in the garden.'

'It's a relative term. Anne Hathaway's cottage isn't exactly
one up, one down.'

The white-painted wooden gate had been sculpted, rather
than sawn. Suzie would not have been surprised if the coiling
finials had ended in horses' heads.

'What do I do?' Nick asked. 'Park here, or drive up to the
door?'

The short drive from the gate ended at a gravelled square at the rear of the house, with garages for three cars.

'It looks as if the front door is round the other side, facing the river. So we'd have to walk round, anyway. There's room here without blocking the road.'

Millie jumped out and ran to caress the woodwork of the gate. Its curves invited the hand to stroke them. When Nick had locked the car, she lifted the iron clasp and swung the gate open with a flourish. 'Wood Cottage. Welcome to my humble abode.'

'Didn't Tamara tell you what it was like?' Suzie asked.

'She might have, once. She didn't talk much about visiting him lately.'

'I suppose it was a bit hurtful for her, if he's got two more daughters.'

There were sounds of childish laughter, even as she spoke.

Suzie wished the drive led directly to the door, but what faced them was clearly the back of the house. On such a bright summer's afternoon, she was nervous of rounding the corner and breaking in on a family party between the house front and the waterside. She wondered if eyes were watching them from the windows.

Millie, too, was looking up, as if hoping for a glimpse of Tamara's face at an upper window.

The gently sloping lawn in front of the house came into view. It was deserted. The laughter must be coming from inside the house. Most of the windows were open. The front door was slightly ajar.

Millie, who seemed to have assumed leadership, rang the bell. Chimes pealed through the house. The laughter stopped. There were light, pattering steps. The door was tugged open, and a very small girl stood before them. She wore a yellow satin dress, with frills down the front and a sash tied in a bow. White patent leather shoes and white socks gave her a curiously formal and old-fashioned look. She wore a cardboard crown.

'Do you want Mummy or Daddy?' Her size was in no way a measure of her self-importance.

'Your daddy, please,' Nick answered.

She toddled away, across the spacious parquet floor of the hall, lit from above by a stained glass window. They heard her calling for him.

Suzie struggled to remember what Kevin Gamble had looked like, all those years ago.

The man who came across the hall towards them was certainly different from the somewhat scruffy, red-bearded, bookish man she recalled, with eyes twinkling behind his glasses. He had had a magic then, which he seemed to turn on like a light for children, enchanting them in the flesh, as well as on the page.

This man – she found it easier to think of him as Reynard Woodman now – was casually, yet immaculately, dressed, in carefully pressed shorts and a crisp short-sleeved shirt. His sandals looked expensive. Gone were the beard and glasses. His hair was sleeker, the red just beginning to grey. It gave him a more authoritative air. The blue eyes, she supposed, wore contact lenses.

He was, she realized with a start, more handsome than she remembered.

He gave them an assured smile. He didn't look like a man in hiding from his fans or persistent journalists. There was a slight twist of surprise in his eyebrows, but no alarm. 'Lovely afternoon, isn't it? Can I help you?'

'I'm Millie,' said the platinum blonde teenager on his doorstep.

'Yes?' It was a question. There was no flicker of recognition.

'Millie Fewings.' There was an edge of belligerence in her voice.

She has no idea, Suzie thought, how much she's changed, even in the last few weeks.

'Tamara's friend.'

Poor Millie. All those memories of picnics in the woods, of make-believe games, of the children's author who had been like an uncle to her.

'Ah!' The realization dawned in his face. 'My dear. I'd never have recognized you. You've grown into a real princess.'

'*I'm* the princess,' said the little tot at his knee.

'Yes, sweetheart.' He ruffled her hair inside the crown, but his eyes were on Millie.

The smile was genuine now. He hesitated for a moment, then swept her into a hug. 'Well, what a surprise! Come in. No, belay that. Let's sit outside and enjoy this marvellous weather. Pet! We've got visitors,' he called back into the house.

He led the way across the lawn to where a wrought-iron table and chairs were set out in the shade of a willow tree. He sat them down. Surprisingly swiftly, a young woman appeared with a tray bearing jugs and glasses. She was fair-haired, in an Eastern European way. From her modest grey dress, Suzie guessed she was a maid. She set down in front of them what looked like jugs of fresh lemonade and Pimms, and a stand of delectable-looking cakes. Suzie sensed Millie's hand reach out, even before she was offered one, then hold back, poised.

As the maid was filling their glasses, another young woman came across the grass. She wore a thigh-high, closely-fitting black dress with shoelace straps, and sunglasses. Her sculpted black hair shone with glints of purple. Running alongside her were the toddler in the yellow dress and a rather taller girl in a pirate outfit.

'My greatest fans,' said Reynard Woodman with a smile. 'The dastardly Persephone, with the eyepatch, and Her Highness Princess Calliope. And this –' twisting to smile up at the woman – 'is my sternest critic. Petronella.'

Now he focused the warmth of his smile on Millie. 'To what do I owe this privilege? What brings you all the way from the marvellous south-west to Burwood?'

'Tamara. I'm looking for her.' Millie turned on the woman in the black dress. 'You're the one I spoke to, aren't you? Petronella Gibson. Did you tell him I'd phoned about Tamara?'

The woman's colour rose beneath the veil of make-up on her cheekbones. She tossed her head but said nothing.

'Pet?' Reynard's voice was surprised. But he controlled it. He wasn't going to risk a domestic row in front of them. 'I'm sorry, Millie,' he went on. 'But Tamara only lives a few streets away from you. I assume you're still in the same house. Why would you come looking for her here?'

'She's missing. She ran away.'

The alarm in his face looked genuine. 'When was this? Why?'

'Ten days ago,' Suzie said. 'She set out for school, but never arrived. But we have reason to think that she was planning to go. We don't think she was kidnapped, or anything like that.'

'Poor Tamara! She never said anything to make me think she was unhappy. Quite the contrary. She comes here occasionally, you know. But it's been . . . Oh, my goodness!' He turned to Petronella. 'This should have been one of her weekends, shouldn't it? Do you know, I never thought. Lisa usually rings me beforehand.'

Either he's genuinely thrown, or he's a very good actor, Suzie thought.

'And you haven't seen anything of her?' Nick asked. 'Or heard from her in the last ten days?'

'Not a word. But, ten days . . .? Surely the Dawsons have called the police? I'm surprised they haven't contacted me before this. It didn't need you to drive all this way. No offence, my dears. Of course, it's lovely to see Millie again. And . . . Suzie, wasn't it?'

Was the warm smile he turned upon her genuine?

'They haven't called the police,' she said.

He jumped up. 'Not called them? Tamara's run away . . . But she's only fourteen. They can't just do nothing!'

Suzie tried to marshal her words. 'Mr Dawson is a headmaster. I expect you know that. Have you met him?'

'No. I can't say I was falling over myself to make his acquaintance.'

'He's a bit of an authoritarian. He's reputed to rule his school with a rod of iron. We think . . . he might have felt it would dent his image, if it got around that his stepdaughter had run away from him.'

'But Lisa? She must be out of her mind with worry.'

'As Suzie said,' Nick put in, 'he's a strict disciplinarian. That includes his wife. She's terrified of him.'

'Poor Lisa!' Was there just a hint of smugness in his voice? 'What a sad business. And poor Tamara.'

The conversation seemed to hang. Where do we go from here, Suzie wondered. 'She's not here?'

'Definitely not.'

'Look,' Nick said unexpectedly. 'They haven't reported it to the police. And I don't think the police would take much notice if *we* did, because we're not related. Dawson has put out a story about her being unwell and going away for convalescence. But you're her father. You said she should have been here with you this weekend?'

'I'm truly sorry I forgot about that.'

'Well, then. *You* could report her missing.'

'Mm. That's a possibility.' He thought it over. 'Do you have any idea why she ran away?' His eyes were intent on Suzie.

'He used to beat her,' Millie said. 'It was bad enough before, but when he found out about . . .' She stopped and turned alarmed eyes to her parents.

Suzie looked into Reynard's concerned blue eyes and made a decision. 'About the baby.'

'I'm sorry?'

'I think, as her father, you need to know this. Tamara is expecting a baby.'

She saw the greyness of shock take over his face. The look of consternation in those eyes. Her heart constricted as she thought how she would feel if someone she hardly knew told her this about Millie.

'Whose?' It was almost a whisper. 'Some pimple-faced schoolboy, I suppose.'

'We don't think so. We're afraid it may be someone older. There's a tennis coach she was rather smitten with. But we wondered if it could be . . . Leonard Dawson.'

Something blazed in Reynard Woodman's eyes then. He hit the table. 'I'll kill him!'

'We don't know that,' Nick told him. 'It's just a suspicion. That sort of authoritarian figure can abuse his power over women and children. Whoever it is, she wouldn't tell Millie. That suggests there was something unmentionable, some of sort of taboo.'

'So you'll tell the police?' Suzie asked.

'I'm sorry. I need some time to take this in.'

'Of course.'

'And you say nobody knows where she is? Could she have gone off somewhere to get an abortion, do you think?' His eyes begged Suzie for an answer.

'No,' Millie put in. 'Absolutely not. We talked about it. That awful Mr Dawson wanted her to have one, and she wouldn't. So he hit her.'

'Poor little sod,' Reynard whispered. 'What made you think she'd come here?'

'You're her father,' Suzie said, a little too crisply.

'Besides,' Millie said, 'she sent me a card. She wouldn't tell me where she's hiding, but it had this picture of Anne Hathaway's cottage. So we guessed she'd be here.'

'Here.' He repeated the word dully, and swallowed. 'No. I very much wish she had come here, but she didn't.'

He sat for a long time, gazing down at his hands on the table.

Nick stirred and rose from his chair. 'I'm sorry. This must have been a bit of a shock for you. I'm sorry we had to be the ones to break it. We'll leave it to you to tell the police, shall we?'

Suzie got up too. 'You can't think of anyone else she might have gone to? In this part of the country?'

Just for a moment, she thought there was a flash of hope in his eyes. Then it faded. 'No. No, I've no suggestions.'

'We'll go, then.' She put out a tentative hand to touch his arm. 'I'm really sorry.'

Calliope turned up her little face to her mother. 'Is Tamara lost?'

'Yes, honey. I'm afraid so.'

Persephone brandished her plastic cutlass. 'Good riddance! She always spoiled things. Daddy was never the same when she was here. I chased her away, didn't I?'

'Yes, sweetie. You're a big, bad pirate. Do you want to feed the swans?'

Petronella led the children down to the water. As she passed Reynard's chair, her hand caressed his neck.

'Please let us know if there's any news,' Suzie said.

Nick took out a business card and laid it on the table. 'I hope you find her.'

Reynard Woodman sat with his head bowed.

Millie swung the white gate shut behind them.

'What do we do now?'

Nick paced the landing stage back in Burwood. From here, they could see along the river to the trees beside Wood Cottage. The house itself was hidden from view. A cruise boat was nudging into the jetty. The summer afternoon was drawing to a close.

Suzie stood back to avoid the disembarking passengers. 'There was something.' She spotted a wooden seat in a quieter part of the waterfront and led Nick and Millie to it. 'I think he was mostly telling the truth, don't you? He really doesn't know where she is. And I don't think he had any idea she was pregnant. But I'm sure there's something he's not telling us. Right at the end, when I asked if there was anyone else round here she might have gone to, I saw his eyes change. It was only a moment, but I really thought he was going to come out with a name. Then it went. He said no, quite definitely. But I think he was stonewalling. There *is* someone. I'm almost sure of it.'

'Not that that gets us any further,' Nick said. He leaned forward to study the river, where the bow wave of the boat was still sending its wash against the bank. 'If he's keeping the name to himself, we'll have to leave it to him. He's her father. It's out of our hands now. And he's said he'll tell the police. That's a weight off my shoulders, I don't mind admitting. I'd have done it days ago, if I'd thought they'd take us seriously.'

'He didn't,' Millie said.

'Didn't what, love?'

'Say he'd tell the police. You two kept asking him. But he never actually said he would.'

'He was in shock,' Suzie said. 'It was a lot to take in at once. Tamara missing. Expecting a baby. And the hints we were dropping that it might not just be a teenage affair.'

'Well.' Nick straightened up. 'I don't know about you two, but I don't feel much like hitting the road again and driving all the way home this evening. How about strolling up to the

Bear and Staff and seeing if they've got a couple of rooms for tonight?'

'Good idea,' Suzie said. 'I'd like that.'

'No!' squealed Millie. 'No, Dad, I don't mean I don't want to stay the night. We've got to. I've just thought who it was he didn't tell you about. I'm an idiot! Why didn't I think about it sooner?'

'Who?' Suzie asked. 'You mean there's somebody else besides her father?'

'Her aunt. You remember I told you? Tamara wasn't so keen on going to her dad's as she used to be. But there was that time she went shopping in Birmingham. Her aunt took her.'

'And where does this aunt live?'

Millie's enthusiasm faded. 'I don't know. Tamara didn't say. But it must be close, mustn't it? If she could come over and visit when Tamara was here?'

'Do you know her name?'

Millie frowned. 'It began with an F . . . Frances! That was it.'

'And her surname? Is she married?'

Millie shrugged. 'You're the one who's into family history, not me. I didn't ask her the details of her family tree.'

'It's a very long shot that she's still Frances Gamble, but we could try. If not . . . Well, we can hardly go round looking for all the women in Warwickshire called Frances.'

'We could get back to Reynard Woodman. Ask him,' Nick suggested. 'Although, if you're right, Suzie, we shouldn't need to. He's already realized she's the next most likely person Tamara would go to. He's probably got on the phone to her already.'

'Would she tell him?' Millie asked. 'It was supposed to be such a secret that Tamara wouldn't even tell *me* where she was. If this aunt wanted him to know, she'd have told him by now, wouldn't she?'

'That *is* odd,' Suzie reflected. 'The girl's in trouble. She's pregnant. She's been beaten, maybe even sexually abused, by her stepfather. She's afraid he's going to force her to have an abortion. And yet she hasn't told her real father.'

'Like there was only one person she thought she could trust,' Millie agreed.

'Steady on,' Nick objected. 'What have you women got against fathers? He seemed a perfectly decent bloke to me. He was really cut up about Tamara. You could see that.'

'Yeah,' Millie said. 'He's a lot different from what he was when he lived with Tamara. But he's still a knockout, isn't he? He's got that gorgeous smile. And when he hugged me, it was just like the old times, when we were little. He was the most fantastic dad then . . . Sorry, Dad! I didn't mean it like that. You're brilliant too.'

'But I'm not the charismatic Reynard Woodman. Which brings us back to the question. If he's such a fantastic dad, why didn't she run to him? And why hasn't she told him she's only a few miles away?'

They walked slowly up the village street.

'Could it be the kids?' Millie said. 'That one in the pirate gear obviously doesn't like her.'

'She seemed to feel her nose was put out of joint when Tamara was there,' Suzie said. 'That Reynard only wanted to be with Tamara. Which makes it all the more curious that she's not there now.'

'Maybe she's scared to tell him she's pregnant,' Nick suggested. 'After her experience with Dawson.'

'He's not like that!' Millie exclaimed. 'You can't compare those two in the same breath. He'd stand by her, wouldn't he? He was, like, really upset for her.'

'Any parent would be,' Suzie said quietly. 'It's not a good situation for a fourteen-year-old.'

'Let alone the man responsible, when they find him,' Nick said. 'If it *was* a full-grown man. A boy might get off more lightly.'

Suzie sighed. 'So, how do we find a woman called Frances, living in a village near here, whose surname may be Gamble, but probably isn't?'

'Do we *have* to find her?' Nick asked. 'I mean, it's some-body's else's job now, isn't it?'

'I wish I was sure of that. I agree the first thing Reynard Woodman will do is get hold of his sister. If he thinks he knows where Tamara is, he probably won't bother to tell the police. He wouldn't need them. But I wish I knew why

Tamara wanted to keep her whereabouts secret, even from him.'

'The cat's out of the bag now,' Nick said, kicking at a cobble in the pavement. 'We've told him everything and pointed the path to her aunt's front door. He'll get there long before we could, even if we did find her address. There's nothing more we can do.'

'So that's it, then? We can go home?' Millie rounded on them, her face suddenly sharp with anxiety. 'Tamara *said* I had to keep it a secret. She wanted me to burn her letter when I'd read it. She didn't even want you to know. And now I've as good as told everybody where she is. She'll kill me.'

TWENTY-THREE

Millie kicked her foot against the pub table. 'It's not fair,' she complained. 'It's bad enough that she's pregnant, and some horrible man may have done it. But now that it's happened, why can't they let her go ahead and have the baby, like she wants? Why do they have to turn it into a melodrama? It's not the first time girls like her have had a baby.'

Suzie ordered a tomato juice and a coke from the bar. She passed the coke to Millie. 'And they've been suffering for it, too, if they couldn't produce a husband. There are still a handful of old ladies in mental hospitals, who were put there just because they were expecting an illegitimate child.'

'You're kidding?'

'No, I'm not. And if it wasn't a mental hospital, it could be a Mother and Baby home where they were forced to work as skivvies, scrubbing floors or doing back-breaking work in the laundry. It was part of the punishment.'

'That's gross. What happened to the men?'

'You may well ask. Of course, most families hushed these things up. I discovered your great-great-aunt Bertha had a baby in the First World War, but no husband. She handed it over to an aunt and uncle who couldn't have children, and they passed it off as their own.'

'There are countries today,' said Nick, coming up to their table with a beer, 'where the woman is stoned to death, even if the child is the result of rape.'

Millie sat open-mouthed. Words no longer seemed enough.

'That's what we're so worried about,' Suzie said. 'The possibility of rape, I mean. We *do* want to nail the man. There's more to the way Tamara's behaving than just being a teenage mum. There has to be a reason why she's *so* afraid of her stepfather.' She reached for her handbag. 'I ought to ring Tom. Report progress. We haven't actually found Tamara, but we've more or less answered the question of where she is.'

She selected his name. It was a few moments before he answered. She heard the excitement in his voice in his first questions.

'Mum! Hi. How are you doing? Did you find her?'

'Not exactly. We found Reynard Woodman in this marvellous Georgian house by the river.' She went on to give him a colourful account of their meeting. '. . . I thought there was something in his face that suggested he knew where Tamara could be. And then, afterwards, Millie remembered she has this aunt. Only, we don't know what she's called, other than Frances, or where she lives. Anyway, I think Reynard Woodman is on to that, though he didn't actually say so. He's probably round at her house by now. So you could say it's sorted.'

'Hmm. Mum, just a thought. You don't think *he* could be the father?'

'Tom! Don't be ridiculous. He writes children's stories, for goodness' sake. He didn't recognize Millie at first, of course, but when he found out who she was, he couldn't have been nicer. He hugged her like she was some favourite niece he hadn't seen for years.'

'And what's that supposed to mean? The fact that he can put the charm routine on teenage girls hardly rules him out, does it? And if he's that great a dad, why didn't Tamara go to him? It looks like she wouldn't even let her aunt tell him.'

'Well, yes. There are some questions that still need answering. But there could be reasons. She's obviously upset about the baby and scared of her stepfather. She's not just toughing it out. It's sometimes harder to talk about personal things with somebody you're close to. If her aunt was somebody she trusted, but just that bit removed, it might have been easier for her.'

'Mmm. But you'd still think she'd want her aunt to break the bad news to Daddy, wouldn't you? Not just put the shutters up, so she's even afraid to email Millie.'

'Tom, you have an overdramatic mind. I thought we were risking falling into melodrama, by suspecting Leonard Dawson of abuse. But at least he has form. For physical abuse, anyway. There's nothing about Reynard Woodman that could possibly justify what you've just said.'

'No? What about this bit in the slinky black dress you described so well? And she's not even the one he left Tamara's mum for. Seems like *he's* got form for sex kittens.'

'But his daughter? That's an outrageous suggestion.'

'You wouldn't have fallen for his charm just a teeny bit yourself, Mum?'

Suzie was aware of Nick and Millie following her side of the conversation, wide-eyed.

'Think of it,' Tom said. 'World-famous author. Adored by millions of children. Gets his under-age daughter pregnant. That's a criminal offence twice over. Can you imagine the publicity? Bang goes a brilliant career.'

She scrabbled for straws. 'She's a minor. They wouldn't allow her name to be published. And anyway, he'd be Kevin Gamble in court. Who'd know he was Reynard Woodman?'

'Ever heard of the Internet, Mum? You can't keep that sort of thing quiet nowadays. You can slam an injunction on newspapers, but the twitterati would have a field day.'

'I think you're being ridiculous.'

'I really wish you'd let me come along. If I'd been there, I bet I could have sussed him out better than you women could. What does Dad say? No, forget that. I guess he'd just think what *he'd* do as a father. And it wouldn't be that. But if you ask me, Tamara has a very good reason to be scared that he might find out.'

'What do you mean?'

'Get real, Mum. He can't let her have this baby, can he? If she won't have an abortion, then he's got to make sure that *something* stops the baby being born. Work it out. Sorry, got to run. Smells like my pasta's burning. I'll check back.'

'He thinks *what*?' Millie flashed outrage.

'Well, let's face it. We're all clutching at straws. Tom's feeling left out, so he just wants to throw in an idea we haven't thought of. One-upmanship.'

'He's just plain silly,' Millie growled.

Nick had his back to them, looking across the courtyard garden of the pub. 'We ought not to close our minds to it, though. It may be a long shot, but it wouldn't be unique. Something has to explain why Tamara's behaving in such an extreme way.'

'Are you blaming it on Tamara now?' Millie protested. 'Of course she's running away from that Dawson man. He beat her.'

'Yes.' He turned back to her with a sigh and sat down. 'That's certainly the most obvious explanation.'

Suzie defended Millie. 'Accusing Reynard Woodman of sexually abusing her is as daft as . . . well, suggesting it was Alan Taylor at Springbrook Church.' She caught the speculative look in Nick's eye. 'Oh, no! What's wrong with you now? I wasn't in a million years meaning Alan *was* a suspect.'

'He's a hit with the kids, apparently. But you were the one who brought his name up, not me.'

She thought of the way those bright brown eyes smiled and then could suddenly deepen with sympathy when the darker things of life crossed his path. As they often did.

'You're probably right,' Nick said. 'All the same, Millie has a point. Tamara did ask her for absolute secrecy. We've been so keen to find her and check she's OK that we've been a tad freer with information than we should have been.'

'He's her *father*,' Suzie exclaimed. 'If her mother can't protect her, he should.'

'It's bit late for second thoughts, anyway. As you said, he's probably on his way there by now.' He sat, twirling a beer mat absently. Then he got up and went to the bar. 'Do you have a telephone directory?'

'Sure. Just a minute.' The publican crossed the corridor to his office and returned with the book.

'Thanks.'

Suzie watched with growing disbelief as Nick thumbed through the pages.

'Gamble. There's just three of them. Not our friend Kevin, alias Reynard Woodman. He's ex-directory, of course. And none of these begins with an F. She's married, then, or has been. You're sure she lives nearby?' he asked Millie.

Her reply was surly. 'How would I know? I wasn't exactly *here*, was I? But Tamara talked about her coming over and taking her shopping once. So I just assumed she didn't live a hundred miles away.'

'Good thinking.' He strolled back to the bar. 'Excuse me. Last time we were here, we met Kevin Gamble's sister, Frances. We promised next time we were in the area, we'd look her up. But we can't remember her surname. You wouldn't happen to know it, would you?'

The landlord put his head round the door to the kitchen. 'Mandy? Bloke here wants to know the name of Kevin Gamble's sister. Can you remember? Didn't she book a table here back in the spring, to celebrate some anniversary?'

'I can't recall it, though,' came his wife's voice. 'Something Irish, was it? O'Sullivan? My hands are all over flour at the moment, but it'll be in the book.'

The obliging publican reached for a leather-bound folder on the shelf behind him. He leafed back through it. Then he swivelled the book for Nick to read. 'Would that be the one? March twenty-fourth. O'Malley? Table for eight?'

'Yes, that's it.' Nick covered the lie with a smile of gratitude. In a few strides, he was back at the table, flicking through the telephone directory more rapidly. 'Keep your fingers crossed it's in her name, not her husband's.'

'Tamara never said anything about an uncle,' Millie said.

'Got it! O'Malley, F.D. The House in the Forest, Little Fairing.' He jotted down the number, then swivelled back to the landlord. 'How far would Little Fairing be?'

'About twelve miles, I should think. Will you be wanting a table for this evening?'

'Could we leave that open? I'm not sure when we'll be back.'

He threw a meaningful look at Suzie and Millie as he strode for the door.

'Nick, what are you doing?' asked Suzie as she caught up with him in the car park. 'We can't just go barging in on them. Not now we've handed it over to her father.'

'You're right. We ought to ring her first. There's just a chance we might catch her before Reynard Woodman gets there.' He got out his mobile and phoned the number he had copied. His voice was sharp with anxiety.

She felt a stab of irritation. All they needed was for Nick to take off down a false trail of suspicion.

'Frances O'Malley? This is Nick Fewings. You don't know me, but my daughter Millie is best friends with Tamara . . . No, look. I know that Tamara doesn't want anyone to know where she is. It was Millie who worked it out. I'm afraid we may have been a bit indiscreet. We were at Reynard Woodman's house this afternoon . . . Yes, her father. We've all been desperately worried about her since she disappeared. Our first thought was that she might have gone to him . . . Yes, I'm afraid he knows now. And we think he might have guessed she's with you . . . Look, I understand your feelings . . . You don't have to tell me anything. We just thought we might have done the wrong thing and that he'll be over to your place . . . Yes, I'm sorry. It was stupid. But, well . . . He hasn't got there yet? Thank God for that, at least. If there's anything we can do . . . No, I quite understand. That's perfectly justified. I'm sorry.'

He pulled a wry face as he snapped the mobile shut. 'She wasn't admitting anything, but from the earful I got, I don't think we're flavour of the month.'

'Nick!' Suzie protested. 'You're just being ridiculous.'

'It's all my fault,' Millie wailed. 'I told him about the card. But he can't mean her any harm. He's Reynard Woodman. He wouldn't.'

Nick ran his hand through his hair. He stood indecisively

in the middle of the car park. 'I wish I was as sure as you are. We've fouled up, big time. We've broken her cover. Or as good as. The only thing we can hope is that Suzie was wrong, and that Reynard Woodman *didn't* twig where she was.' He juggled his car keys. 'On the other hand . . . if he does show up, and there are just the two of them . . .'

He reached a sudden decision and made for the car. After a moment's exchange of furious looks, Suzie and Millie hurried after him.

'I'm not sure if you should come,' he said.

Suzie got in, without stopping to argue. Millie did the same.

'She'll deny it,' he said, starting the engine. 'The only thing she has to do is tell him Tamara's not there. What can he do?'

'What would he *want* to do?' Suzie demanded. 'Nick, you and Tom are being outrageous. What does it matter if he *does* find out where she is? I'm sure he could warn Dawson off a lot better than his sister could.'

'I wish it didn't matter if people found out. But Tamara evidently thought it did. And, from the sound of it, her aunt does too. So let's just hope we get there before he does.'

TWENTY-FOUR

'Which way?' Nick asked as they headed out of the pub car park.

'Pass me the road atlas, will you? And that Ordnance Survey map.' Suzie turned to Millie in the back seat. She checked the location of Little Fairing. 'Back to the main road, then left.'

A summer landscape of the English countryside flew by them. A glimpse of a cricket match, white figures on a tree-lined field. Half-timbered cottages, whose crooked walls added to their selling price, rather than diminishing it. Newer houses, flocking round the desirable waterside like recently-hatched ducklings.

She turned to the Ordnance Survey map for more detail.

'Got it. It's even marked on the map. "The House in the Forest". Wonder if that's where Reynard got the idea for his book from. Now, there's a small town coming up. Take the right fork in the centre. Little Fairing's the next village.'

Her mobile rang.

'Hi, Tom.'

'I'm guessing you're checking out that aunt's address. Right?'

'As a matter of fact, we're on our way there now. The House in the Forest, Little Fairing. I'm not for a minute accepting your ridiculous suggestion that Reynard Woodman's our culprit. But your father seems to think it's a possibility. And having come this far, we'd like to check that Tamara really is fine. Well, as fine as she can be, in the circumstances. At least then I can tell Lisa I've seen her.'

'And you think this Woodman bloke has sussed where she is, too?'

'I'm only guessing. He didn't say so.'

'Watch yourselves, then.'

'What ever do you mean?'

'Rich, famous man. An inconvenient truth. He may not be as crude a bully as Dawson, but I bet he can find his own ways of shutting people up.'

'He's a children's author, for heaven's sake, not a Mafia boss.'

'Yeah. You're right. I reckon that's why Tamara should be scared.'

'Tom! Look, I'm not going on with this conversation. I'm supposed to be navigating. We'll be home tomorrow.' She snapped the phone shut and put it back in her bag.

Tomorrow. Back to everyday life. This whole peculiar day behind them – meeting Reynard Woodman and his new family, in their riverside luxury. The aunt ahead, in her lonely house in the woods. Tamara's hideaway. Some questions answered, but not the most important ones. Who was the father of Tamara's child? What had sent her running away here?

'Straight through the village,' she said, hastily getting her bearings as Little Fairing sped towards them. 'Then left at the next crossroads. It's all on its own. The Gambles obviously like their privacy.'

The wood was bounded by an old brick wall. Nick slowed. An unmade track led off to their left through the trees. They could just glimpse the house between the branches. Not Tudor, by the look of it, but mellow red-brick.

'You're not going to drive up to the door, are you?' Millie's voice came from the back seat. 'It's not going to be much good her aunt telling Reynard she's not here, if we all pile in. He'll know she's lying.'

'This is madness, anyway,' Suzie told them. 'Surely her father's the very person she needs right now?'

Nick clenched the steering wheel. 'It may not look like it to you, but I'm trying to be rational. Tamara's here, and not at her father's, for a reason.'

'The girlfriend? Those kids? There are lots of reasons why she might prefer an aunt living by herself. And if she really is afraid of Dawson, somebody needs to warn him off. Somebody with more clout than we have.'

'I wish we'd stayed at home,' Millie said. 'Tamara was all right with her aunt. All we've done is mess it up.'

'That's all I need,' Nick said. 'You were the one who was dying to come.'

'She's right,' Suzie said. 'I feel ridiculous with this cloak-and-dagger stuff, but it will be even more embarrassing if Reynard Woodman catches us here, prying into his family business.'

'I can't see a car outside the house.' Nick was peering up the track.

'It was all a wild goose chase. He isn't coming. He probably rang his sister and she told him no.'

'You didn't speak to her. It's not just Tamara who's scared. Her aunt is too. At least, that's the only way I can explain how mad she was with me. With us.'

'With *me*,' said Millie. 'I told him. But he is her father.'

'I'd pretty well filled him in on the picture before that,' Suzie said. 'About her being pregnant and running away.'

'But you didn't say about the card and Anne Hathaway's cottage. That was me. I led him here. But I'm sure she'd want to see him. I would.'

'He's not coming,' Nick said. 'He'd have been here by now.'

All the same, he drove a little further on, past the entrance. Outside the boundary wall, trees crowded down to the roadside. He nosed the car along a smaller path, where branches shielded it from the road.

'You stay here. I'll check the house out. If the coast's still clear, I'll knock and see if I can sort things out with the aunt. I'd feel easier in my mind if we had some definite news about Tamara. There's been too much guesswork.'

'If you're going to see Tamara, I'm coming too!' Millie had her seat belt off and was opening the door.

'There's no saying the aunt will let us in, even if Tamara is here.'

'She's more likely to let me in than you.'

Suzie sensed that Nick was on the point of refusing her. Then he hesitated. 'All right. But do exactly what I tell you. I'm going first. You stay behind the wall. If I signal you that it's OK, you can come.'

He did not refer to Suzie. She followed them, the tall figure of Nick ahead, with his wavy black hair, the slight figure of Millie with her blonde crop.

They picked their way through the trees, avoiding the road, until they came to the brick wall surrounding the house.

'Wait here,' Nick ordered Millie. 'Suzie, have you got your mobile? I want you to watch the road. If you see Woodman's car turning in, or stopping on the road, ring me immediately.'

He climbed the wall easily. Trees grew close to the house, but some had been felled to leave wider spaces. Nick flitted from one to the next, drawing nearer to the brick house.

The summer sun had not yet set, but it was slipping down into an almost invisible bank of violet haze. It was duskier under the trees. There was a glow of light in one of the down-stairs windows. Perhaps a reading lamp.

Suzie watched Nick position himself behind the substantial trunk of an oak, almost opposite the window. He peered care-fully around it. Then he drew back into hiding and waved to Millie.

So Reynard wasn't there.

In a moment, Millie was over the wall and running to join him. Suzie hesitated, then decided she would have a better view along the track to the road if she climbed over too.

She wished she had left her shoulder bag in the car, but she could hardly abandon it here. She slipped the strap over her head, so that it hung more securely across her body. She was not unused to scrambling over moorland tors. Soon she was dropping on to soft leaves the other side. The only significant damage was to the leather of a good pair of sandals.

She crouched and faced the road. Nothing yet.

Nick and Millie were now making their way openly to the front door. What Nick had seen through the lighted window had given him confidence.

Reynard wasn't coming, then. She must have been wrong about that flash of intuition she thought she had seen in his eyes. He hadn't suspected whom Tamara might be with. She felt a great relief. It wasn't for Tamara's safety. She hadn't been able to bring herself to share Nick's suspicion. It was not like the fear she had felt confronting Leonard Dawson. She would have been shaking with nerves if she were watching for *his* arrival. What she feared if Reynard Woodman found them here was extreme embarrassment. The Fewings family, caught behaving like children in an Enid Blyton mystery.

A wider slice of light showed as the door opened. Suzie turned her head from the road to watch. A tall, red-haired woman in a blue smock stood eye to eye with Nick, listening to his story. Then she bent her head to look down at the smaller figure of Millie. It was too far to be sure of her expression. She ushered them inside.

Warmth coursed through Suzie. It was all right. That must mean Tamara was there. They had done what they set out to do. They had found Tamara. Millie would be reunited with her. The two girls would be hugging each other, pouring out their separate stories. Presently, someone would probably come out to invite Suzie in. They would talk for a while, discussing Tamara's future. Then the Fewings would go back to the Bear and Staff for the night, and home tomorrow. Mission accomplished.

She was just about to turn her attention back to the road when her eye was caught by a brightness beyond the house. The sun had slipped below the bank of cloud. She gave a little gasp of surprise. She had not realized, as they navigated the twisting roads, how close they had come back towards the river. Through the widely-spaced trees at the back of the house, she had glimpses of golden light on the water.

Then she remembered why Nick had left her here. She was supposed to be watching the road. However melodramatic she thought he was being, she supposed it was prudent to keep an eye open. She could at least give Aunt Frances and Tamara some warning if Reynard was on his way.

She had a moment's guilty panic. Might he have turned into the track while her attention had been on the river behind the house?

The road was shadowed, on the edge of the wood. Nothing moved.

As she watched, a beam of light probed through the trees. Suzie stiffened. Her hand went to the mobile in her bag. She opened it and found Nick's number. Her thumb was poised to confirm, just in case.

The headlights came on, passed the entrance to the track and zigzagged away. She relaxed.

It was a long five minutes before the next car approached. It, too, drove on.

She glanced back at the house. It was hardly fair of Nick to leave her out here in the woods. It was obvious by now that Tamara's father wasn't coming. And what if he did? He *should* know.

When she resumed her watch, the road was harder to see. In those few minutes, the sun had set. She was conscious of things stirring in the twilit wood. There were rustlings among the leaves.

A low, amused voice spoke behind her left shoulder. 'Well, Suzie! It seems the Fewings family are determined to meddle with other people's business.'

She jumped up, spinning round, to find herself face-to-face with Reynard Woodman.

TWENTY-FIVE

For a horrified moment, the spy-thriller nature of the evening convinced Suzie that he was holding a gun to her.

Then sanity returned. She saw nothing but mocking laughter in his light-blue eyes.

A hot flush suffused her body. She could not begin to explain why she was crouched in the woods outside his sister's house. Mercifully, he did not ask.

'So, great minds think alike. You've obviously worked out, too, that if Tamara wasn't with me, she must be at Fran's house.'

She nodded, her mouth too dry to speak.

Belatedly, she became aware of the mobile still clutched in her hand. She dared not look down at it. She must just hope that Nick's number was still the one selected. It seemed foolish now to be carrying out her instructions. But her thumb felt for the button and pressed it. She slipped the phone into her dress pocket, under cover of her shoulder bag, and hoped he would not notice the movement in the shadow of the trees.

'Were you waiting for someone?' At last the question she had been dreading. 'I'm sorry if I surprised you. Cars are such a carbon-inefficient way of travelling when we have the river, don't you think?'

Only then did she look past him. It was twilight in the wood, but still clear evening light over the river. She saw the trim, white lines of a motor launch against the bank.

Embarrassment deepened, as she pictured how he must have come walking up through the trees to Frances's house, until he saw the light blur of her dress as she crouched by the wall. What must he have thought?

'Shall we go in? I can't tell you how upset I am about Tamara, after what you told me. Poor little sweetheart. You know these things happen to girls, but you never think it will be your kid. You've got a daughter, Suzie. I'm sure you can imagine how gutted it makes me feel. I'd like to get my hands on the boy and thrash him.'

No mention that it might not be a schoolboy. Suzie cast her mind back. She was almost sure they had voiced their suspicion of Leonard Dawson.

They walked towards the house. Reynard chatted, without apparent embarrassment.

'Luckily, she doesn't have to go through with it. I can afford to have it dealt with in the very best clinic. Emotionally painful, of course. But in time she'll thank me for it. We don't want to mess up the rest of her life, do we?'

'She won't,' Suzie said. 'Millie says Tamara's refusing to have an abortion.'

'*What*?' He stopped and faced her. His expression had changed. She read alarm.

'Didn't I tell you? That's why we're afraid Leonard Dawson would beat her. He'd want to hush it up. But she already thinks of it as a human being. She doesn't want to kill it.'

He snorted. 'She's bound to be emotional just now. Who wouldn't be? I'll talk to her. Father-daughter stuff. I'm sure she'll see reason. Can't have her saddled with a baby at fourteen. Think what she'd be giving up. Her whole future.'

They had reached the steps. There was the sound of a door opening. Frances O'Malley stood in the porch. The flood of light illuminated a stone dragon on one side of the threshold, a troll on the other. Moths circled the lamp above her red hair.

'Well, Kevin.' The name jolted Suzie. She had used it herself once. But now it subtly diminished the image of the celebrity author Reynard Woodman. She sensed from Frances's tone that he was her younger brother. 'It's been two years since you deigned to set foot in my garden. To what do I owe the honour of this unexpected visit?'

So he hadn't phoned to ask her if Tamara was here. Instead, he had come slipping along the river in his launch to surprise her. And Tamara.

The first spasm of doubt crossed Suzie's mind.

'As a matter of fact, I came to see Tamara. I'm sorry to sound rude, my dear, but you'll understand how shocked I am at the news. It's bad enough to put herself in the club, at her age. But running away from home is a bit over the top, even given that she doesn't like that louse Dawson. I'm here to do my fatherly duty and sort things out for her.'

'Tamara's not here.'

The words came as a jolt to Suzie, as well as to Reynard. They both stopped, the somewhat strained smiles wiped from their faces.

Suzie's eyes flew to Nick, who had appeared behind Frances. His sober expression gave nothing away.

Her eyes questioned him. Tamara wasn't here? What about that angry phone call Nick had had with her aunt? Hadn't it meant what they thought it had?

He looked past her.

'But I think you know where she is.' Reynard's voice sharpened.

'I know that she's pregnant, and she's run away from home, yes. Mr Fewings has just told me. I gather they went to you first. And you gave them the same answer I have.'

Suzie looked from brother to sister. Which should she believe?

'That's right. They turned up at my place this afternoon.'

'If you thought she was with me, it's taken you a while to get here. It's nearly nightfall.'

'Hardly. Just because you choose to live in such a gloomy place in the forest. Like a witch's house. It's only just past sunset. Light enough to take Tamara back with me on the boat.'

Suzie saw the startled look Frances sent towards the river. But she turned back to her brother with a different question.

'I suppose you've told the police she's missing?'

'Isn't that being a teeny bit melodramatic, my dear? I thought she was with you.'

'And now that you've found she isn't, shall I ring them, or will you?'

Suzie was aware of tension crackling in the atmosphere as brother and sister faced each other. Her thoughts were racing. Where *was* Tamara? Had she been here? Was Frances bluffing?

What had happened when Nick picked up her call? He refused to meet her eye.

Belatedly, a new question insinuated itself into Suzie's mind. Her mouth opened to ask: 'Where's . . .'

Nick shot her a look of such intensity that she stopped before she could say 'Millie'.

'Sorry. Nothing.'

'Would you like to come in?' Frances said, with a lack of sisterly warmth. 'I expect we could all use a coffee. Is Petronella with you?'

'She's on the boat. I don't think we need to call her. She'll be fine keeping an eye on it.'

As they trooped indoors, Suzie caught the troubled glance that passed between Nick and Tamara's aunt.

She was hardly surprised to find that Millie was not in the sitting room.

The atmosphere was awkward. Frances served coffee and cake. As she accepted a slice, Suzie was aware that she and Nick were sitting on the edge of their seats, unable to relax. Reynard Woodman, however, leaned back on the cushions, smiling. That seemed strange to Suzie. Anxiety would be more appropriate. It was almost as if he were playing a game now. He had looked genuinely upset when he first learned that his daughter was pregnant and nobody knew where she was.

It was a relief that the author's composure scotched Tom's wild notion that Reynard himself was the father of Tamara's child. That would certainly have been a disaster, for him, as well as Tamara. He was still endeavouring to be as charming as he used to be, in the days when he took Millie and Tamara on picnics in the woods . . .

No, don't go down that path.

She wrenched her thoughts away, to sense that Frances and Reynard – or Kevin, as his sister still called him – were locked in a sibling rivalry they had conducted from childhood.

'Let's take this slowly,' Reynard was saying. 'The Fewings, Nick and the charming Suzie, came here because they believe you know where my daughter is. Just as they came to see me this afternoon.'

'As I pointed out, you told them she wasn't with you. They believed you. So why shouldn't they believe me when I tell them Tamara's not with me?'

'Because she has to be somewhere. I'd have worried myself stiff, imagining a much darker scenario. That she was wandering the streets of London, or some other big city. That she'd fallen into the hands of some undesirable character who'd offered her a bed. Even, God forbid, that she'd committed suicide. But Millie, bless her, says Tamara sent her a card. That she was safe and well, and being sheltered by someone she apparently trusts. So I ask myself, who else could that be but her favourite aunt? Living in a conveniently secluded house, not too far from Anne Hathaway's cottage, which was depicted on the card?'

Suzie glanced at Frances just in time to catch the twitch of alarmed annoyance at the mention of the notelet. It was a clue she had overlooked when she gave it to Tamara. As the Fewings themselves had failed to see its significance, until Prudence had identified the picture.

They had come to the right place, hadn't they? She wished desperately that she could ask Nick what had happened between Frances inviting Nick and Millie indoors and her own panicked speed-dialling Nick's number.

Nick and Millie. For the first time, her thoughts leaped on to a different track. The fact that neither Tamara nor Millie was in the room had come as more of a relief than a surprise. Yet where *were* the girls?

She listened for girlish voices from a room upstairs. But that was nonsense. If they were up there, they would be waiting in tense silence, desperate to hear what was going on down here. Frances would not be putting up this valiant defence of Tamara's privacy if the girl were not frightened of being discovered, even by her own father. Why? Was it just her traumatic experience with Leonard Dawson which had made her so scared of men?

Of men in general? Or this particular man?

It was hard to believe.

Her phone rang, making her jump. She pulled it out and glanced at the screen. Tom. She snapped it off. She couldn't handle his suspicions just now.

'Sorry,' she said to the others.

She watched Reynard Woodman's relaxed pose on the sofa. But his sister seemed immune to the crinkle in his eyes when he smiled.

She had lost the thread of the conversation. The red-haired couple were still sparring with each other.

'How long are you going to sit on my sofa before you get it into your head that I'm not harbouring your daughter? Poor Petronella will be starting to get chilly on that boat. If you're not going to invite her in, shouldn't you go and relieve her boredom?'

'Pet knows she's a lucky woman. She'll wait till I come.'

'God's gift to the female sex.' Frances rolled her eyes.

'Success is a well-known aphrodisiac. I have to plead guilty.' The warmth of the smile he shot at Suzie disarmed the apparent conceit.

But she was growing edgy. Why *wasn't* he more worried?

A disconcerting thought entered her mind. Until now, she had believed that Frances was lying through her teeth when she said she was not sheltering Tamara. But what if it were true? What if it had been Reynard who was lying, when he told them Tamara was not with him at Burwood?

She turned to study the man on the sofa beside her more closely.

But it didn't make sense. Why, if he knew where Tamara was, would he come all this way to Little Fairings in his boat at dusk, to see if Tamara was here? If she was in his own house, he wouldn't have needed to ask Frances.

Unless – a new, darker, thought insinuated itself – he wanted to create an illusion of innocence. To divert suspicion from himself.

Suspicion of *what*, for heaven's sake? Giving refuge to his own daughter? What could possibly be the harm in that?

Before her mind could take her any further down that alarming road, Reynard asked the question she had been hoping he would not.

'And while we're trying to clear up this mystery about where Tamara is, what's happened to the delightful Millie?'

He turned to look her full in the face. The laughter was

gone. The light-blue eyes locked on hers, demanding an answer.

She had no excuse ready.

Nick came to her rescue. 'We left her back at the Bear and Staff. She's feeling a bit under the weather. Queasy stomach, I'm afraid. Didn't want to risk another car journey.'

'I'm *so* sorry. Do give her my love.' The sympathetic smile was back. 'I do hope it's not the same reason Tamara is . . . unwell.'

She saw by the compression of Nick's lips how he was controlling his anger. For a moment, she sided with him.

'I think not. And I don't find Tamara's condition a laughing matter.'

'Oh, no. It's definitely not that. She's my daughter, remember. But, do you know, I don't believe you. Millie's here, isn't she? With Tamara. And the two of them are either in this house, or not very far from it. So which of you is going to take me to them?'

No one met his eye. Frances rose and began ostentatiously collecting the cups and plates.

For a while, Reynard sat on, wilfully ignoring the hint. Then he stood up and confronted his sister. 'Since you insist that Tamara is not in your house, you won't mind if I look upstairs.'

'That's an outrageous suggestion. You most certainly may not.'

They remained locked in an unspoken confrontation. Suzie realized that the rangy Frances was slightly the taller of the two. She had that air of the older sister. There was a confident authority towards him, which even the self-possessed Reynard found it hard to face down.

After moments of tension, he relaxed and smiled. 'Very well. You can hardly wonder that I'm not a frequent visitor here. You couldn't claim to make me feel welcome. But at least you won't object if I visit your bathroom before I leave.'

The smile he gave her was not the warm, eye-crinkling laughter that made Suzie's heart skip a beat. She saw a clever little boy, calculating how to outwit his authoritative big sister, and releasing a smile of pleasure at his plan.

Her certainty of his innocence faltered.

Her gaze flew to Frances. She couldn't let him go upstairs, could she? And she could hardly escort him to the bathroom, like a security guard with a prisoner in transit. What would he find, up there on the landing? Two girls, huddling in a bedroom, terrified of discovery? An empty bedroom, all too obviously inhabited recently by a teenage girl?

But that scenario depended on the supposition that Tamara really had found refuge here, and was not, after all, at her father's house. Was Reynard bluffing, to throw them off the scent? Whose protestations of ignorance should she believe?

Or were they both telling the truth? Was Tamara in some different hideout altogether?

And if she was not here, then where was Millie?

Frances's smile was broader than her brother's, but equally lacking in warmth.

'Of course. You'll find a cloakroom in the hall, to the right of the stairs.'

A shadow passed quickly over Reynard's face. He kept his smile in place with an effort.

As he made his way into the entrance hall, Nick followed him. Through the open door, Suzie saw Reynard head for the foot of the stairs. His head went up. Listening? Then he turned away and made for the cloakroom Frances had indicated.

Despite her doubts, it was a relief to see Nick's tall figure stationed at the foot of the stairs.

What now? Frances and Reynard were engaged in a cat-and-mouse game. But why? Supposing Tamara had fled to Frances, why was her aunt so determined to act as the gate-keeper, beyond whom her brother might not pass to reach his daughter?

Tamara was desperately in need of a loving parent. What harm could it do for her father to share her burden?

She had not wanted to think it, but the sick realization of the dark lives some children endure came creeping over her again. The same black thoughts she had nursed about Leonard Dawson. But no, surely not Reynard Woodman? He was a completely different character. A children's hero, sharing their dreams, spellbinding, even if he had grown just a little bit too pleased with his own success. She could not imagine him violating any child, let alone Tamara.

There had to be some other reason for Tamara's fear.

Reynard was back in the hall, saying a polite goodbye to Nick. He ignored his sister. But he shot that crinkling smile through the doorway at Suzie. 'Goodnight, Suzie. Lovely to meet you again. I do hope Millie will feel better in the morning.'

The porch light shone on his red hair as he walked out between the dragon and the troll, on either side of the door.

His final sentence unnerved her. How sincere was it? She suspected he knew Nick had been lying to him. That Millie had come with them. That she was probably with Tamara, either in this house, or somewhere near.

She found she was trembling.

TWENTY-SIX

Nick did not immediately come back into the room. He stood at the front door, watching Reynard make his way through the wood. Then he went outside. The river was at the back of the house. Nick would have to walk round the corner to make sure that Reynard was really going back to his boat.

Where else would he go?

Restlessly, she got to her feet. She and Frances stood in silence, waiting.

At last, Nick came back. It was almost dark under the trees, beyond the porch light.

'He seems to be heading back to the river. What now?'

'I don't trust him. He gave in just a shade too easily for someone who's always been used to getting his own way.'

'Where's . . . Millie?' Suzie asked. The real question was still too delicate to voice.

Frances looked startled. Then she smiled. 'I'm sorry. I forgot you were one step behind Nick. The truthful answer is, I'm not quite sure. When I knew you'd been to see Kevin – I'm sorry,

I can't bring myself to call him by that ridiculous pen name
– and that you'd told him about Tamara's card, I thought it
wouldn't take him long to guess where she was. I've sent her
out of the house until the coast is clear. A little hideaway of
mine. Then when Millie showed up with Nick, I knew how
much Tamara would love to see her. I let her out by the side
door.'

'So both girls are out there? In the woods?' Fear was rising.
She remembered the shock of Reynard coming up behind her,
while she had been watching the road.

'I have to say, I had a moment of panic when I found Kevin
had come by boat. Millie would have been screened from the
drive, but not from the river. Well, not the whole way. I'm
assuming he *didn't* see her, or he wouldn't have come to the
house and found you. But it must have been a close thing.'

'So the girls don't know he's here?'

'Don't worry. When you rang Nick, he relayed the warning
to Millie's mobile. So, yes, they're both out in the woods,
somewhere. I only hope Millie's found Tamara and that she
knows he's close. And that Kevin doesn't decide to do some
night manoeuvres of his own.'

'You're talking as though it would be a terrible thing if he
found her,' Suzie protested. 'Would it really be so bad?'

All the warmth went out of Frances's eyes. 'Yes.'

The single word chilled Suzie.

'Is there anywhere we can keep an eye on his boat?' Nick
asked. 'Make sure he leaves?'

'There's a veranda at the back. Built precisely to give a
good view of the river. Shall we?'

She led the way through a back door to a wooden deck with
comfortable chairs. She didn't switch on any more lights. They
sat in the dusk, on cushions that were just beginning to feel
the damp of the night air.

Through the trees, Suzie could make out the launch in the
paler grey over the river. There was a light in the cabin.

'No sign of him going,' Nick said after a while.

'That's what I was afraid of. He doesn't give up easily. To
do him justice, that's why he's got where he has. Single-
mindedness. He's always had talent, but he's worked for years

to become the overnight success people think he is. It means a lot to him. Success.'

They were talking quietly, but Suzie was still afraid to ask the question that was uppermost in her mind. Where were the girls?

Nick must have been feeling the same. He murmured, 'Do you think I should go looking for them? See if they're OK?'

'I wouldn't,' Frances said. 'I don't trust Kevin further than I could throw him. He's not waiting on the river just to enjoy the calls of the night birds. He thinks when the coast is clear, we'll do just that. Lead him to her.'

Suzie ventured a question that was almost a whisper. 'Why is it so important that he doesn't find her?'

Frances turned to her. It was impossible to read her expression in the dusk. 'She didn't tell you? No. Then I don't think I should breach her privacy, either.'

It opened the door on Suzie's darkest fear.

Her voice trembled slightly as she asked, 'What do you think will happen if he does find her?'

Frances did not answer for a while. Then she sighed. 'I'm his sister. It's hard for me to say this. But, as I said, he's single-minded. I'm frightened he'd do whatever it takes to ensure her silence. To preserve his career. Tamara might meet with an unfortunate accident.'

Her fingers drummed on the wooden arm of her chair.

'You mean, he'd *kill* her?' Suzie breathed.

'Oh, he wouldn't use that word. He'd rationalize it somehow. I wondered why he didn't leap into his car straight away and drive over here. When I knew he'd come by boat, it made sense. You know how it is with teenagers. Their minds can't keep pace with the speed their limbs are growing. A clumsy move on the boat. Pitching over the side. A frantic search in the dark. They find her too late, of course. Must have hit her head going down. He'd convince himself, as well as everyone else. He's a very good storyteller.'

Nick broke the silence. 'You have to tell me where they are. I'm having kittens thinking of those two alone in this wood in the dark, while *he's* around.'

'No,' Frances said. 'That's why he's waiting. I'm kicking

myself now for sending Millie to her. I thought it was too late now for Kevin to arrive tonight. But he's clever. He could see you were lying about leaving Millie at the pub. He knows Tamara's here.'

'All the more reason they need protection.'

'Shouldn't we call the police?' Suzie asked.

'And tell them what? We suspect my famous and much-loved brother of being about to murder his daughter? They're going to ask why.'

It came out as a reluctant whisper. 'To avoid being arrested for incest with a minor? That's rape.'

France's eyes widened. But she neither confirmed nor denied it.

Suzie winced. 'Yes,' she admitted. 'We had the same problem when we thought it was Leonard Dawson. Who would have believed us?'

'We have to tough it out for a while.' Frances was suddenly decisive. 'Until his boat leaves. Then we'll need to think fast what to do.'

'What if he doesn't go? He could stay there all night.'

'Look,' Nick said, with sudden decision. 'I'm going down to that boat. I can't bear the thought that he might have sloped off into the woods without us seeing him. It's getting darker by the minute. What if he creeps up and finds them on their own? We can only just see the bows from here. He could have got them aboard already, while we've been sitting here.'

'I'll come with you.' Suzie jumped to her feet, glad to have something to do.

Frances stood too, looking away into the woods. It was becoming harder to distinguish one tree from another. 'Maybe when it gets fully dark, I could risk going to get them. I only wish their hideaway was further from the river. I hadn't planned for this.'

Suzie turned, startled. 'Could he see it from his boat?'

'He might. If he looked in the right place. Let's hope he hasn't. It'll be fully dark in a while, but there'll be a biggish moon later. I might have a couple of hours to get them out without his seeing. As soon as it's safe, I'll need to drive them somewhere further away, but I can't think where. Give me your mobile number, Nick, and I'll ring you when we're far enough away to breathe easily.'

'Then we need to get to that launch. He won't be able to get ashore if he knows we're watching him. If we're not too late already.'

Nick set off, striding down the gentle slope towards the water.

Suzie hurried after him. The trees were widely spaced below the house. The grey of the river was merging with the fields beyond. She could just make out the white bows of the launch. The rest was hidden by bushes. The cabin light still glowed.

They came out on a wooden landing stage. The trim launch lay alongside. The waterside was very quiet. Across the river came the snort of an animal she could not identify. A cow, a horse? There was no sound from the boat.

'Are you looking for someone?'

The voice startled them from the far end of the landing stage. A figure stood up from the bollard where he had been sitting, half screened by tall rushes. Reynard Woodman, hands in pockets. His smile in the twilight seemed assured.

'You.' Nick's usually easy tone was decisive. 'There's no need for you to remain here. Frances has made it clear you're not welcome.'

'*Frances*?' Reynard mimicked him. 'It hasn't taken you long to get on first name terms with my sister. Let me put it, at the risk of considerable understatement, that I've known her longer than you have. We have our differences. Sibling rivalry. Especially lately. I fancy she envies my success. But we understand each other. She's made her point. She has the upper hand for the moment. Tamara came to her, not to me. A woman thing, you see. But if I let Fran cool off, and I go back suitably humble, she'll see it my way. She always does, in the end.'

Suzie found she was crossing her fingers. This was a dangerous conversation. It would be so easy for Nick to admit Tamara's presence at the house without meaning to.

She took the initiative. 'Frances has already told you Tamara's not here. You're wasting your time.'

'Oh, Suzie.' His tone was gently reproachful. 'You're no

better at lying than your husband. She's here, all right. And Millie. Not actually in the house, perhaps. But . . .' He looked meaningfully around at the wood behind him. 'I don't remember the layout, but I do know Fran has a number of rustic bowers, gazebos, what have you, where she can sit and enjoy the great outdoors. *The Secret of Humbledown Forest* wasn't entirely my own invention, you know. This was always a magical place for children. Mine used to love it. Great place for hide-and-seek.'

Suzie followed his eyes to the darkening acres of foliage and tree trunks. She could imagine how it would be in daylight. Sunlight dappling the floor between the trees. Winding paths. Perhaps there would be unexpected statuary in a glade round the next corner. Cousins of that stone dragon and troll in the porch? Wind chimes on the branches? A yew tree clipped into the semblance of a castle?

Her eyes travelled upwards. She caught her breath. Immediately, she regretted it, hoping she had not given herself away. There was something there. She was almost sure of it. To the right of the house, but higher, where the wood swept up over a mound fronting the river. A glimmer of white. A summer house, perhaps?

Could this be Frances's 'hideaway'? Were the girls there?

Fear clenched her throat. How could Reynard not have seen it?

It was overlooking the river, well hidden from the road and the track. Frances had expected her brother to come by car.

She was sure the others must hear her heart hammering in her chest. Every instinct made her want to race up through the trees and warn the girls.

Instead, with a tremendous effort, she turned back to the men on the landing stage. 'Hide-and-seek? I don't think your daughter's playing games. She's in a serious situation. Wherever she is, I hope someone's looking after her.'

'How very maternal. It's a pity her own mother couldn't have done that for her.'

'Tamara was frightened of her stepfather. He beat her.'

'There certainly seems to be something in her home circumstances she was running away from, poor sweetheart. I gather

from what you said that she doesn't even want her best friend
Millie to know where she is. Rather curious, don't you think?
You know what teenage girls are like. Perpetually on the phone
to each other. All the gossip, the heartbreaks, the secret plans.
But not with Millie. I wonder, why was that?'

'Tamara was probably afraid she might inadvertently write
or do something which would enable her to be traced,' Nick
said. 'Which, in the end, she almost did.'

Reynard seemed to ignore him. He spoke directly to Suzie.
His voice was more serious now, deep with sympathy. 'Nick's
very concerned about Tamara, isn't he? I remember when the
girls were small, he was always very ready to include her in
your family outings. Tamara, poor love, has conceived a child.
And she won't tell anyone whose it is. Especially Millie. Think
about that, Suzie.'

The bottom seemed to drop out of Suzie's stomach. She felt
as though she was falling down a dark pit. It was an outrageous
suggestion. One which had never even crossed her mind. And
yet . . .

Nick had been very concerned, even angry, when he heard
about Tamara's pregnancy, right from the first. She had
assumed he was imagining how he would feel if it were
Millie. He'd been quick to put suspicion on to others. The
coach Dan Curtis, Leonard Dawson. Even, for a moment,
Alan Taylor at church. It had been his decision, before she
had thought of it, to come racing up to the Midlands to find
Tamara.

She shook her head wildly, as though she'd blundered into
a spider's web. 'That's preposterous! How dare you even
suggest such a thing?'

'For two pins –' Nick's voice was steely – 'I'd knock you
off this landing stage into the river. That's a libellous
suggestion.'

'Not libel, dear boy. I haven't put it in writing. Slander, for
the spoken word. But I'm beginning to guess what slanderous
scenario you and Frances have been cooking up behind my back.
Does she suspect *I'm* the father? Is that why she won't let me
see Tamara? That really would be monstrous. My own daughter.
And just when she's in desperate need of a caring parent.'

Suzie felt her cheeks flaming and hoped the dusk would hide it. That *was* what they had been imagining. She had tried to tell herself how unlikely that was. But Nick and Tom had persuaded her. And Frances's behaviour had seemed to confirm it.

What if they had got it completely wrong?

Should she apologize?

Her mind scrabbled for something that would defuse the situation. 'You know, there are stories of runaways from the past that have haunted me. There was an apprentice. John Ching of Marwood, "having a base-born child now chargeable upon the parish", did a runner. The Overseers of the Poor were offering a guinea to anyone who caught him. They even advertised his description, right down to his left cheek scarred by the King's evil – that's smallpox.'

'Suzie!' Nick protested. 'Is this really the time to bring up family history?'

'It's just that there were children then, desperately unhappy, running away. And people hunting them down. And he was already marked for life. Even if we find Tamara, she'll be scarred now.'

In the silence that followed, they could hear the current whispering along the hull.

Then she heard Nick's feet shift on the boards, his catch of breath.

'Where's Petronella?' he asked.

Only then did it strike Suzie. All the time they had been talking on the landing stage, there had not been a sound from the launch. Lamplight glowed through the curtains of the cabin. There had not been a flicker of movement inside.

'Ah, Pet.' Reynard smiled in the dusk. 'I really couldn't tell you. But as I told you before, Pet knows which side her bread is buttered on. She's remarkably good at seeing that I get what I want.'

TWENTY-SEVEN

Suzie's body froze. Thoughts ricocheted around the walls of her mind. She didn't know what to believe now. She had almost convinced herself that Frances had made a horrifying misjudgement of her brother. That Reynard was indeed a concerned father, desperate to find his daughter and give her what help he could. She had even, God forgive her, allowed herself a moment of doubt about Nick. Frances was right about one thing: he *was* a persuasive storyteller.

But what did his last words mean, accompanied by that mocking smile? Words that were capable of a chilling meaning.

Pet? Where *was* she?

And where were the girls?

Only one possibility formed itself in her mind. Pet must be in these woods, intent on doing whatever Reynard wanted.

What *did* he want?

She stared at him wide-eyed. Could he really be the father of Tamara's baby?

The consequences crept coldly through her brain. That Tamara and her unborn baby would quietly disappear from his life – that charmed life of the best-selling author, the children's hero, the genial wizard. *The Secret of Humbledown Forest.* The image of everything wholesome and innocent.

Tamara's baby could shatter that.

How long had Pet been gone?

She realized she was staring into Reynard's eyes. He must read her shock.

Fear released her muscles. She turned for the wood. Nick was a jump ahead of her. He was already off the landing stage and on to the grassy bank.

Reynard laughed softly. 'For a couple who were so adamant that Tamara wasn't here, you seem remarkably keen to check on her safety.'

'If you harm one hair of her head . . .' Nick swore.

'Or Millie's,' Suzie choked.

He spread his hands, as if to demonstrate his innocence. 'I simply want my daughter back. Is that so terrible?'

Again, doubts checked Suzie's nightmare.

But Nick was setting off at a swift pace. He seemed to be heading for the house, though. To check with Frances where she had hidden the girls? To put Reynard off the scent?

She ran after him.

Nick waited until the hawthorn bushes screened them from the boat. He drew her aside. 'Wait here. I need to know if he leaves the boat. Or if Petronella comes back, with or without Tamara.'

'What can she do? She's not very big, and there are two of them.'

'I haven't the faintest idea. But whatever it is, I don't think it's going to be good for Tamara's health.'

She pulled him to her, smelling the sweat of the day from his warm shirt. She whispered, 'Did you see it? Over there, on a little hill in the wood. Something white. It could be a summer house. I wondered if that was the hideaway Frances was talking about.'

'I missed that,' he murmured. 'But it's worth a try. Quicker than going to the house. I wish I knew how much of a start she had.'

'Hurry. I'll ring you if anything happens here.'

She hadn't wanted to stay. It was scary, being so near the boat. Knowing that Reynard was still there, but not understanding what was in his mind.

A little breeze got up, rustling the reeds.

It was ridiculous to be frightened for herself. A pregnant Tamara might be a threat to the fantastic house of cards he had built from his fiction. The fame, the wealth, the admiration. But Suzie was no more to him than a suspicious woman, no longer young. Just Millie's mother. And how many 'accidents' could he get away with, she told herself bravely.

She imagined Nick running through the trees in the almost-dark. Was he heading for the right place? Who would he find when he got there? Was he already too late?

For the second time that evening, Reynard Woodman's voice shocked her.

'Poor Suzie. He's left you alone in the dark, has he? With a man he suspects of having violent intentions? Not very chivalrous.'

His smile gleamed white in the reflected light of the river. There was a softness in his voice. It sounded like pity.

A flicker of resentment ran through her. Why *had* Nick been so ready to run off and leave her alone in the twilight?

Reynard seemed to understand that. 'Wouldn't you like to come aboard and do your sentry duty in comfort? I could rustle up a gin and tonic for us both.'

'It's not dark,' she said, like a quarrelsome child.

It was true. There was still some light over the river.

Blood pounded in her throat. She did not want to go on board with him. Even though her fear of him was irrational.

'Oh, Suzie. Isn't this all just a tad ridiculous? We're old friends.'

He was putting her own thoughts into words. And it was the old friendly smile, though she could barely see the crinkling around his eyes.

But she was afraid of that smile now. Afraid that she would succumb to its magic, as so many people did. Millie, Tamara, the black-haired Pet.

Scolding herself for being an idiot, she turned without replying and began to walk away. Nick had told her to watch the boat, but she couldn't. She dared not stay, alone with Reynard Woodman, while night closed in around them.

Suzie sped up the gentle slope with what dignity she could manage. She felt a mixture of guilt and frustration. Nick had set her to watch the boat. They had to know if Reynard left it, or Pet came back. Most of all, if Pet returned with Tamara. Her mind recoiled from thinking what *that* might mean.

But she was too afraid, and too humiliated by her own fear, to stay with Reynard. It made her hot to think that, even now, he was probably laughing at her. He had outwitted her, the clever red fox. She could barely admit to herself how much she still wanted him to think well of her. To earn that smile.

It was easy to see how he could enchant so many millions of fans.

He had been mocking her fears. He knew what she thought he had done. Instead of exploding with rage, he had poked fun at her.

It was not the way a guilty man would behave. Was it?

She had no clear idea where she was going. The path twisted round bushes and trees. She came round a corner and almost stumbled over something grey in the grass.

She bent over and let her hand trace its contours. A stone dwarf peered up at her. The twilight made enigmatic shadows of his eyes. He was grinning at her.

What did she really know about the Gambles' tangled relationships? It was all guesswork.

Like her family tree. It might all be a fiction. It only needed one undiscovered family secret. A child whose father was not who the records said he was. It must have happened. She would never know.

She must get control of herself. Nick was depending on her. She must find a higher spot from where she would have a view of the river and watch the boat from there. It was growing harder as the dusk deepened. But if she did not retreat too far, she should still see movement on the landing stage, where the light lingered longest along the river.

She set off again, angling closer towards where she thought the summer house was. Now that she was in the wood, she could no longer see it. The upward slope was all that guided her. She must stop as soon as she came to a clearing that overlooked the river.

She was conscious of her own rapid breathing, of the rustle of foliage as she pushed up the narrow, half-overgrown path. It seemed to be getting louder.

It was only slowly that she realized it was not just the sound of her own progress. Someone was rushing through the bushes ahead. Feet thudding on the path. Whoever it was, was running towards her.

She leaped aside, crouching to hide until she could see who it was. Petronella? Running from what? Her heart raced as she pictured the possibility of the scene the young woman might have left behind. Why was she in such a frantic hurry to get away? Suzie's mind screamed that Nick had found the summer house too late.

A hurtling figure came clearly into sight through the shadows. The glimmer of a pale T-shirt. Short white hair.

'Millie!'

Suzie leaped upright, blocking the path so fast that her daughter cannoned into her.

Millie screamed, in the second before her brain caught up with reality. 'Mum?' she gasped. 'What are you doing here?'

Suzie gripped Millie's arms. 'Where's Tamara? Why have you left her on her own? What's happened?'

Millie shook her head, fighting for breath. 'I never found her. Frances told me . . . how to find the summer house. She said Tamara was hiding there. But I got lost. All these twisty paths. And . . . and there are these spooky things. I bumped right into one. It was hanging from a tree. A giant bat. I didn't know it was made of willow, did I? I nearly died of fright. And it was getting so dark. All I wanted to do was to get back to the house and Dad.' She clutched her mother. 'Will she be all right? Has Reynard come? Does he know she's hiding?'

'Yes. I'm afraid he's guessed. But it's all right. He's down at the boat.'

'The *boat*?'

'Didn't you know? No, of course you didn't. Frances was expecting him to come by car, but instead, he and that woman Pet took the boat. It's down at the landing stage.'

'But he's not coming to look for her?'

'He came up to the house. Frances wouldn't tell him anything, so he went back to his launch. Only . . . Pet isn't there. We've a horrible feeling she's up in these woods, searching for Tamara. And she's probably seen the summer house. Nick's trying to get to it first. I just pray he does.'

'Why? What would she do?' Millie's eyes shone wide in her pale face.

'I don't know. Whatever she thinks will help Reynard's career.'

'Mum!' Millie's fingers clenched tight around Suzie's arm.

TWENTY-EIGHT

'We have to hurry.'

The knowledge that Tamara was alone shocked Suzie. In the anxious minutes before she met Millie, she had been consoling herself that there was little Petronella could do against two girls. The news changed everything.

'Do you know the way?' Millie panted. 'I lost it.'

'Sort of. Did Frances tell you to look for this white summer house?'

'Yes. She said it looked a bit like a Greek temple.'

'Then I'm sure that's what we saw. To the right of the landing stage, on a little hill. Nick's heading for it.'

'I hope he had more luck finding it than I did,' Millie complained. 'The paths keep twisting and forking.'

Suzie increased her pace. But Millie was right. It was hard to keep her sense of direction.

'Should have brought my knapsack. I always carry a compass on the moor.'

'Ow!' Millie had collided with something in the gloom. 'I've stubbed my toe.'

Suzie's brain was working fast. It was becoming harder to see where they were going. Outside the wood, the long summer day had not completely faded, but here they were stumbling through a different world. Branches reached out to claw at them. Shadowy undergrowth masked the cavities around tree roots and uneven stones. It would be so easy to miss a fork in the path and lose the summer house entirely. She wondered if she dared call out to Nick.

But who else might hear her?

A sudden clearing surprised her. The air was lighter. She had the sense of trees retreating. But the path ended in grass. Could she find it again on the other side? There was a dark clump of bushes in the centre, masking her view.

Millie pushed through the leaves to overtake her. 'Come on, Mum!' She plunged forward. And screamed.

Appalling images raced through Suzie's mind of what Millie might have found. She dashed after her.

She stopped short, aghast at the different horror which confronted her. These were not bushes in the centre. And it was nothing like what she had imagined.

Rearing in the half light in front of her was a leg. A crooked leg whose joint was almost on a level with her eyes. Beyond it was another. And yet more. A gigantic dark body hung suspended between the many splayed legs. An enormous spider.

Millie was clutching her, shivering uncontrollably, trying to drag Suzie back.

'Mum! It's horrible! Is it alive?'

Suzie tried to still her own pounding heart. 'No. Don't be silly.' She put out an unwilling hand and felt the crooked leg. 'Look. It's just another willow sculpture. It's quite clever, really. I wonder if Frances makes them.'

'It's sick! Why would anyone want to put something so gross in their wood?'

'I dare say it just looks a fun thing in daylight.' Is that true of this whole evening? she wondered. Will we wake up in the morning and wonder how we could ever have believed the sensational ideas that are frightening us now?

But Tamara was terrified of something. Both day and night.

'I'm getting disorientated. I think we have to get round to the other side of this spider. The path should go on from there. I only hope there isn't more than one choice.'

Rationality did not entirely take away her reluctance to pass that massive brooding figure. It had been fashioned in realistic detail. Head and thorax, prominent eyes. Eight rearing legs. The raw materials of the forest had been fashioned into something much more sinister.

'Help me,' she said to Millie, when they had rounded it, giving it a wide berth. 'Can you find anything that looks like another path? I really don't want to get lost and have to blunder through the trees.'

'Listen!' Millie said suddenly. 'What was that?'

Suzie held her breath. The evening bird-calls had fallen silent. Then, distant but urgent, she heard a shout.

'*Tamara*! *Look out*!'

'That's Nick! Something's happened. Quick!'

She dashed into the trees towards the call. Her desire to find a proper path was forgotten. She plunged through bushes, avoiding at the last moment tree trunks that rushed towards her in the gloom. Her feet caught in looping brambles, sending her pitching forwards, almost to the ground.

'Wait!' she gasped to Millie.

They listened again. There was nothing now.

Desperately hoping that she had got the direction right, Suzie ran on again. The slope was rising. She could only pray that she not been wrong about the origin of that single cry. That this was the mound on which the summer house stood. That Tamara and Nick were there. And no one else.

The sky was grey above her now. She snatched at hope. The trees had been felled around that white building glimpsed from the river.

It was there, up in front of her. Glimmering in the dusk. Faintly Grecian. A little building with a pillared porch.

She stopped to draw breath.

Millie whispered beside her. 'That's it, isn't it? Where she's hiding?'

'*Was* hiding. Why did Nick shout to her like that?'

They scrambled up the last incline.

Slowly, Suzie mounted the porch steps. She peered inside. 'Tamara?' her voice asked softly.

Nothing stirred. No sound of frightened breathing.

Millie joined her. 'It's me, Tamara. Millie.'

There was no answer.

'She's not here.' Millie turned on Suzie, accusingly.

Suzie nerved herself to go inside and feel the shadows.

There were plastered walls, a cold stone floor. Suddenly, she recoiled, thinking she had touched something living. But it was only the softer feel of cloth. There was a line of serrated metal. A zip.

'She *was* here,' said Suzie, backing out. 'There's a sleeping bag.'

'Then where *is* she? And where's Dad?'

Suzie turned. The river glistened faintly below them, like a snail track winding between woods and fields. More clearly than she had expected, she picked out the white of Reynard's launch, the gleam from the cabin. To her immense relief, there was no sound of the engine starting. Petronella must not yet have got Tamara to the boat. If that was her plan.

But would she have still wanted to, knowing the Fewings were in pursuit? Might she have felt driven to act more quickly than faking an accident on the river?

On a sudden impulse, Suzie dashed around to the back of the summer house.

A broader track led down through the trees, towards the unseen road. Even as she stared down it, Suzie caught a glimpse in the dusk of a running figure. Dark top, lighter trousers.

'There she goes!' She pointed.

'Who?' Millie cried. 'Tamara . . . or that Petronella woman?'

The thought flashed through Suzie's mind that she was supposed to be watching the boat and Reynard. But the drama that mattered was right in front of her. Whoever this was, she was running away from the river.

Suzie did not make a conscious decision. Her feet were flying down the mound. She was aware of Millie sprinting beside her, pulling ahead.

The track that cut through the trees on this side of the hill was broad. For a few blessed moments they were running in grey half-light, not the darkness of the woods. Yet as they plunged lower, it became harder to distinguish the pale trousers of that racing figure in front of them.

Then the ground levelled out and the shadows were upon them again. The broad ride separated into smaller paths, forking in all directions.

Suzie came to a panting stop. Millie had plunged down the path most directly in front of them. Suzie could hear the sound of her daughter's progress as she pushed through the leaves.

Nothing else. Tamara – or was it Pet? – was too far ahead to be heard. Or else – her mind shrank violently from the thought – Pet had caught up with Tamara and stopped the sound of her running.

There was a new sound in the trees to her right. She spun round, tense and fearful.

The tall figure that broke out of the bushes was, she realized suddenly, the one she most wanted to see.

'Nick!'

He came to an abrupt halt. 'What the hell are *you* doing here? I thought you were watching the boat.'

It was not the welcome she needed, but she flew to him, all the same. She clutched his bare arms and felt the sweat of his running. 'I heard you call out to Tamara. Why? I met Millie. We saw someone running from the summer house.' It came out as ragged and incoherent as her breathing.

'I caught sight of Petronella climbing the hill. I wasn't near enough to stop her. All I could do was shout out to warn Tamara. I saw her make a run for it. I was trying to catch up, but I lost them.'

'That way,' Suzie said. 'Towards the road. One of those paths into the trees. Millie ran on ahead of me.'

She could see Nick thinking swiftly. 'You take the left fork,' he ordered. 'I'll go right. With luck, we'll make contact with each other when we get to the road. If one of us hasn't over-taken them first.' He darted a swift kiss at her. 'Take care of yourself.'

'And you.' She fled again.

The wood was doubly scary the second time, and on her own. Darker still, lower down. She lost the path almost imme-diately. She was dodging through tree trunks, hoping against hope she was running straight and not veering in a circle. She longed to stop and listen for others running. But the figure she had seen was a long way in front. She had to catch up.

She prayed that Millie was safe, plunging recklessly ahead on her own.

She gasped as a branch caught her across the face. She struggled free.

The wood was silent.

What if she had run too far? What if Tamara was crouching in some gully, waiting for the sounds of pursuit to move beyond her? How could they find one frightened girl in this vast darkness?

Petronella had seen her fleeing. How close was Suzie behind them?

There was a sudden brilliance of light between the branches. It was seconds before her panicked mind could make sense of it. The light swept past and disappeared.

'The road!' She heard herself gasp the word aloud.

Her eyes had been dazzled by the passing headlights. She stumbled on blindly through the trees. She did not see the ditch until she tumbled into it. The leaf mould at the bottom was damp and sticky. Then there was a bank to climb before she felt the solid familiarity of tarmac.

She stood uncertain. If Tamara had got this far, what would she do? On the far side, there was the glimmer of open fields. She listened for sounds, of pursued or pursuers. The rustle of leaves mocked her. She could not tell whether it was a breeze in the branches overhead or someone running hard further away.

Even as she wondered what to do, another set of headlights swept towards her. She shrank back. It was foolish to think that the car could be personally threatening, but she had an overwhelming feeling that she did not want to be seen.

The car sped past her without stopping, then slowed for the bend. She watched the tail lights disappear.

Moments later, there was screech of brakes. It seemed to go on for ever. Then, silence fell, except for the sound of the engine, still running but stationary.

Suzie's shocked brain took seconds to catch up with the possible meaning.

'*Millie!*'

She remembered her slim blonde daughter sprinting ahead of her, plunging into the woods alone. Had she come dashing out from the trees, while Suzie, clumsier, had fallen? Straight out on to the road, in the path of the car sweeping round the bend?

It seemed impossibly far to that curve in the road. Her feet would not pound the tarmac fast enough. Her breath was ragged, almost sobbing.

Even before she rounded the bend she heard the voices. High and agitated. At least two, a man's and a woman's.

She raced into the scene, brightly lit by the standing car's headlights.

She still could not see what lay in front of the bonnet. A young man standing over something. The woman was almost hidden as she knelt on the road.

Suzie could only see the feet that protruded beyond the nearside wheels. Trainers.

Millie had been wearing trainers.

She felt physically sick.

She had not realized that she had stopped running. She forced herself to walk forward. Past the dark rear of the car. Into the beams that illuminated the road in front.

The girl lay face downward. Wavy dark hair tumbled about her head. Not Millie.

Tamara.

Guilt swallowed up the first wave of selfish relief. Guilt, and pity.

The young man was talking fast. 'Is she all right? I jammed the brakes on as fast as I could. It was my first emergency stop. I didn't even stall the engine.'

She read the shock in his voice, gabbling inconsequential things. Probably a newly qualified driver.

He knelt beside the body. The headlights shone full on his face.

'Tom!' she cried, incredulous.

The woman looked up. 'She's still breathing, thank the Lord.'

The unmistakable Pennsylvanian accent of Prudence.

TWENTY-NINE

Incomprehension paralysed Suzie. She must have passed from reality into waking dream.

Prudence had a practical hold on the situation. 'Get your

emergency services,' she ordered Tom. 'I don't know the number.' She turned her face up to Suzie. 'And don't you blame Tom. He slowed right down for that bend. We couldn't see a darn thing outside the headlights. She just came rushing out on to the road. And he's right. He did a really good stop. Couldn't help hitting her, but it might have been worse. He didn't run over her.'

Tamara stirred and moaned.

'Should we move her off the road?' Suzie asked. Other questions whirled through her head. How could Tom and Prudence possibly be here, in rural Warwickshire, when she had left them more than a hundred miles away?

'No, I think we'll just get her into the recovery position until we see how bad she's hurt. Could you get in the car and find those – what do you call them? – those lights that flash on and off.'

'Hazard lights.'

'Right. And there's a coat of mine on the back seat.'

As she turned to obey, Suzie was relieved to find that Tom had got control of his panic. He was talking crisply into his mobile. '. . . Just west of Little Fairings. We must be pretty close to a place called The House in the Forest.'

She set the orange lights flashing and came back with Prudence's jacket. The other woman had turned Tamara's head sideways. Her face looked ghostly in the artificial light, between the heavy waves of dark hair.

Suzie knelt beside her and eased the jacket under her head. There was a panicked skip of a heartbeat as she felt the stickiness of blood. 'It's all right,' she said, forcing a smile. 'Just lie still. The ambulance is on its way.' She took the girl's hand.

'How are you feeling?' Prudence asked. 'Do you have a pain anywhere?'

'My head hurts.'

An enormous relief took hold of Suzie. Tamara's speech was slurred, but at least she was alive, conscious, coherent.

She felt ashamed that part of her terror was not just that Tamara would die, but that Tom might have killed her.

She realized she was shaking.

'Now, before you get mad with Tom,' Prudence said, 'let's

just get one thing straight. The hire car's mine. I got this idea. If I'm flying out of Birmingham airport tomorrow, Warwickshire is kind of on my way. So why not? Well, I was having kittens, having to fly back to the States not knowing how this all was going to turn out. It was my idea to bring Tom along as the second driver.'

'But how did you find us?'

'Seems you told Tom where you were headed. Since then, he's been imagining goodness knows what, when you folks weren't answering your phones.'

Suzie had a guilty memory of seeing Tom's name on an incoming call and switching her mobile off. 'No, sorry.'

'We covered the distance in pretty good time. He drives well, your Tom.' She bent over Tamara. 'What were you running away from?'

'Someone . . . up to the summer house . . .' Tamara's speech was heavy with silences.

Suzie squeezed her hand. 'Nick was coming to help. Did you know it was him?'

'Someone else . . . woman . . .'

'Petronella,' Suzie said softly.

She felt the spasm of the girl's hand within her own.

'It's all right. She's not here. She can't get you now. You'll be safe in hospital. We'll look after you.'

Tamara's eyes closed. Suzie tapped her cheek. She had a feeling you weren't supposed to let the victim of an accident drift into unconsciousness. She shouldn't have blurted out the most frightening subject.

'Millie's here,' she said. 'We were coming to find you. We talked to your aunt. She's nice, isn't she? Millie guessed you might be staying here.' She spoke as lightly as if Tamara had just come away for a summer holiday.

'Millie?' Tamara murmured.

A new fear grasped Suzie. Where *was* Millie? She had gone running ahead into the darkness of the woods.

Tom called sharply: 'Someone's coming!'

Suzie twisted round, trying to see past the dark bulk of the hire car. She couldn't hear the expected siren of the ambulance, or see flashing lights. Through the purr of the engine they had left running she began to make out the sound of footsteps crackling through the undergrowth.

'Tom!' Nick's voice made the same incredulous cry she had herself.

Nick came running into the shaft of light. There was someone with him. A slight blonde figure.

Millie let out a small scream and dropped to her knees beside Tamara. 'Is she dead?'

'No.' Suzie's reassurance was for Tamara, as well as Millie. 'She's going to be all right.' She hoped it was true.

Nick cast a look round the scene. 'I can't begin to imagine what's going on here. Explanations later. Have you called the police?'

Police? The word rang oddly in Suzie's mind. It was the ambulance they needed, wasn't it?

Tom's voice was emphatic. 'Too right. We should have done that long ago.'

Suzie heard the catch of Nick's breath.

'What's *that*?' he asked. He was staring into the wood at the roadside, shading his eyes from the glare of headlights. As she followed his gaze, Suzie caught the glimpse of something pale through the lower branches.

That running figure had been wearing light-coloured trousers. She glanced down. Tamara's jeans were black. It had been someone else they had seen. Someone chasing Tamara. Someone who was lurking even now to watch this unplanned outcome. To take the news to Reynard.

'Pet!' she cried, leaping up. 'Get her!'

Nick and Tom leaped for the bank and plunged into the wood. The dim shape that must be Petronella wheeled and darted away.

Suzie threw an anxious look behind her. Millie and Prudence were kneeling beside Tamara. The ambulance was on its way. She gave in to the desire for action and scrambled over the bank herself.

It was bafflingly dark beyond the headlights. But Petronella's trainers betrayed her progress as they swished and crackled through the leaves. Nick and Tom charged after her. Suzie sped in their wake.

She heard Pet cry out. The sounds of trampled leaves and snapping twigs gave way to human shouts.

'Lie still,' Nick ordered. 'You're not getting away with this. A girl may die because of you.'

Might she? Suzie's initial relief had been founded on so small a thing. That Tamara was conscious.

She stumbled upon them, almost cannoning into Tom. The two men were stooped over a small, prostrate figure.

'The police are coming,' Tom grunted as he struggled with her. 'Dad, have you got something to tie her wrists with?'

'I'll get her shoelaces,' Suzie offered.

She knelt in the damp leaves and felt for those trainers. Pet kicked once as Suzie's hands closed round her ankle. Then she lay obstinately still, refusing to move her foot.

It was fiddlesome work, unthreading the laces, when she had only the feel of her fingertips to guide her. As she moved to the second leg, Suzie's knuckles connected with something hard. She finished her task and handed the laces to Nick. 'Try these.'

She heard, rather than saw, him twist Pet's arms behind her and lash her wrists. It was reassuring to have Nick and Tom with her. Not to be alone in the dark wood, fearing what or whom she might meet. Or to be on the riverbank with only the mocking charm of Reynard for company. She shivered.

As she sat back on her heels, she remembered that moment when, instead of the soft fabric of Pet's trousers, her hand had met something harder under the cloth.

On an impulse, before her mind made sense of the memory, she reached out in the gloom. Her eyes had adjusted enough to see the pale fabric clothing Pet's legs. Her hand closed round it. She felt the long pocket of cargo pants. Yes, there was something under the cotton. Something long, narrow and hard. She ripped open the Velcro and drew it out. 'She had this.'

Nick still had hold of Pet, though she had stopped struggling.

It was Tom who took the bar from her and examined its shape. 'That feels very like a monkey wrench. What was she doing, charging through the woods with one of these in her pocket?'

In the silence, a tree creaked overhead.

Nick said quietly, 'I don't think we need to guess what would have happened if she'd caught Tamara. If she'd refused to come back to the boat, there was another plan. More risky than a simple drowning, but a risk this young lady was prepared to take for Reynard Woodman.'

Petronella said nothing. Suzie could hardly see her face in the near darkness. She tried to remember that immaculately groomed and made-up young woman on the lawn beside the river this afternoon. Now she lay in the mud, among damp leaves, with twigs twisted in her hair.

Nick was hauling her to her feet. He and Tom took her arms, one on each side. They were marching her back to the road.

'Why just her?' Suzie said. 'Why isn't Reynard here?'

'Deniability,' Nick snorted. 'This silly woman would do anything for him. As if he'd keep her, anyway.'

Pet gave a bitter little laugh. The headlights caught the toss of her head. 'Oh, he will. I know too much.'

'You won't be able to blackmail him. Once you come before a court, everyone will know what he's done.'

'Will they? You really think that girl will talk?'

Suzie's mind did a somersault. Tamara had fled her home, not even telling Millie why. She could not bear to confess to anyone what her father had done to her. Even now, no one had actually *said* Reynard was the father of Tamara's child.

And Tamara was lying injured on the road. At the very least, a head injury. And who knew what besides?

The blare of a siren cut through the shocked quiet around the car.

THIRTY

The flashing blue light that screamed towards them was too low. It was not the reassuring bulk of an ambulance but a police car. Two officers got out. A man and woman, both young. Suzie watched the man come towards them, glancing nervously at Tamara on the ground in front of

Prudence's car. She could see he was thinking of the emergency first-aid he had been taught, should he be the first at the scene of an accident, and hoping he would not be called upon to use it.

It was his colleague who knelt swiftly beside Tamara. Prudence answered her questions about the girl's injuries briefly and practically.

The policeman drew an audible breath of relief. He turned his attention to the rest of them. 'Constable Martin. And that's my colleague, Constable Eve Tandy. You reported a traffic accident and –' his young face took on an expression that struggled with disbelief – 'an attempted murder?'

His wary gaze took in the slight form of Petronella, closely guarded by Tom and Nick.

'That's right,' said Tom. 'I was the one who phoned you. Tamara ran out in front of our car. But we were on our way to help her. Mum and Dad and Millie had come to look for her after she disappeared and we were scared—'

The constable held up a placating hand. 'Just hang on there, sir. I'll want statements from all of you. You're . . .' He consulted his notebook. 'Tom Fewings, right? Who's this young woman? Why is she tied up like that?'

'Citizen's arrest,' said Nick. 'We suspect her of having designs on the life of Tamara Gamble. We found this on her.'

The constable's eyebrows shot up at the sight of the wrench. It looked bigger, uglier in the full glare of both sets of headlights.

A palpable relief washed over the group as the sound of a second siren brought the ambulance speeding smoothly to a halt. Suzie felt some of the terror drain from her as the green-overalled paramedics, in their yellow jackets, jumped out. One had an emergency kit in her hands. Tamara was still alive. She had crossed that dangerous gap between the accident and the arrival of professional help. She was no longer the Fewings' responsibility.

It was selfish to think like that. Tamara had no one else here.

Frances. For the first time since she and Nick had left the house for the landing stage, Suzie suddenly thought of Tamara's aunt. Had she been sitting in the House in the Forest all this time, waiting for full darkness to fall so that she could spirit Tamara away? Wondering what was happening in the meantime? What her brother was doing? Why none of them had come back?

'Do you have Frances's number?' she asked Nick.

She saw his guilty start. He reached for his phone.

The paramedics had finished their examination of Tamara. They were putting a neck brace on, getting ready to ease her on to a stretcher to transfer her to the ambulance.

'Can I come too?' Suzie asked. 'I'm not a relation, but Millie here is her best friend. She knows me.'

'Good idea,' said the female paramedic. 'I'm Betty, by the way.'

'Suzie. Suzie Fewings.' She glanced anxiously at PC Tandy. 'You'll be wanting statements from all of us. But I don't like to think of her going to a strange hospital without somebody she knows. Not after what happened this evening. We're getting a message to the aunt she's been staying with.'

'Go ahead,' said the policewoman. 'From what I've picked up so far, I think I should come too. I don't think she's fit to be questioned yet, but someone should be on hand in case she does want to talk. And you've said enough to make me think I should keep an eye on her safety. There seem to have been some fairly strange goings-on in these woods this evening.'

'It's a complicated story. But there's something else. Someone else. You'll find a motor cruiser on the river on the other side of the wood, if he's not already taken fright and headed back to Burwood. Kevin Gamble. Otherwise known as Reynard Woodman.'

'The author? I loved his books when I was a kid. How does he fit in with this?'

'He's Tamara's father. I can tell you what I *think* he's done. But only she knows the truth.'

'Let's hope she makes it, then.'

The words shocked Suzie out of the warmth of relief she had felt when the emergency services arrived. Could Tamara still die? She shot a fearful look at the girl's still, white face.

They were lifting the stretcher gently into the ambulance. Suzie was about to climb up after it.

Millie sprang forward. 'I want to come too.'

The paramedic Betty turned round from the ambulance's interior. 'Sorry, kid. This is an ambulance, not a coach excursion. We've got enough on board as it is.'

'That's not fair!'

Constable Tandy looked back at her colleague, at the group around the hire car, now a possible crime scene. At Petronella, now handcuffed. At Tom, who had been driving. At Nick and Prudence and the indignant Millie.

'I hope he's called for backup. This is only his second week on the job.'

Hunched in the back of the ambulance, PC Tandy took Suzie's statement. Suzie was aware how circumstantial and incoherent it must sound. Tamara's reluctance to name the father of her child. The Fewings' fear of Leonard Dawson's role. His refusal to report her missing. The glamorous tennis coach. The scared schoolboy Justin Soames. Their failure to contact Tamara's father. And the notelet, with Prudence's inspired guess that led them to the House in the Forest and Tamara's aunt. But not before they had misinterpreted the evidence and called on Tamara's father and Petronella. Their converging on Frances's house; all of them hunting the elusive and frightened Tamara.

All the time she was talking, Suzie was aware that Tamara herself was lying only an arm's length away. She could not be sure how conscious the girl was of what was being said about her. The occasional moan suggested she was still awake. It might be the pain of her injuries or emotional distress.

Only Tamara could tell them the truth about her baby. Unless she was willing to testify, no one could be brought to court.

She might die before that.

Her thoughts were broken into by a sudden tension in the ambulance. Betty was bent over the recumbent figure of Tamara. The motherly paramedic called to the driver, 'Brad. She's haemorrhaging.'

'I'm doing my best.'

The ambulance was speeding through the late evening traffic

on the outskirts of a town, siren blaring. Suzie undid her seat belt and moved to kneel beside the stretcher.

In the dim light she saw the stain where Betty had pulled back the blanket from Tamara's legs.

'She was pregnant,' she said.

The other woman's eyes met hers. 'Maybe just a threatened miscarriage.' Then her expression sharpened with awareness. 'She looks very young.'

'She's fourteen.'

'So maybe it's just as well, as long as she pulls through safely. We'll be at the hospital in a few minutes.'

Tamara stirred on the stretcher. She gave a little cry. 'The baby! Will I lose it?'

Suzie's hand closed round hers. 'Don't worry about a thing. We're almost at the hospital. They'll look after you.'

Tamara had started to cry. 'I don't care what they say. It's *my* baby. I want it.'

Betty was preparing an injection. It would be some sort of sedative, Suzie guessed. All she could do was hold Tamara and stroke her face. The needle slipped in. A few moments later, Tamara's anxious face softened. Suzie felt her limbs relax.

She turned her face up to Betty. 'You heard her. Tell them to try and save the baby. She knows the problems, but she'd already made up her mind. It was because they wanted her to have an abortion that she ran away from home.'

She felt the huge responsibility of Tamara's future in her hands. And that of the unborn child. It would be so easy for a well-meaning doctor to put an end to it now. Would Tamara thank her for this intervention? Or would there come a time when she regretted she had not taken the easy way out?

Suzie thought about the tiny, partially-formed baby and what it might become. She remembered Tom and Millie, newborn. The inexpressible wonder of it.

Then reality kicked in. How would Tamara explain its parentage to the child? She opened her mouth to pull back from that too-confident instruction. Then changed her mind again.

Had Johan Clayson wished she might lose the baby, before Adam was born? Had she taken steps to procure a miscarriage, from some eighteenth-century wise woman? How did she feel when she held Adam in her arms and knew that calumny would always follow them?

She had not lived long to bear her share of it.

Suzie struggled with her fear. It was illogical to think that Tamara's story would mirror Johan's as closely as that.

This was the twenty-first century. Modern treatment would save Tamara. If necessary, the Fewings would stand by her and her child.

Or would she prefer to be with her aunt? Away from the tyrannical Dawson . . . but so close to her father, if Suzie's darkest fears about Reynard Woodman were true?

The ambulance swung off the road, the siren silenced. Moments later, it pulled up at Accident and Emergency. With practised speed, the stretcher was lowered to the ground. Nurses and porters were already waiting to speed it inside. Suzie and Constable Eve Tandy were left as bystanders.

Suzie's mind sprang to life again. 'Quick. There's something we need to do.' She ran down the corridor after the retreating stretcher party. She caught the nearest nurse. 'She's having a miscarriage. At least, we think she is. It's really important. She wants this baby, but if it can't be saved, can you . . . I don't know what you do with a foetus, but can you keep a . . . a sample? For DNA. In case there's a criminal prosecution.'

The nurse looked startled. Then she took in Constable Tandy's uniform. 'OK. I'll tell the doctor.'

Tamara was gone, through the swing doors. Suzie and Tandy looked at each other.

'Coffee,' said the constable. 'Or tea. With sugar. No arguments.'

THIRTY-ONE

Suzie came to with a start. She looked around her, disorientated, and felt a sharp pain in her neck. She had fallen asleep in the hospital waiting room.

Around her, in various aspects of weariness, were Nick, Tom and Millie. Prudence was asleep beside Suzie.

Sometime in the night, Constable Tandy had been relieved. In her place sat Detective Sergeant John Smithens. In contrast to the fit young woman, he was middle-aged and rather plumper than Suzie thought a policeman should be. She tried to imagine him running down Petronella as she fled through the woods. He would have been unlikely to catch her. But he had a genial, fatherly look about his side-burned face. Someone Tamara might feel reassured to find at her bedside when she was able to talk.

If she could trust any man now.

Maybe it would have been better if Constable Tandy had stayed, even though she was only a beat-pounding, uniformed officer.

Still, the arrival of the Detective Sergeant meant that the police believed they were dealing with something more than a traffic accident.

Doors swung open and Frances O'Malley came through. Her tall, rangy figure bore little family resemblance to the curvaceous Tamara or Frances's sprightly brother Kevin, otherwise Reynard. Only their red hair linked brother and sister.

Frances's face was gaunt with tiredness. She looked at their expectant expressions and said, 'She's lost the baby.'

'And Tamara?' The question was wrenched from Suzie.

Frances sighed. 'All right, under the circumstances. She's still sedated.'

So the very worst had not happened. This was not going to be Johan's story.

Yet Suzie felt the wrench of bereavement, even at second hand. She caught Nick's eye and, before he could speak, snapped, 'Don't you dare say, "It's all for the best"!'

Nick looked startled. 'But think of the problems it would have caused. Not just any teenage pregnancy, but *this* one. She's spared that.'

'It was still a baby. *Her* baby,' said Millie. 'That's what she told me. Can I see her now?'

Sergeant Smithens rose. 'I'll need to take a statement from her when she comes round.'

'Of course. Though I'm not certain how much she'll tell you.'

The unspoken question hung heavy over the room.

Prudence was awake now. She straightened her crumpled summer suit and fished in her handbag for a powder compact. She touched up her make-up and patted her hair, as a soldier might check his combat-readiness.

'Well, I guess this story was never going to end happily. But at least she's safe. I just couldn't fly back to the States and not know whether you guys had found her, and that nobody got hurt.'

Hurt, thought Suzie. Tamara can never really get over the hurt that's been done to her.

As though she read her thoughts, Prudence reached out a hand and clasped Suzie's knee. 'It could have been a whole lot worse than it is. If you hadn't arrived when you did . . . If this Petronella character had caught up with her . . .'

'They can't prove anything, can they?' Tom cut in. 'She didn't actually *do* anything. They didn't get her aboard his boat. All you've got is that she was carrying an offensive weapon. Nothing at all on Reynard Woodman.'

'I think you may be wrong there,' said the detective sergeant. 'Your mother was quick-witted enough to make sure the hospital kept the evidence. If the father is who you think it is, we can prove it.'

'They can do that?' Tom asked. 'While it's still that small? It's got separate DNA from its mother?'

'Oh yes. From the day it's conceived.'

There was silence, as the implications of this sank in.

'You good people really ought to go home and get some sleep. I'm the only one who's getting paid overtime.'

'It's not exactly home,' Nick said. 'It's the Bear and Staff at Burwood. And we haven't booked a room for Tom. Still, I dare say we could smuggle him in.'

Prudence yawned. 'I guess I ought to be heading for Birmingham Airport. I can't tell you how sorry I am to be leaving you folks. You've been so good to me.' She patted her capacious handbag. 'I've got so many memories in here. Photographs of all the places you took me to. The farms, the church, and that

Dissenters' graveyard.' She hugged Suzie. 'I'd never have gotten to that one without you. I didn't tell you. I tracked it down after you left. Meeting Lane. No meeting house there now, more's the pity. But there's still the burial ground, with a wall around it. Someone still goes in there and cuts the grass some. Not too much. They let the wild flowers grow. It was kind of peaceful, just sitting there and knowing Johan had come to rest at last.'

She stood up more briskly. 'I'm going to get the folks back home together. I'll tell them the whole story. The highs and lows. You know how shocked I was when I found our great Adam Clayson was a bastard? I guess I can make them see it differently now. What it was like if you bore a child out of wedlock in those days. How she came right out and named the father. And shamed him, I shouldn't wonder, a married man his age. And little Adam, starting out from next to nothing, to do all he did. I only wish Johan could have lived to see it. Her son, the great timber merchant in Pennsylvania and founder of the Presbyterian chapel at Come-to-Good. But she found her own peace in Corley, God rest her soul.'

Suzie hugged her back. She herself had warmed to Johan's unfolding story. She envied Prudence's ability to talk about her faith without embarrassment. She made a decision that she, too, would find the Dissenters' burial ground and leave flowers there.

Meanwhile, another girl lived on, without her baby.

'You guys just have to come to Pennsylvania and let me show you around my place. I'll take you to Come-to-Good. And, Tom, thanks for getting me here. I've given your police my statement. That accident was absolutely not your fault. Anybody else driving might have killed the girl.'

'Thanks.'

Suzie saw relief relax her son's face and blessed Prudence for that.

One last round of hugs. Then the warmth and enthusiasm of the American woman was gone, leaving the waiting room a thinner place.

'Sergeant Smithens is right,' Nick said. 'We could all use a few hours' sleep.'

*   *   *

Suzie and Millie were back at the hospital at mid-morning.

Frances was sitting beside Tamara's bed. She got up when she saw them. 'Good. I could do with some coffee. I'll leave you to it.'

Tamara looked at them ruefully, her head half turned away. She greeted them quietly, but seemed unwilling to talk. Some of her thick brown hair had been shaved away, and there was a large plaster where her head had hit the road.

Millie, for once, was finding it hard to come up with the usual girlish chatter. 'Does it hurt?'

Tamara nodded, and winced.

Suzie filled the awkward silence. 'They say you haven't got concussion. That's good news. There's severe bruising down the side where the car hit you, but nothing broken. You were lucky.'

'Lucky.' The girl's voice was flat.

'I'm sorry!' Suzie put out an instinctive hand to touch her. 'That was crass of me. I was talking about physical injury. I know you wanted that baby. In spite of everything.'

'He was mine. I don't care what anyone says.'

'Yes. I know.'

'The chaplain came in this morning. She was nice. I'm sick of nurses and doctors telling me it was all for the best. *She* didn't. She said if I went along to the chapel this morning, after their service, I could light a candle.'

'Would you like to do that? Can you walk?'

'Just about.'

'I can get a wheelchair for you.' Millie sprang up.

'No. I can do it.'

Millie, somewhat nervously, helped her off the bed. Tamara was already fully dressed. Frances must have brought her fresh clothes.

'We passed the chapel on our way down the corridor,' Suzie said. 'It's not far. I think their service finishes at eleven.'

'She asked if I'd like to come to it. But I couldn't face all those people.'

'That's understandable.'

They helped her walk the short distance to the chapel. The room was light and airy, lit by two tall windows on either

side. An embroidered banner hung from the front wall – a
white dove descending in billows of scarlet fire. Pentecost,
Suzie remembered. The coming of the Holy Spirit.

The last of the little morning congregation was drifting
away. A young couple stood talking to a small, bespectacled,
grey-haired woman. Her eyes went past them to Tamara and
she smiled.

Tamara limped forward and sat down on one of the chairs.
The couple made their farewells and moved out.

The chaplain did not come directly to them. She turned to
face the tall golden cross in the middle of the front wall. For
a time she stood before it, hands folded. Then she bowed her
head and turned to greet them. 'Tamara. I'm glad you came.
And these are . . .?'

'My friend Millie, and her mother Suzie.'

'It's good to know Tamara's got friends here.' Though her
smile was welcoming enough, her concern was focused on
Tamara. 'Would you like me to say a prayer for the baby?'

Tamara nodded.

The woman led the way forward. To one side of the steps
up to the communion table there was a bank of tea lights.
Some of them had been lit. Each, Suzie realized, must represent
a prayer someone had made. A thanksgiving, a memorial.

The chaplain prayed in a clear, quiet voice. She seemed to
have no doubt that this was a real child they were speaking of.
Someone who, even in this tiny, unformed state, mattered to
God, and to its mother. She lit a taper and handed it to Tamara.

Suzie stole a look at Millie and was surprised to see tears
on her face. Millie had wanted to stop going to Springbrook
Church under its old minister. Would it have made any difference if she had known Alan Taylor? But she would remember
today and be moved by it.

The little flame sprang to life. Tamara stood back.

The chaplain handed her a white rose. 'Go in peace, and
the peace of God be with those you love.'

'Thank you.'

The police-station car park was quiet on a Sunday afternoon. The
Fewings emerged into the sunshine.

'Is that it?' asked Millie. 'No more questions? We're free to do what we like?'

'Unless there's a court case,' Nick said. 'Yes, they're finished with us.'

'But there must be, mustn't there?' Tom protested. 'They can't get away with it.'

A blue BMW slid quietly into the visitors' car park and stopped. Reynard Woodman got out. He was alone.

The Fewings stopped dead and stared at him.

Reynard advanced towards them, his red hair glinting in the sunlight. There was a foxy smile about his mouth. His clothes looked dapper. His maroon jacket had a velvety sheen. There was a blue-and-white spotted bow tie. 'Suzie, you look quite shocked to see me.'

'I thought . . .'

'That I'd be locked up, like poor Pet? I'm afraid your slander machine isn't quite powerful enough to touch me.'

'You nearly killed Tamara,' Millie broke out.

His eyes widened in surprise. So did his smile. 'Did I hear you right, Millie? My information is that Tom was driving the car that knocked her down. I was a half a mile away, on the river.'

'It wasn't my fault,' Tom growled. 'She ran out in front of me because your Pet was chasing her with a monkey wrench as long as my forearm. I don't imagine she was acting entirely off her own bat.'

'Oh, but she was, the sweetie. Do you really think I'd sanction anything as crass as that, even if, for some strange reason, I'd wanted to get rid of Tamara? I can assure you, I could think of a much more subtle plot than that. I haven't won the book prizes I have for nothing.'

'You were going to get her on to your boat, weren't you?' Suzie was finding it difficult to speak. 'A drowning. Impossible to prove it wasn't an accident.'

The fiery eyebrows rose. 'What a lively imagination you have. And not a shred of proof.'

Nick cut in. 'Mercifully, she's still alive. But the police are well aware of what nearly happened. If you lay a finger on her in future . . .'

'Now why would I want to do that? My own daughter.'

'Because you got her up the duff, that's why!' Millie cried. 'And you're her father.'

'That's a ridiculous suggestion. And anyway, Frances informs me she's lost the baby. It seems Tamara doesn't want to talk about whatever schoolboy oik it was that fathered it. No case to answer. You can all go home and stop worrying.'

Suzie's voice was steely now. 'Tamara doesn't need to talk.'

'How so? I should have thought she was the only witness to its paternity.'

'Because, small though it was, the foetus had quite enough DNA for the hospital to send a sample for testing.'

She watched his face turn white. For long moments nobody said anything.

Then Reynard Woodman tugged at his bow tie, as though it were choking him. He strode past them into the police station, where Petronella was still being held.

'Will they take him to court?' Millie asked. 'Can they get it into the newspapers, without Tamara's name coming out? I want to see his photograph plastered all over the Internet, so that everybody knows what he's done. I want them to sweep his horrible books off the library shelves. I hope he spends years in prison, and that he's on the sex-offenders register for the rest of his life.'

'Some of that may happen,' Suzie said. 'He'd be prosecuted as Kevin Gamble, though. And there probably would be restrictions on reporting, for Tamara's sake. But the police will certainly keep tabs on him when he comes out. I doubt if they'll let him go on living with Calliope and Persephone, if they're still under age by then. Poor little things. I don't know what will happen to them if they've got enough on Petronella to send her down. But the fact is, she didn't actually *do* anything to Tamara.'

'So he could get away with it? I mean, he could still be the great Reynard Woodman, and hardly anybody but us would know what he'd done? Just the police and the judge? He could even go on writing books in prison.'

'If Tamara wants to keep this quiet, I'm afraid that could happen.'

'I'm not so sure,' said Nick. 'Rumours get around. If his publishers hear a whisper of this, they're going to think twice about investing big money in someone whose sales could crash if he turns into a hate figure. Even if that never actually happens.'

'Knowing him,' snorted Suzie, moving towards the car, 'he'll invent another pseudonym. Get a different publisher. And make a second fortune.'

'It's not a fair world,' said Millie.

'No one ever said it was.'

THIRTY-TWO

'I've taken all his beastly books off my shelves and binned them. I couldn't bear to lie in bed and look at them.'

Suzie looked up from her laptop. Millie stood belligerently in the doorway to the conservatory. She looked, Suzie thought with a smile, suddenly childish again, despite that sophisticated blonde haircut. 'You could have given them to my charity shop.'

'It gives me the shudders to think of little kids reading them and thinking what a wonderful person he is.'

'You don't think it's possible that someone could be a bad person and still write good books?'

'Are you trying to make excuses for him? I saw the way he smiled at you. He thinks he can magic anyone into doing what he wants.'

'He magicked you once.'

Millie kicked at a chair. 'I know. And I keep thinking what might have happened if he hadn't left Tamara's mum. Imagine if he'd stayed here, and I'd kept going to their house. I hate him for making me feel like that.'

'Don't!' Suzie found the thought unbearable.

'And there's something else,' Millie muttered. 'That Dan Curtis at the club. He gives me the creeps now.'

The doorbell rang.

'Get it, will you?' she asked Millie.

Next moment, Alan Taylor walked into the conservatory. He was wearing an open-necked shirt, instead of his dog collar. He gave her a broad grin. 'Can I sit down?'

'Of course. Would you like a cup of coffee?'

'No thanks. I can't stop. But I've got some good news to report. At least, I hope you'll think it's good.'

'About the Dawsons? That was quick.'

Suzie had rung him the day before, after they got back from Burwood. They had left Tamara with her aunt, her future still uncertain.

'No time like the present. I told him what had happened. And I didn't mince words. What Tamara went through, and what could have happened to her, were a direct consequence of the way he treated her. It nearly led to her death. That shocked him. But he understands straight talking, I'll say that for him.'

'You were braver than we were.'

'He's not fundamentally a bad guy. It's just that his moral code is different from ours. I wish I could get him to see that the light of the Gospel shows up those punitive bits in the Old Testament he's so fond of in a whole new way. We're living in a new era. Christ moves us on, from law and punishment to grace and mercy. He thinks I'm a dangerous liberal. But it's scared him. I've warned him what will happen if he uses violence on Tamara again. Or Lisa. I'm not putting either of them in danger, even if it means the end of his career.'

'He has other ways of bullying, besides hitting her,' Millie said.

Alan turned his face to her, thoughtfully. 'You're right. The three of them are going to need help. And friends.'

'I shouldn't have just left Lisa to him,' Suzie said quietly. 'She only lives round the corner. What worries me more is that it was us who told Reynard about Tamara's pregnancy. Without us, he wouldn't have known she was carrying his child.'

Tom stepped in from the patio. 'You should worry? *I* was driving the car.' His deep-blue eyes were still troubled.

Alan looked at them steadily. 'We can't all have the wisdom

of Solomon. Everything you did was because you cared for
her. She knows that.'

'She's coming home to her mum, then?' Millie asked.

'At the end of the week.'

'Terrific!' Millie sparkled with delight.

'And you'll tell me straight away if you're worried about
her?'

'You bet I will.'

He rose to go. 'It won't be easy. For any of them. They'll
need people like you around.'

When he had gone, Suzie turned back to her laptop, where
she had been checking an overflowing in-box. 'Look at this,'
she cried. 'It's just come in. It's from Pru.'

The others gathered round her. Nick came in from the garden
to look over her shoulder.

'She must have written this almost as soon as she got home.
Look, she's attached a picture.' She clicked on the
download.

They were looking at a long, low, white building. The clap-
board walls had a distinctively American look. On one end of
the roof was a small structure with a bell. The photograph
might have been taken a century ago. Men in their Sunday
best, with bowler hats. Women in blouses with leg-of-mutton
sleeves, whose dark skirts reached the ground. Girls in white
starched pinafores. Boys in tight jackets. At the bottom of the
picture was written: *Come-to-Good*.

'Adam's chapel,' breathed Suzie. 'The one he founded, right
back in the eighteenth century, after he'd started to make his
way in the timber business. Johan could never have imagined
that, when she had to stand barefoot in a white sheet and
confess her sins before the whole village. Not bad for a "base
child".'

AUTHOR'S NOTE

The people, places and institutions in this book are fictitious. But I am indebted to many real-life people and organizations who have done so much to help my own family history research in ways which have inspired this book, or have given me other advice. They include the following:

Devon Record Office: www.devon.gov.uk/record_office.htm

Westcountry Studies Library: www.devon.gov.uk/index/community/libraries/localstudies

Genuki genealogical website: www.genuki.org.uk

Access to Archives: www.nationalarchives.gov.uk/a2a

Arthur Warne, *Church and Society in Eighteenth-Century Devon*. David & Charles, 1969

Eve McLaughlin, *Illegitimacy*. Varneys Press, 2009

National Archives: BT 98 (information on crew lists)

Tom Davy, for his talk to Devon Family History Society conference

Brenda Hopkin, for the Clarkson-Clayson research

Mary Evans, for advice on dialogue

While I have given free rein to my imagination here, many details owe their inspiration to people and places in my own family history research:

Adam's baptism record – baptism in 1727 of Jane Nosworthy, daughter of Jane, a base child. St Andrew's, Moretonhampstead, Devon.

Birth of William Eastcott – Mary Arscott, baptized one month after the marriage of Sarah Arscott to William Lee. St Michael's, Doddiscombleigh, Devon.

Elizabeth Radford's marriage after her father's death – Jane Nosworthy of Moretonhampstead, who bore one child out of wedlock, and married Walter Hutchings one month after her father's death, when she was six months pregnant.

Charlotte Downs and her illegitimate children – Elizabeth

Bushell of Deal, Kent, mother of three illegitimate children.

Adam's apprenticeship indenture – indenture of Thomas Mathews of Chulmleigh, Devon, 1737.

The lease on Hole – lease for Rose Barton, Rose Ash, Devon, between George Smith, knight, and Henry Eyme alias Zeale, yeoman, 1616.

Corley Barton – Rose Ash Barton, Rose Ash, Devon.

Norworthy – Great Wooston Farm, Moretonhampstead.

The stone barn – Laployd, Bridford, Devon.

The theft of gooseanders – Manor Roll of 1510 for Morchard Cruwys, Devon.

The shift from Clarkson to Clayson – this is not recorded in the south-west, but it is in Kent.

The bastardy bond – John Turner of Chulmleigh for Mary Baple's child, 1758.

The runaway apprentice – John Pook of Berry Pomeroy, Devon, 1776.